On the outside, Lauren Fairfield appears the very picture of cool, contained nobility and blueblood British sophistication. Inside, however, she longs for Tom, the charming rogue she loved—and lost.

Now a sinfully handsome, yet socially unschooled, would-be gentleman has arrived in London—and Lauren nearly swoons when she realizes it is her Tom, grown to magnificent manhood. He has come to claim his lost title as Earl of Sachse . . . and to fulfill an oath once made by two young lovers beneath a long-ago moon, a scandalous promise no proper lady would dare honor.

Lauren could never love a staid and stifling lord, and Tom's future is the aristocracy. So she will teach him their ways before she exits his life forever. But the wildness she adored still lives in Tom's heart—and he will not rest until he proves to the proud, resisting beauty that "forever" is a promise that *must* be kept. . . .

By Lorraine Heath

PROMISE ME FOREVER
A MATTER OF TEMPTATION • AS AN EARL DESIRES
AN INVITATION TO SEDUCTION
LOVE WITH A SCANDALOUS LORD
TO MARRY AN HEIRESS • THE OUTLAW AND THE LADY
NEVER MARRY A COWBOY • NEVER LOVE A COWBOY
A ROGUE IN TEXAS

If You've Enjoyed This Book,
Be Sure to Read These Other
AVON ROMANTIC TREASURES

LORRAINE HEATH

Promise Me Forever

An Avon Romantic Treasure

AVON BOOKS
An Imprint of HarperCollinsPublishers

This is a work of fiction. Names, characters, places, and incidents are products of the author's imagination or are used fictitiously and are not to be construed as real. Any resemblance to actual events, locales, organizations, or persons, living or dead, is entirely coincidental.

AVON BOOKS
An Imprint of HarperCollins*Publishers*
10 East 53rd Street
New York, New York 10022-5299

Copyright © 2006 by Jan Nowasky
ISBN-13: 978-0-06-074982-8
ISBN-10: 0-06-074982-2
www.avonromance.com

First Avon Books paperback printing: April 2006

Avon Trademark Reg. U.S. Pat. Off. and in Other Countries, Marca Registrada, Hecho en U.S.A.
HarperCollins® is a registered trademark of HarperCollins Publishers Inc.

Printed in the U.S.A.

10 9 8 7 6 5 4 3 2 1

*With my heartfelt appreciation
to Robin Rue,
who is everything an author
could wish for in an agent.*

Chapter 1

London
1880

"They say he's devilishly handsome."

"They say he's frightfully *uncivilized*!"

"No surprise there. He's American, after all."

"Not quite. He may have grown up in America, but his blood is as English as yours or mine."

"Thank God for small favors, I say."

"I've heard he has more money than the queen."

"I daresay he'll need every ha'penny in order to secure himself a suitable wife. Quite honestly, who among us has any desire to marry a *savage*?"

Who indeed? Sitting within her stepfather's

drawing room, having contributed not a single word to the ludicrous conversation based on speculation and the latest round of gossip, Lauren Fairfield couldn't help but think that her four uninvited guests were doing exactly what they claimed they wouldn't be caught dead doing: entertaining the notion of marrying a *savage*. If not marrying him, then at the very least gleefully consorting with him. Their eyes were filled with mischief, their cheeks were flushed, and they were studying her as though they thought she had firsthand experience at being ravished and might advise them on the best recourse for pursuing the possibilities.

She hardly knew how to respond to these ladies who had been among the first to accept her into their prestigious inner circle. They were known to swoon upon occasion, at will, their performances worthy of a standing ovation. And why not? They'd held numerous swooning parties in their youth, so they could hone their skills. It was, after all, expected: to be so delicate and fragile that one was always in danger of being broken, to leave no doubt in gentlemen's minds that the men were the stronger of the sexes. It was a ghastly way to live, keeping one's true self hidden behind a screen of expectations that transformed into obligations.

When the looming silence became rather uncomfortable, Lady Blythe reached out and lightly touched Lauren's hand. "Oh, you must forgive us, dear friend, if we offended you by referring to the barbaric nature of Americans."

"We meant no offense," Lady Cassandra concurred. "One wouldn't know by your mannerisms that you're American, and thus we always seem to forget that you are. Which is a grand compliment, I would say."

The other two young ladies in attendance bobbed their heads and murmured their agreement. Like them, Lauren wore the latest fashion: a slenderizing skirt that accentuated her tiny waist and narrow hips. She was grateful the bustle had at last disappeared from fashionable clothing, but she suspected that Ladies Blythe and Cassandra missed it. Their hips weren't well suited to the narrower skirts. A cruel thought that was most unlike Lauren. Perhaps she hadn't quite lost her American mannerisms as much as they thought.

Or perhaps she was simply too weary to extend the proper courtesies. The ladies had arrived right on her heels, after a particularly challenging day, and Lauren had barely had time to greet her stepfather, the earl of Ravenleigh, before she found herself in the role of hostess, since her mother and sisters had gone out for a bit of afternoon shopping.

"I'm deeply flattered that you hold me in such high regard," she finally responded, more out of habit than anything else. She and her sisters had spent hours practicing their replies to insincere compliments, so *they* at least appeared sincere. Sometimes she felt as though her life had become an elaborate play, scripted, rehearsed, performed, words spoken because they were the predictable response. She'd recently taken to doing the unpredictable, and while she was doing it in secret, it still brought her a measure of satisfaction to be doing it at all.

"As well you should be," Lady Cassandra acknowledged. "I daresay nothing is worse than a crass American. While you, dear friend, pass as English with no effort at all."

No effort? Had the lady forgotten how often they'd rolled their eyes at her when she'd first arrived in London? How they'd grimaced at her drawl, snickered at her poor choice of words? How often she'd been the object of hurtful gossip, because she hadn't known the difference between an earl, a duke, or a marquess, and had once— upon being introduced to a knight—asked if he would show her his suit of armor? Did Lady Cassandra have no idea as to how often Lauren had fallen asleep on a pillow soaked with her tears?

Why every aspect of Lauren's behavior was an effort: to sit properly, walk properly, speak properly . . . to remember titles and correct forms of address, to know when to curtsy and when to smile at a gentleman, how to subtly flirt without being brazen, how to tamp down boldness. Always, always to comport herself as the most refined in polite society, above reproach, rumor, or innuendo.

She'd practiced, studied, observed, and emulated until she was no longer an embarrassment to herself or her stepfather. Until all her American idiosyncrasies were buried so deeply that she thought she was in danger of never again finding them. Until she'd become, as Lady Blythe had alluded, so near to being the perfect English lady that few remembered the uncultured family Ravenleigh had possessed the audacity to bring back with him from Texas when he'd gone to visit his twin brother, Kit Montgomery.

Until she feared that she might have even lost herself. Although she'd recently begun to take actions to rectify that possibility, she could only hope that she hadn't waited until it was too late.

"So tell us," Lady Blythe prodded with characteristic exuberance, "did you ever meet the latest Earl of Sachse?"

Ah, at last, the true purpose behind their visit: to discover what *she* might be able to reveal about the man who had only a short time ago arrived on England's shores to claim his rightful title.

Lauren was quite unclear regarding the particulars. She'd been too involved with her own plans to give the rumors much credence or attention. Still, she was aware that London was all a titter about the earl who had been lost in America and only found a short time ago. Everyone had believed that he'd died of illness when he was but a boy—after

all, almost twenty years earlier his mother had
made that very claim, and no one had reason to
doubt her, especially in light of how much she had
grieved over the loss of her only child. Recently,
however, a letter had been discovered that revealed the astonishing truth: The lad was alive, to
be returned to England upon his father's death.

Lauren thought the true miracle was that
Archibald Warner, a distant cousin who'd been
granted the title, had actually possessed the decency to hire private investigators to search for the
rightful heir. She knew many lords, having once
tasted the power, influence, and prestige granted
to them by virtue of their exalted position, would
have held on to it until the devil was tossing snow-
balls in hell.

"I never had the pleasure of meeting him," Lauren confessed. "But, then, America is an extremely
large country. The chances of our paths crossing
are astronomical."

"But it's rumored they found him in Texas,"
Lady Cassandra said. "Surely that increases the
odds of your knowing him, since you lived there
for a time."

"Texas is a big state, the biggest in the nation,"
Lauren told her. "So I doubt where they found
him makes any difference to the chance that we'd
met. And as you say, I lived there for only a short
time."

With the discussion turning to odds, she wondered if they'd made private wagers as to whether or not she knew the newly discovered earl. It seemed these people bet on everything. Last Season, the majority of the wagers had centered on whom the Duke of Kimburton would favor with a marriage proposal: Lady Blythe or Miss Lauren Fairfield. By the close of the Season, he'd chosen Lauren, which in the end had turned out to be a rather unfortunate selection on his part.

When faced with the reality of staying in England forever, Lauren had been unable to accept his earnestly delivered proposal. As a gentleman, he'd graciously accepted her refusal, but it was rumored that he had no plans to come to London for the coming Season. Pride and all that. She deeply regretted that she'd hurt him, caused him embarrassment, because of all the English gentlemen she'd met, he'd come closest to claiming her heart.

Lauren was actually surprised that Lady Blythe, having failed to gain Kimburton's final favor, had seen fit to pay a visit this afternoon. Of course, the opportunity to learn a bit more about the new earl was apparently a strong enough incentive for Lady Blythe to forgive her rival almost anything. That and the fact that Lauren surely wouldn't be any serious competition for her in the new Season. Having turned down the duke's offer, Lauren knew it unlikely that any other man would favor her with his attentions, and while she acknowledged that she'd miss the flirtations, she was looking forward to the freedom of pursuing her other endeavors more earnestly.

"Besides, it has been almost ten years since I lived in Texas. If he and I had met, I doubt I'd remember, especially since he most likely wasn't introducing himself as Sachse."

"I daresay he certainly wasn't. Apparently, he had no earthly idea that he was titled or that he had anything at all waiting over here for him," Lady Cassandra said.

"Can you imagine your mother abandoning you in America, of all places?" Lady Blythe asked. "Simply leaving you there among the *heathens*?"

She spoke *heathens* as though referring to a delightful dessert glazed in chocolate, and Lauren was beginning to have her suspicions confirmed: These ladies weren't nearly as put off by the American-raised peer as they were letting on. As a matter of fact, as she'd observed earlier, excitement and anticipation danced within their eyes at the mere mention of the mysterious lord.

"From what I overheard, his mother didn't actually *abandon* him," Lady Cassandra said. "She turned his upbringing over to a well-connected family in New York, and I've read that New York is quite modern."

"Regardless of its reputation, it's not London, and, therefore, hardly a suitable environment in which to raise a future lord. Besides, the investigator didn't find him in New York, so who knows what sort of improper influences he may have encountered along the way. I can't help but wonder what the earl's mother was thinking when she left him abroad."

"I think she was hoping to protect her son," Lady Anne said quietly before shuddering. "Richard knew the old Earl of Sachse and could barely tolerate the man."

Richard was her brother, older by a good many years. The Duke of Weddington. A man Lauren had seen at only one ball. Apparently, he didn't tolerate balls well either. His prestige, however, guaranteed that his sister was embraced by all, in spite of the fact that she was quite young, having only recently had her coming-out.

"But America?" Lady Blythe emphasized. "Surely she could have found someplace nearer to home, where he could have gained an appreciation for all he would inherit."

"Whether she could or couldn't is moot," Lady Anne said. "The fact remains that she *didn't*. We can't know exactly what she was thinking; we can only know what she did."

"Is he a hateful creature like his father, do you suppose?" Lady Blythe asked.

"I've heard he's nothing at all like his father," Lady Priscilla announced. Lady Anne's closest and dearest friend, one seldom seen without the other, she was the authority on all things, her word always taken as gospel rather than gossip.

"Has anyone actually set eyes on him?" Lady Blythe asked.

The ladies looked at each other as though wondering who'd been peering in windows, again with an excitement about them at the possibility that one of them had done the forbidden. Behavior was so strictly controlled, and while Lauren had grown accustomed to it, there were times when she desperately wanted to break free of the societal restraints.

"I might have seen him," Lady Priscilla finally volunteered, her cheeks reddening with her confession.

All the ladies except Lauren gasped and inched up on their seats toward Lady Priscilla, as though they might catch a glimpse of the elusive earl still mirrored in her expressive eyes.

"Where?" Lady Blythe asked.

"Do tell all," Lady Cassandra urged.

"Yes, quickly, before I expire from the anticipation."

"I haven't much to tell really. My spying of him happened in Hyde Park yesterday morning. He was riding the most beautiful black. horse."

"Who gives a fig about his *horse*. What of him?" Lady Cassandra asked. "Was he beautiful?"

"I could hardly tell. He wore only black. Black greatcoat, black hat. A very wide hat, at that, so I couldn't clearly make out his features. I believe he was dressed as I've heard cowboys described.

And here's the most interesting thing . . ." She leaned forward, drawing the other ladies closer, and lowered her voice to a conspiratorial whisper. "As he rode by, his coat billowed, and I do believe I saw a pistol pressed against his thigh!"

"No!" Lady Blythe exclaimed.

"Yes!"

"How intriguing."

How ridiculous, Lauren thought. To carry on so about the newcomer when there were lords aplenty. Their interest in him stemmed only from the fact that he was new, not yet tested. She'd been in that position once. She didn't envy him what he would suffer as all of London took their measure of him. No doubt he would be found wanting. After all, he'd not been properly groomed for the role he would be expected to play in their society.

"You're familiar with cowboys, aren't you, Lauren?" Lady Blythe asked.

Lauren felt an unexpected pang in her heart as the question unlocked memories that she'd long ago banished. She was surprised that after all this time, all these years, they could still be so powerful, stir such intense yearning.

"Yes," she finally admitted. "I've known cowboys, but it's been many years, and I was a young girl, so my memories might be tainted by my youth and inexperience. My mother is constantly reminding me that we tend to remember things as being much more pleasant than they actually were."

Her mother's incessant reminders usually followed one of Lauren's frequent announcements that she'd like to return to Texas.

"Tell us what you remember," Lady Cassandra demanded.

Lauren remembered a lazy smile that had made her heart race, brown eyes that reminded her of a puppy that had been kicked once too often and was now afraid to trust. She remembered a defiant stance and a challenging expression in a face that should have looked younger than it did. She remembered coal black hair, long and shaggy, always in need of a trimming. Dirty hands and worn, dusty clothes, a tall, lean body that was agile and surprisingly strong.

"Come now," Lady Blythe urged. "Don't torture us so. Tell us what a cowboy is like."

Lauren relented only because she thought it was the quickest path to clearing her drawing room of their presence. She felt the beginning of a headache and longed to lie down before she had to begin preparing for dinner.

"He's respectful," she said. Although hers hadn't always been.

"He tips his hat to the ladies." Although hers never had.

"He's short on words." Hers usually wasn't.

"To cross a street, any street, he'd rather ride his horse than walk." Or he would have if he'd owned a horse.

"Quick to smile, slow to anger." Although his smiles had always been slow in coming, the corners of his mouth taking their time to hitch up as though they enjoyed the journey as much as they did getting to their destination.

"They adore women." Hers had especially. All women, young and old, fair and plain. He never discriminated.

She released a self-conscious laugh. "At least that's what I remember about a cowboy." Her cowboy.

"Oh, I like the adoring women part," Lady Blythe said. "Our gentlemen tend to take us for granted, I believe. Even when they go through the proper motions, they do so simply because it's expected, not necessarily because they desire to put forth the effort. All a man truly cares about is that a woman is perfectly capable of quickly providing an heir and a spare. Frightfully unromantic."

"On the other hand, cowboys aren't quite as refined as the gentlemen here," Lauren admitted. "Their gifts tend to be bits of hair ribbon, or flowers stolen from someone's garden in passing, or lines of atrocious poetry."

"But if the gifts are given from the heart . . ." Lady Anne's wistful voice trailed off.

"Well, I daresay this cowboy lord won't be stealing flowers," Lady Blythe interjected. "As I said, it is rumored that he is quite well off. Even without his inheritance, supposedly he is to be envied."

"Envied?" Lauren repeated. "Envied because he achieved success through hard work? Envied because he must now leave behind what he knows and live in a country that is far different from that with which he is familiar?"

"We are not *that* different," Lady Blythe said. "Besides, what is to be envied is his wealth."

"Which he earned."

"And his most fortunate wife shall have the pleasure of spending."

"Earlier you were of the opinion that he'd have difficulty securing a wife," Lauren reminded her.

Lady Blythe smiled as though she were suddenly superior. "One never knows. When a man has enough coins in his pockets and a title as well, a good deal that one might find distasteful can be overlooked."

"Although one can't deny, as Miss Fairfield reminded us, that he *earned* his money. Terribly unfortunate that," Lady Cassandra said.

"But he earned it before he knew he was an earl," Lady Blythe said, "so surely it is a forgivable offense."

Lauren found herself feeling incredible empathy for the man, who undoubtedly was about to have a strange new life thrust upon him as she'd once had one thrust upon her. Perhaps she would seek him out and advise him to return to Texas as quickly as possible, before he was shaped and molded into an aristocrat, blending in with everyone else, no longer his own man with his own thoughts, opinions, and dreams.

He heard her voice—surprised that he could identify it after all these years. It had changed slightly, he couldn't deny that. Grown softer, with a gentler timbre that could lure a man in before he realized he was well and truly captivated.

That's how Thomas Warner felt. Captivated.

And he sure as hell didn't want to be.

There wasn't much in life that Tom dreaded, but he'd been dreading this encounter from the moment that it had dawned on him that sooner or later it would come to pass. He'd put it off as long as he could, and now that it was about to happen, he was torn between wishing it had come along sooner and wishing that it had never arrived.

While the butler—in a snit because Tom didn't have a proper calling card—had gone to inform the Earl of Ravenleigh that Tom had come to call, Tom had been standing in the entry hallway, cooling his heels, waiting. But he hadn't been doing it patiently. Being accustomed to giving the orders and having them obeyed without question, he wasn't used to waiting on any man.

Then he'd heard the voices, talking almost too fast to decipher . . . then her voice. She'd lost a good bit of the slow drawl that had once been music to his ears, but he could still hear it when she spoke certain words, like a memorable chord wafting off a fiddle. So he found himself listening intently for the familiar.

He'd eased over to the doorway, leaned against the doorjamb, and just . . . spied on them. A gathering of women, so intent on their visiting that they weren't noticing him. He remembered times in his life when he'd yearned for a woman's presence with such longing that he'd thought he'd die from the wanting. Not only her touch, but her fragrance, her softness, the comfort she could offer.

He knew it was wrong to stand there, knew he should announce his presence, but he wasn't sure what would happen once Lauren saw him.

Did she even remember him?

When he'd never been able to forget her?

Chapter 2

<figure>❧◦◦☙</figure>

Ten years earlier

"I saw what you did."

Sitting against the back wall of the general store, Tom Warner peered out from beneath his dusty, battered hat and squinted at the young gal standing before him, legs akimbo, fists planted on her almost nonexistent hips. She sure was a pretty thing, with eyes the color of bluebonnets in spring and hair the shade of the full moon that looked down on him while he slept. "So?"

"You stole those crackers."

Tom shoved the last of his bounty into his mouth, chewed, and swallowed, wishing he had some milk with which to wash them down. "What crackers?"

Her jaw dropped, and she began to blink those startling blue eyes of hers. "So you're a liar, too?"

"What do you care? It ain't your store."

"But it's wrong to steal and lie about it."

Lord save him from the self-righteous. "It's only stealing if you take something when you got the money to pay for it. Besides, I was hungry."

She furrowed her brow. "You ain't got no money?"

"I've got a bit"—two bits as a matter of fact—"but I'm saving it for an emergency."

"Being hungry is an emergency."

"Nah, it ain't." He shoved himself to his feet. He was considerably taller than she, so she had to tilt her head back to look into his eyes. He liked the way she kept watching him. "I been hungry lots of times. Something always comes along."

"You mean you always steal something."

"I mean the Lord provides."

"Are you a preacher?"

"Hell, no."

She gasped, her eyes growing even wider. "You're not supposed to cuss."

Hell wasn't really a cussword, was it? He'd used far worse words in his day. *Might be fun to use one now, see her get more riled.*

"Well, damn," he said, taking pleasure in her horrified expression. "What's left to a man if he can't steal, lie, or cuss?"

"You ain't a man," she said indignantly.

"Close enough. I'm almost sixteen."

He reached into his shirt pocket, pulled out a paper and a pouch of tobacco, and slowly rolled himself a cigarette. He stuck it between his lips. While she watched, mouth agape, he flicked his thumb over a match, the strike causing it to ignite. Touching the flame to the cigarette, he inhaled deeply. Smoking always took the edge off his hunger. Course, stealing the makings wasn't as easy as stealing crackers, but sometimes a man simply needed a challenge.

"You ain't supposed to smoke in the presence of a lady without asking permission," she said, a scolding tone to her words that would have had him turning on his bootheels and walking away if she wasn't so pleasing to look at. He wasn't partial to being chewed out, didn't see much point in tolerating it.

Blowing out the smoke, squinting through it, he gave an exaggerated look around the area. "I don't see no lady around here."

"I'm a lady."

"You're just a kid."

"Am not. I'm a young lady, almost fully growed."

"Let me see."

She blinked rapidly, her nose no longer pointing at the sky. "What do you mean?"

"I mean, let me unbutton your bodice. Let me see if you're almost fully growed."

She blinked again, shrugged, and thrust her chest toward him, a dare in her eyes that astounded him. "All right."

Sweet Lord in heaven! She was going to let him do it. He dropped his cigarette to the ground and mashed it with the toe of his worn boot. His mouth grew so dry that it was as though he'd chewed the tobacco instead of inhaling it. He wiped his suddenly damp hands on his trousers, then reached for her bodice, embarrassed that his hands were shaking so badly that he could barely get his fingers to work. But he was determined not to stop, because he desperately wanted to see what he'd been growing more and more anxious to see in the past few months. A woman's bosom. Well, a girl's bosom in this case, but a bosom was a bosom. Hell, if he'd known it was this easy to get a gal out of her clothes, he would have asked one long ago.

"Lauren Fairfield, what in the world is going on back here?"

The tartly delivered question almost had his skin running out of there without him in it. Once he quickly recaptured his breath, he realized her mama—the woman looked too much like her not to be—must have come around the corner without him noticing, and he was only one button closer to seeing paradise. Survival kicked in, but before he could duck and dart away, her mama sent his hat flying into the dust, got hold of his ear, pinching hard, which brought him up short. "Ow!"

"Have you been smoking back here?" her mama asked.

"No, ma'am. Only him. He didn't ask me first. And he cusses."

The girl stopped her explanation there, lowered her gaze, and Tom wanted to kiss her for keeping her mouth shut about his worst transgressions. With her lips pressed tightly together, he stood a good chance of not going to jail. They didn't arrest people for smoking or cussing. But if she'd revealed that he'd stolen as well . . .

"If your pa were still alive, he'd beat this boy to within an inch of life for taking liberties with you, but since he's not, it's left to me to take care of this matter," her mama said, grabbing her daughter's arm and tugging harder on Tom's ear.

Prison might be better after all. He followed after them because the woman gave him no choice, not if he wanted to keep his ear, and he was right partial to it. It matched the one on the other side of his head.

They rounded the corner of the building, her mother trudging through the alley, pulling them both along behind her. She turned the next corner. "Marshal!"

Ah, hell, could his luck get any worse? The marshal was leaning against the front of the general store, his forehead pressed to the wood.

"Just past noon and you're already drunk," her mama chastised.

The man twisted his head slightly and stared at them. Tom had never seen such pale blue eyes.

"I saw you coming out of the saloon," her mama continued. "I don't know why the people of this town saw fit to make you marshal, or why I'm turning to a womanizer with this problem. Reckon because I got no choice." Without releasing her hold on Tom's ear, she somehow managed to thrust him toward the marshal.

"Ow! Ow! Ow!" Tom cried, wincing. Dang, but the woman could pinch.

"I want him locked up for the night."

Tom tried to look on the bright side. At least he'd get a hot meal and a cot.

The marshal finally spoke. "My apologies, madam"—the man talked so danged funny that Tom almost burst out laughing, but he decided that considering the spot he was in, it was to his advantage to keep quiet—"but I can't—"

"You sure can, and you'd better. Take him!"

The marshal wrapped his hand around Tom's arm and pulled him away from the woman. "What's his offense?"

"He was unbuttoning my Lauren's bodice, try-ing to . . . take advantage of her innocence. She's only fourteen."

Fourteen? Holy hell! She *was* just a kid. Tom had figured she was closer to his age, had just called her a kid to rile her.

The marshal gave a brisk nod. "I shall handle the matter posthaste."

"See that you do, or I swear I'll have the town council throw you out of office." She trudged away, pulling her daughter behind her. The gal glanced over her shoulder, giving Tom a look that said she was as sorry at the way they were parting as he was.

"Who was that termagant?" the marshal asked.

Judging by the man's prissy voice, all soft and elegant-sounding, Tom didn't think he was from around there. He looked to be a dandy. Tom was pretty sure that he could outrun the fella. And he wasn't exactly sure what a termagant was, but based on the way the man had asked and the way Lauren's mother had been scolding the man, Tom didn't think he was issuing any compliments.

"The Widow Fairfield," Tom answered, figuring it was the only name that suited her if her husband was dead and the gal was Lauren *Fairfield*.

"How old are you, lad?" the marshal asked.

Tom angled his chin defiantly. "Fifteen, and I ain't afraid of jail."

"I'm not going to put you in jail for being curious, but wait until you're sixteen before you unfasten any other bodices. Make certain the woman is older or a sporting sort who is willing to take money to satisfy your natural curiosity." The marshal released his hold. "Now, be off with you."

Tom didn't have to be told twice. He ran around the corner, down the alley, and around the other corner, coming to a stop behind the store. He snatched up his hat, crammed it on his head, and gently scooped up what remained of his cigarette. He could finish it off that night when his stomach started rumbling. Unless he could find something more to eat. He wondered what they tossed out behind the saloon.

"I see you're still stealing."

Tom finished off his cracker, before squinting up from his favorite sitting spot behind the general store. There she was again. Lauren Fairfield. Dressed in blue, a row of buttons up the front that went clear to her chin. Had to be durn near choking her.

"Took up drinking, too," he said, with a grin.

He liked the way her eyes got so big and round whenever he shocked her.

"So you're still lying, too, I see."

"Ain't lying. Found a half-empty bottle out behind the saloon last week. Finished it off."

"What'd it taste like?" she asked, obviously curious.

Like piss, but he didn't tell her that because she might ask how he knew what piss tasted like, and he sure didn't want to reveal that sorry aspect of his life. So he settled for, "I've tasted better."

"You're supposed to take off your hat in a lady's presence and stand up."

"You sure care a lot about manners."

"Everybody does."

"I don't."

"How come?"

"Can't see that there's any advantage to 'em."

"Not getting your backside whupped is an advantage."

"Who's gonna whup my backside?"

"Your parents."

"They're dead."

Of all the things he'd said to her, that comment seemed to shock her most of all.

"You're an orphan?"

He shrugged.

"Where do you live?"

He shrugged again.

"Is that why you steal?"

"You sure ask a lot of questions." He squinted at her. "What do you know about that marshal?"

"That Mama don't like him. Or his friends."

"He talks funny."

"He's from England. He and his friends moved here right after the war, to help with the harvesting of the cotton, on account of so many of the menfolk got killed."

England. He didn't know anyone from England. He was sure of it. Still, the way the man talked tickled something at the back of his memory. He couldn't get it out of his head, but then he couldn't seem to get Lauren out of his head either. He'd been taking her to sleep with him, her and that one unbuttoned button.

"Why do you care about him?" she asked.

"I don't. Just curious. Something tugging at my memory. Can't rightly put my finger on it."

"I'm sorry my mama got you in trouble with him."

With his thumb, he tipped his hat off his brow. "He let me go as soon as your mama was gone. Didn't have to spend the night in jail after all."

She smiled. "I'm glad."

Lord have mercy. His heart kicked painfully against his ribs. When she smiled, she got downright beautiful. "You still fourteen?"

She laughed lightly, and somehow managed to take his breath away at the same time.

"Course, silly. Why are you asking?"

" 'Cuz it's my birthday, and I wanted to buy me a present."

Her eyes and smile got brighter. "What are you gonna buy?"

"An unbuttoned bodice."

She furrowed her brow, narrowed her eyes, and pinched her mouth. "Didn't think you had any money."

"Told you I had a bit."

"Thought you were saving it for an emergency."

The way his heart was hammering . . . "It is an emergency."

"My mama sure was mad—"

"That's 'cuz I didn't know that I had to pay." He scrambled to his feet, removed his hat, and pulled the quarter out of his pocket. "The marshal said it was all right for me to do it if I paid for it."

"Why are you so set on unbuttoning my bodice?"

" 'Cuz I ain't never seen a bosom before, and I heard fellas talking about what a fine sight it was."

She took on a mulish expression, so he unfurled his fingers to show her what he was willing to offer this time.

"What fellas?" she asked.

"On the orphan train."

"You rode on the orphan train?"

He nodded. "All the way from New York. Not to here, of course. I walked here, didn't much like the family what took me in."

"How come?"

"Just didn't. You want this two bits or not?" he asked impatiently. He didn't want to think about all that had happened after his folks died. He wanted to have a good memory of his sixteenth birthday, something he'd be thinking about if he lived to be a hundred.

She skewed up her face, which he thought should have made her look ugly, but it didn't. It just made him want to tease her more, to keep her lingering around.

"All you want to do is unbutton my bodice?"

He nodded, his mouth suddenly so dry that he didn't think he'd be able to talk if he had to.

"You can't touch nothing," she said.

"I won't," he forced out through the knot forming in his throat as his anticipation built. "I'll just look."

"I guess there's no harm in just looking."

"None at all."

She held out her hand. He dropped the coin in it, wishing his didn't look so dirty to him all of a sudden. After setting his hat aside, he wiped his hands on his trousers and cursed them for starting to tremble again. He hated to think how badly they might be shaking if he got to touch more than buttons. Not that he would touch more than she'd given him permission to. He might be a thief, a liar, a cusser, and—most recently—a drunk, but he wasn't a scoundrel. Well, maybe he was a little. The unbuttoning might be walking right up to the line, but he wasn't going to step over it. A man had to have some principles.

Holding his gaze, she lifted her chin. He swallowed hard, wishing she didn't have so *many* danged buttons. The first one seemed to take forever to slip through that tiny little loop. It parted to reveal the tiniest bit of her throat. He stopped breathing. Moved his fingers to the next button—

"Lauren Fairfield!"

Before he could make a move to escape, his ear

was held in a painful grip, and he was dancing on his toes, trying to stop the agony. How could a woman inflict such torment with a pinch?

She was hauling him around the building before he could work up a protest.

"Marshal Montgomery!"

Sliding his gaze to the side, because she wouldn't let him turn his head, Tom caught sight of the marshal, standing by the telegraph office. She marched Tom across the dusty street.

"Madam—"

"He was doing it again. Unbuttoning my Lauren's bodice."

The marshal glared at him. "I told you—"

"I turned sixteen today," he hastened to explain, "and you said I could have a look-see if she was willing to take money. I give her two bits."

"You told him he could unbutton my daughter's bodice if he paid her?"

"Not exactly. He misinterpreted my instructions," the marshal tried to explain.

"You worthless son of a bitch!" she yelled as she thrust Tom toward the marshal. "I want him in jail and you along with him. I'm going to the town council."

Tom watched her march off, righteous indignation in every determined step. Lauren was looking over her shoulder at him, worry in her expression that caused his chest to tighten. It had been a long time since anyone had worried about him.

"What's your name, lad?" the marshal asked.

"Tommy." He preferred Tom, but he'd learned that people cottoned up better when he used a version of his name that made him sound younger, more innocent. A Tommy they might protect. A Tom they'd cart to jail.

"Where in God's name are your parents?"

"Dead."

The marshal sighed heavily. "Come with me."

Dang it. His ploy had never let him down before. He jerked up his chin defiantly. He'd gotten out of many a scrape of late by bluffing. "I ain't afraid of jail."

"I'm not taking you to jail."

The marshal walked along the boardwalk, his steps echoing over the planks. Tom recognized the sound of anger when he heard it. He might really be in trouble. He thought about running, but he was so danged tired of running. And if he ran, he might never see that blue-eyed gal again.

The marshal shoved open the door to the saloon.

"You gonna lie and tell 'em I'm old enough to drink?" Tom asked, hopefully.

The marshal gave him a steely glare. The man wasn't as much of a dandy as Tom had thought. He was usually pretty good at figuring fellas out, but this one confused him.

Tom shrugged insolently. "I reckon you ain't."

"Wyndhaven," a man said as he slowly walked

over, leaning heavily on a cane. Tom recognized him as being the owner of the saloon. He talked the same funny way that the marshal did. "What have you got here?"

"A lad with no parents and too much time on his hands. What can I do with him?"

The saloon owner looked Tom over. Tom clenched his jaw. He hated being looked over, measured, judged.

"Know anything about cattle, lad?"

"I know it all," Tom said confidently, defiantly. He knew what happened when a fella was found lacking. He got a sound beating.

"You don't know a bloody thing, you little liar," the saloon owner said, "but you will before the month is out."

"What are you going to do with him?" the marshal asked.

"Put him to work for the Texas Lady Cattle Venture."

By nightfall, Tom had a full belly, a soft pallet on which to sleep, and for the first time in a long while, hope for a better life.

Ten years later he'd come to thank the man responsible. It had been Ravenleigh—Viscount Wyndhaven at the time—who'd offered him a chance back in Fortune. As fate would have it, it hadn't been the marshal to whom Lauren's mother had kept turning Tom over—it had been the man's twin brother, come for a visit. And when he'd left

Fortune, he'd taken Lauren's mother, Lauren, and her sisters with him.

Tom wasn't sure if he made a noise or Lauren simply sensed his presence, but she rose gracefully—so gracefully—turned to face him, then stilled as though suddenly encountering an unknown danger.

Sweet Lord in heaven! She'd grown more beautiful than he'd imagined. And he'd done a lot of imagining about her over the years. And he realized with a startling clarity so sharp that it almost doubled him over that he hadn't come to thank Ravenleigh. He'd come for something else entirely. But he had too much pride to go begging, too much pride to admit how much her silence had hurt him. But not so much pride that he wouldn't take what he was owed.

Lauren had heard the smallest whisper of movement, had assumed the tea she'd requested earlier had finally been brought by a servant. But when she rose and faced the door, her breath caught painfully in her chest. She was barely aware of the other ladies gasping, one of them squeaking.

Tea hadn't arrived. A cowboy had.

And she would have recognized him anywhere.

Tall, whipcord lean with a loose-hipped stride that hinted at no hurry to arrive, he boldly crossed over to her, confidence brimming in every step, a man with a mission. The thud of his bootheels hitting the polished parquet floor echoed through the room. He clutched his black hat in his large, weathered hand, while his dark brown eyes held her captive.

His midnight black hair, more tamed than she'd ever seen it, brushed the collar of his white shirt, almost hidden beneath his simple black jacket. A black silk tie was knotted into a limp bow at his throat. His mustache was a new addition, as thick as his hair, framing the upper bow of his mouth and the sides that spread wide as he bestowed on her one of his slow, sensual grins.

She didn't think it was squinting at the unforgiving Texas sun and wind that had carved lines into his face, at the corners of his eyes, across his brow. It was harsh living, and probably hard playing. He'd never been one to do things in half measure. For all the changes that she noted, it was what remained the same that made him so recognizable.

He gazed at her as though she belonged to him. Once upon a time, perhaps she had.

He was the last person she'd ever expected to see again, the one person she'd given up hope of ever seeing again. Perhaps he was a mirage, a figment of her imagination, a faint hope that she'd held on to when she'd thought she'd given up completely.

Except when he stopped directly in front of her, his scent—leather, tobacco, a touch of whiskey, a bit of dust—stirred to life forgotten memories of nights spent with him beneath the stars. He was real. And he was there. At long last, he was there. She could scarcely believe it.

Her heart was thundering so hard that she was certain everyone could hear it, could see it pressing against her chest with each forceful beat.

"Tom?" she finally whispered.

"Hello, Lauren." His voice was a deep rumble, raspy, sensual, which shimmered through her and touched all the lonely barren corners of her heart.

"What in the world are you doing here?" she asked.

"I've come to collect a debt."

A debt? What on earth was he talking about?

"My goodness, Tom, who owes you—"

"You do, darlin'."

Chapter 3

Lauren stared at him, his words registering but hardly making any sense. The only thing she'd ever owed him . . .

Good Lord! After all this time he'd come here to collect what he'd failed to collect in Texas? Her unbuttoned bodice? Had the man taken leave of his senses?

"You can't be serious?"

"Deadly."

Tom watched as disbelief washed over her delicate features, to be quickly replaced by defiance. He couldn't explain why it pleased him to see the obstinate jut of her chin, the pressing together of her lips in disapproval, especially when it wasn't her disapproval he'd come for. Somehow she always managed to bring out a bit of the devil in him.

"You're him, aren't you?" one of the ladies asked, before Lauren could sting him with a sharp reply.

Tom turned to the woman who'd spoken and wondered why he didn't find her blond hair and blue eyes as attractive as Lauren's. In some ways she was prettier, but in all ways that mattered to him she was simply ordinary. Still, he wasn't in the habit of ignoring women. They were too rare in Texas for their presence to be taken for granted, so he grinned. "And who would that be, darlin'?"

"Oh." She released a tiny giggle, and her eyes began blinking faster than a hummingbird's wings. Clearly flustered, she took a deep breath. "The Earl of Sachse."

"Of course, he isn't," Lauren said. "He has business dealings with my stepfather. Isn't that the real reason you're here, Tom? To bring Ravenleigh the latest news about one of the Texas Lady ventures?"

Tom knew that as the enterprise had grown to include more than cattle, Ravenleigh had become an investor, a partner with his brother and his two friends, Grayson Rhodes and Harrison Bainbridge. Tom was also well aware that the men had kept Ravenleigh informed of his progress, his success, and while it had never been official, he'd often felt as though they had adopted him.

"I told you the reason I was here," he said to Lauren.

"Surely you didn't travel all this way for something as trivial—" She stopped abruptly, as though remembering that she had a drawing room filled with ladies who might find his reason a tad scandalous. Tom knew all about the damage a scandal could cause. Every Englishman he'd ever met had some sort of scandal associated with him that had resulted in his exile to Texas.

"I never considered anything about you trivial," Tom said, watching as vibrant red slashed across Lauren's cheeks. He hadn't remembered her being one to embarrass so easily. But then it didn't take much looking to realize that she was no longer the girl who had challenged him outside the general store. She possessed a poise, a calmness, a grace that she'd lacked in her youth. She was the epitome of a lady, and he wasn't quite certain how he felt about the obvious changes, wondered if the changes in him were as clear to see.

"Please, you simply must join us," the hummingbird urged, again before Lauren could respond, and he realized that he should have waited before approaching her, waited until he could get her alone. After all these years, she deserved that consideration. They both did.

"Please," one of the other ladies implored. "We would love to have you join us."

How could Tom say no to such an earnestly delivered invitation, when such expectation hovered in the room, as though staying would fulfill their every wish?

"I appreciate the invite." He sat on the offered chair, bringing up one leg, putting his ankle on his knee, placing his hat on his thigh.

With her delicate brow furrowed, Lauren stared at him as though she didn't quite approve of his posture—or perhaps she was still having a difficult time believing he was there. But then he was having a difficult time believing it as well. He wondered if it would be inappropriate to ask her to step outside for a minute so they could talk in private. He had ten years of questions that needed ten years of answers. But even as he considered the possibility, he knew the required resolution: of course it would be inappropriate to take her aside. The one thing he had learned regarding the women in England was that a man wasn't allowed to be alone with one—no matter how innocent his intentions.

With an almost imperceptible shake of her head, as though accepting his presence, she made introductions without fluster, as though cowboys with daring declarations were known to barge into her drawing room every afternoon. The hummingbird was Lady Blythe. The dark-haired woman was Lady Cassandra. The younger ones were Ladies Anne and Priscilla.

"Are you a cowboy?" Lady Blythe asked.

"Yes, darlin', I am."

She ducked her head and peered over at him, batting those long eyelashes again, appearing inordinately pleased. He'd always enjoyed showering attention on the ladies, but he was accustomed to having to work a little harder to get any sort of results.

Leaning over, Lauren touched his hand, and desire speared him clear down to his bootheels. She'd always had an effect on him, but it had never been so strong, so sharp, so immediate.

"These ladies . . . their fathers are all peers. You should address them with a bit more formality," she said.

"I, for one, don't mind that you called me darling," Lady Blythe said. "I've never before had a gentleman call me darling."

He gave her a broad grin. "I find that hard to believe, darlin'."

Lady Blythe released another tiny giggle that was almost a sigh. "It's true."

"Then I'm thinking that you're living in the wrong place, because fellas would be lining up to call you darlin' back in Texas."

"Truly?"

"I'm not one to lie."

"Since when?" Lauren asked.

The anger, hot and furious, roiled through him, and it was all he could do to keep it harnessed, as he slid his gaze back over to her. "Did you want to start counting off false words spoken—in front of your company? If so, I'd be only too happy to oblige."

She looked as though he'd fired a bullet into her heart, but he wasn't about to apologize or take the words back. She was the one who hadn't kept the promise they'd made.

"Tom!"

The familiar cultured voice echoed between the walls. Tom came to his feet, hand outstretched, as the Earl of Ravenleigh crossed the room. He didn't look much different from when Tom had seen him last. A few more wrinkles across his brow. His hair might be graying a bit on the sides, but it was barely noticeable against the reddish blond strands that were combed back.

The man shook his hand, his light blue eyes twinkling. "It's good to see you, lad."

"You, too, sir."

"I had no idea you were planning a trip to our side of the world. You should have sent word, so I could have made arrangements to meet you. Do you need a place to stay?"

"No, sir, that's taken care of."

"Excellent." He turned to address the women in the room. "Ladies, excuse my interruption."

"Not at all, my lord," Lady Blythe said. "It's always a pleasure to see you."

"An equal pleasure to have you in our home." He gave his attention to his stepdaughter. "Lauren, please notify Cook that we'll have a guest for dinner. You will stay for dinner, won't you, Tom?"

"Yes, sir."

"Splendid." He clapped Tom on the arm. "Join me in the library, so we can talk for a bit and have some refreshment. I want to hear about all your adventures, and I want a firsthand accounting of how my brother and his friends are doing in that hellish place you call Texas. Letters leave much unsaid."

Tom nodded to the women. "Ladies, it was my pleasure to make your acquaintance."

Lady Blythe looked as though he'd issued her a personal compliment, her smile wide, her eyes back to blinking quickly.

Tom tipped his head slightly toward the girl who had left him behind. "Lauren."

Then he followed the earl out of the room, wondering how Lauren truly felt about his staying for dinner.

"You simply must tell us everything!"

"However did you meet him?"

"Who is he exactly? If he's not the earl . . ."

"Are all cowboys so handsome?"

"Is it possible he's Sachse? He didn't exactly deny it."

"Well, he didn't confirm it either."

"He was so intriguing. Regardless of who he is, we must see that he is invited to an upcoming ball."

"I daresay I shall speak with my mother post-haste about the possibility . . ."

Lauren was dizzy with the circle of comments and questions, could barely take in who was saying what. They didn't seem to be truly seeking answers, until Lady Blythe pointedly asked, "Lauren, you obviously have a history with this man. How did it feel to see him again?"

Suffocating silence suddenly dropped down on her, and Lauren couldn't tell them the truth. He did what he'd always done: confused her, excited her, infuriated her. All these years, she thought she'd gotten over him, thought she'd forgotten about him as easily as he'd forgotten about her. All it had taken was seeing him again to stir the memories and unwanted emotions back to life. How could she possibly answer their questions?

She'd risen to her feet when her stepfather had made his appearance. Now she turned her attention away from the door and finally faced her guests, hoping that she successfully masked all the emotions reeling through her. She'd had years to practice for this moment.

"Ladies, I don't wish to be an ungracious hostess, but the company is unexpected, my mother is out shopping, and I must see to the plans for the evening in her stead. I beg your forgiveness, but I must ask you to take your leave."

The ladies quickly stood.

"Of course," Lady Blythe said. "We understand,

but please, do tell us . . . what is this mysterious debt that he has come to collect?"

"A coin," Lauren hastily answered, wanting to halt the direction of the conversation, and if at all possible get these women out of the house quickly. "I owe him a coin."

"He came all this way to collect a coin?"

She forced herself to smile. "I know it seems rather ridiculous—"

"I find it intriguing. I daresay that his presence shall make the Season most interesting," Lady Blythe said.

Oh, dear Lord, surely Tom won't be here long enough to become embroiled in the Season. Though if he were searching for a wife, she doubted he'd find a better marriage market on earth than the one that was about to take place in London. She quite suddenly didn't want to contemplate the scenario of his hunting for a wife.

"Ladies, please, you must excuse me. I'll have Simpson see you out."

Hurrying across the marble-floored hallway, she caught the butler's attention. "Simpson, please have the ladies escorted to their carriages, while I inform Cook we are having an unanticipated guest for dinner."

Trusting him completely to see to her orders, she didn't wait for his acknowledgment but walked in a daze through the various familiar rooms, explaining to different servants that adjustments needed to be made for the evening meal. When she was sure that everything would be handled to what she was certain would be her stepfather's high expectations, she gathered up what little courage remained to her in order once again to face her past.

She walked down the hallway to the library, a room she'd always found comforting, a place where the family had spent many a night reading. It was the one room that reminded her of Texas, because her mother had always read to them in the evenings when they'd lived in Fortune. She'd continued enjoying the practice, but she had many more books from which to choose. But then Ravenleigh always had so much more of everything. It was one of the reasons her mother had never been able to understand Lauren's discontent.

Taking a deep breath to calm her frenzied nerves, Lauren strolled into the library. She thought she should have found the pleasant memories associated with this grand room comforting, but everything faded into insignificance with Tom's overpowering presence. How could he take up so much space, when he was doing little more than sitting in a leather chair opposite her stepfather, both men holding a glass of amber liquid? Whiskey, no doubt. Liquid courage. Lauren could have used a good swallow of some courage herself at that precise moment.

Setting the glasses aside on the small, round

marble-topped tables beside each chair, the men stood. The walls and ceiling seemed to swirl, move out and move in, until she was disoriented, uncertain, afraid that she might actually swoon. She could hardly wrap her mind around the reality that he was there.

He was there. Tom. Tom, who'd promised to write and never had. Tom, who'd promised to come for her and had finally arrived . . .

To collect a debt.

If she wasn't so devastatingly disappointed, she'd be infuriatingly angry. Although in total honesty what could she have said if he had told her that he'd come for her? She saw shadows of the boy he'd been, but could she truly say she knew this man well enough to traipse halfway around the world with him?

He'd grown taller, broader, but it wasn't the physical changes that she found so disconcerting. It was the confident aura that surrounded him, a man who had been shaped by the fires of hell into uncompromising steel. She didn't need to know the path of his past in order to recognize the results of his journey.

"I'm sorry to interrupt," she finally managed, wading through the incessant questions and doubts that plagued her.

"Nonsense," her stepfather said. "Tom was just sharing some fascinating news. Please join us."

As though in a fog, she walked over to her stepfather and sat in the chair beside his, facing Tom. He *wasn't* the boy she'd left behind in Texas. His attentions back then, while scandalous, had still held a certain measure of innocence. She didn't think this man, with the deep creases in his face, carved by sun, wind, and hard work, and the sharp edge in his eyes, held any innocence at all. Yet he was still her Tom. Whatever it was that had first drawn her to him was still there, perhaps not quite as obvious, but she sensed that it was still a part of him. That for all the rules he'd broken and the scandalous behaviors, he possessed an undeniable goodness deep down inside where it mattered the most.

"What's the fascinating news you were sharing?" she finally asked.

Tom looked to her stepfather as though he expected him to announce it, whatever *it* was, as though it was too difficult for him to speak again. Dread began to creep through her. What could have possibly happened to cause such hesitation?

When her stepfather did nothing more than study them as though slowly coming to a realization that he may have missed something important along the way, Tom—looking incredibly uncomfortable—leaned forward and planted his elbows on his thighs. It was a posture so typical of Tom, that it caused an unexpected ache in Lauren's heart.

He rubbed his hands together as though he

thought he could conjure up the words like some magician, then clasping his hands so forcibly they made an audible clap, he unflinchingly held her gaze. "That lady in the drawing room guessed right."

"That you're a cowboy? That's not a very difficult guess to make. One doesn't even have to look closely—"

"No," he said cutting her off, grimacing. "The other. That I'm the Earl of Sachse."

She heard the words, but they made no sense. Oh, she understood what they meant, the meaning was clear enough, but that they were coming from Tom . . . more importantly that they *applied* to Tom . . .

She shook her head. "You're the Earl of Sachse?"

He nodded slowly. "Yes, ma'am."

She thought of the ladies in her drawing room and their interest in the new earl. She considered the compassion and empathy she'd felt for him, not realizing he was a man she knew . . . or at least a man she'd known when he was very young.

Lauren stared at him, this man she'd carried into her dreams since she was fourteen. No, it wasn't he whom she'd carried. She'd carried a sixteen-year-old youth. Did she even know this man? Had she simply imagined that a part of him remained the same?

Overwhelming disappointment slammed into

her as the true reason for his arrival hit her square
in the chest. She hadn't been a deciding factor in
his decision to come to England, hadn't been any
factor at all. He hadn't come for her. He hadn't
even truly come to unbutton her bodice. He'd
come to England because he had obligations. Because he was a damned earl!

She was merely an afterthought, if even that.
Whatever desperate hope she'd held on to that he
would one day again be hers burst into a confla-
gration, leaving her with nothing except scorched
ashes.

"You're Lord Sachse?" she clarified again, her
voice raspy and dry.

Tom slowly nodded.

"Why didn't you acknowledge it when Lady
Blythe—"

"Because you were so sure I wasn't, and it was
the easier path. I didn't want to get into explaining
my present circumstance with an audience of
strangers listening."

"Your present circumstance? You say that as
though you're expecting it to change."

"I'm aware that it won't. But that doesn't mean I
didn't wish it would."

"So that's the reason you're here. To claim your
title." She was incredibly proud of herself for keeping her voice even, for not revealing even a hint of
the devastation she was feeling with the painful
realization that he hadn't come for her. After all

this time, she'd been unrealistic to think he would.

"The reason I'm in *England*." He left unsaid, but the look in his eyes communicated clearly, that it wasn't the reason he was now *there*, at Ravenleigh's house. He was there to claim a debt that no reasonable man would expect a woman to pay.

She glared at him, hoping to signal her displeasure at his boldness. He hitched up a corner of his mouth in familiar challenge. Why did everything about him have to seem familiar, yet foreign at the same time? Why couldn't she simply forget about the history that not only joined but separated them?

"You told me your parents were dead," she reminded him.

"I thought the folks I was living with were my parents. They never gave any indication that matters were different. The past few months have . . . unraveled everything I believed." He shook his head. "I have no recollection of my life here, in this country, of my true mother and father. I stare at my mother's portrait . . . I want to remember her, but I can't."

She couldn't imagine not having any memories of her parents. Her recollections of her true father were vague. She'd been so young when he'd marched off to war, but she did have memories of him, frayed with time, but still there.

"I'm sorry that your life has been turned

around," she heard herself say, her sympathy true. She was only too familiar with the awful reality of suddenly living a life that was so very different from what one was accustomed to, to what one expected. "I can't imagine how difficult it is suddenly to have all these responsibilities thrust on you."

"The responsibilities don't bother me. I'm used to handling more than my share there. It's just the finding out that I belong to a life I'd never given any thought to that's not to my liking. I considered ignoring the summons, but as the investigator explained it to me, I had no choice in the matter. Whether I wanted it or not, everything waiting over here for me was mine."

"The law is quite clear in that regard," her stepfather said. "One can't turn away from one's responsibilities toward a title."

"So you're stuck here, in England," she said.

"You say that like it's a bad thing," Tom said.

"Lauren's never been happy here," her stepfather said.

Astonished by his comment, she looked at him.

"Don't look so surprised," he said quietly. "It's my single regret: that I was unable to bring you the happiness you deserve."

Her emotions still raw from the reality of Tom's arrival, her stepfather's heartfelt words caused tears to sting her eyes. She desperately wanted to acknowledge the comfort, the love, the acceptance that he'd always given her. She shook her head. "You can't blame yourself. There's nothing you could have done differently. I simply wasn't meant for this life."

"But you adjusted, you learned, and while you might not have been happy, you did succeed in mastering all the intricacies of our life. Tom is in need of someone to teach him all the English *trappings*, as he's referring to them. We were discussing the possibility of you tutoring him."

"What about Lady Sachse? The old earl's widow," Lauren said. "She did an exemplary job teaching Archibald Warner."

"And fell in love with my cousin during the process," Tom said. "She recently married him."

"I didn't know."

"The ceremony didn't take place in London. She left all this behind, without looking back."

A woman who had achieved what Lauren had only dreamed about: leaving all this behind and never looking back. She suddenly felt a kinship with the woman. The way Lady Sachse had waltzed through London, Lauren had never guessed that she wasn't happy with the life she led. How many other ladies weren't?

"You might talk to my cousin Lydia. She's the Duchess of Harrington now, and she absolutely adores the rules. She's even published a book on the subject of manners. *Blunders in Behavior Corrected*. It's apparently quite popular among the

American heiresses who are looking to fit into London society. You can purchase it at any bookshop."

"I've never been one for reading. I prefer being shown. I'd rather you be the one doing the showing."

"I'm afraid that my present schedule gives me very little time," she said.

"I wouldn't need much," he said.

She smiled sadly. "You have no idea, Tom. There are so many rules, so many things to learn. It would take months, and I don't have months to give."

"What's so important that it can't wait?"

"For some time now, I've been making plans to return to Texas."

Chapter 4

L auren's announcement hit Tom like a solid punch to the gut that would have caused him to stagger if he'd been standing. He wasn't prepared to have her exiting his life so soon after he'd walked back into hers.

Ravenleigh looked equally startled, but before he or Tom could question Lauren further, joyous laughter echoed outside the room just before the door opened and three women—smiling brightly, obviously happy—traipsed in.

Joining Ravenleigh as he came to his feet, Tom thought the older woman was Lauren's mother, but she in no way resembled the harsh woman whom he'd avoided at all costs back in Fortune, a woman he'd never seen smile. The two ladies accompanying her had to be Lauren's sisters. He had a vague recollection of them, but even without that memory, he would have recognized the strong family resemblance: blond hair, blue eyes, and delicate features. Her sisters had grown into beauties, but they still paled in comparison to Lauren. He recognized that all women always would because they always had.

"I take it you had a successful outing," Ravenleigh said.

"Yes, indeed," one of the younger ladies acknowledged, her blue gaze shifting to Tom with obvious interest.

"You remember Tom, Mama," Lauren said.

For the briefest moment, he thought he saw fear reflected in her mother's blue eyes, just before she angled her chin defiantly, a gesture that Lauren had long ago begun to emulate. "Yes, of course. What in the world brings you to London?"

She surprised Tom by speaking with a refinement that she hadn't before, not quite British, but almost. He wondered if a day would come when he'd sound as foreign to himself as everyone around him did now.

"He's come to claim his title," Lauren said, before Tom could respond. "He's Lord Sachse."

Her mother looked at Tom as though he'd suddenly sprouted a set of horns. He shifted his stance, wishing he didn't feel so incredibly uncomfortable under her scrutiny. The woman had always had a knack for making him feel as though he was doing something he shouldn't. Usually because he had been.

"Well, isn't this a surprise," her mother finally said, tonelessly.

"I daresay that's an understatement," one of her sisters announced. "You're the talk of the town. Everywhere we went today, people wanted to know if we knew the new Earl of Sachse." She laughed lightly. "We had no idea that indeed we did."

"You might feel as though you know him," her other sister said, "but I must confess that I have hardly any memory of him. I'm sorry, my lord." She curtsied. "I'm Amy in case your recollection of me is as vague as mine of you."

Tom bowed his head slightly, acknowledging— and he hoped—appearing refined at the same time. "I remember you."

Lauren's other sister gave him a coy look. "And me, my lord. Samantha. Do you remember me as well?"

"Yes, ma'am, but you don't have to call me 'my lord.' "

Samantha smiled warmly. "I'm afraid we do. It's one of the rules you see. Rule number three, I believe."

"The rules are numbered?" he asked incredulously.

"She's teasing," Amy said. "There are so many

rules that Lauren took to numbering them shortly after we arrived here. I think she got to number thirty-five before she declared it a hopeless task and stopped."

"Did you know you were an earl when we knew you?" Samantha asked.

"No."

"You must tell us everything. We shall, no doubt, be the envy of the Set."

Tom despised revealing his ignorance, but he figured it was less embarrassing to display it among folks who'd known him in Texas than around those who hadn't. "The Set?"

"My apologies, *my lord.* I'd forgotten how strange everything can seem at first. The Set. The Marlborough House Set. Fashionable people with whom the Prince of Wales keeps company. Marlborough House is his London residence, of course, and hence responsible for the name associated with those with whom the prince is intimate. They love gossip. And now that we know who you are"—she gave him an impish smile—"I suspect we shall be even more sought out for any juicy tidbits we can provide."

He wasn't at all sure that he liked the sound of that possibility. He hadn't been there long, but he'd already figured out that he was fodder for gossip.

"I would think the last thing this family would need is more gossip," their mother said.

"That's the point, Mama," Samantha said. "The gossip won't revolve around us any longer—"

"Spreading gossip often backfires, Samantha," her mother said, her gaze darting between Tom and Lauren, as though she feared the gossip might run closer to home than she wanted. "We need to prepare for dinner."

"I've invited Tom to join us," Ravenleigh said.

It was strange that Lauren's mother suddenly looked defeated. She gave Tom what he was certain was a forced smile. "Yes, of course. We'll be delighted to have you. Come along, girls, we need to prepare ourselves."

It didn't escape his attention that unlike her daughters, she wasn't prone to refer to him as my lord. He suspected she still viewed him as the callow youth she'd known in Texas.

As her mother ushered all her daughters out of the room, Lauren gave Tom a parting glance, similar to the ones she'd given him on the street in Fortune. He supposed some things never changed. A mother issuing orders was always a mother to be obeyed.

"Let's finish our drinks, shall we?" Ravenleigh suggested.

Nodding, Tom sat in the chair, took his glass, and sipped on the whiskey that Ravenleigh's brother had sent him from Texas. It was good to taste the familiar when everything else around him was far too foreign. He leaned forward, elbows on his knees, holding the glass in his hands, studying the amber liquid. "You seemed surprised by Lauren's announcement that she was making plans to return to Texas."

"Quite."

Tom lifted his gaze, hoping the man might be a bit more forthcoming.

"I'm sorry, Tom"—Ravenleigh shook his head— "Sachse. I can't elaborate, as I have no idea how she's planning to accomplish this feat."

Tom nodded, wondering if he might get a chance to talk with Lauren alone before he left. How long had she been planning to return to Texas? What exactly was it that she'd missed? Obviously it wasn't him if she was still planning to return now that he was in England.

"Do you see much of my brother these days?" Ravenleigh asked, effectively steering their conversation off the path that Tom would have preferred it stay on.

Kit Montgomery was becoming a legend, his daring exploits and pursuit of justice rivaled by few. Once the marshal of Fortune, he remained a partner in the various Texas Lady ventures and a man for whom Tom had a great deal of respect.

"I don't see him much since he became a Texas Ranger and moved to the western part of the state," Tom admitted.

"He thought the drier climate might help his wife's health improve," Ravenleigh said. "I suppose it has."

"All I really know are the rumors floating

around. Montgomery is getting quite a reputation as a lawman. I hear they're writing another book about him."

Ravenleigh chuckled. "It seems an odd twist of fate for a man who was sent to Texas because of the scandals he created here at home. My brother and his friends have done remarkably well for themselves."

"I can't argue with that."

Ravenleigh studied him for a minute. "Kit and his friends kept me apprised of your various accomplishments. You've done extremely well for yourself by all accounts."

Tom nodded, gazed back at his glass. "Considering the odd journey my life has taken. I'm comfortable in Texas. I can't say the same for this stretch of the world."

"You'll adapt and grow accustomed to it. I have no doubt about that."

"You gave me a leg up when I needed it. I owe you for that."

"Yes, well, I owe you for my present family. If not for your misconduct, I might have never met my Elizabeth."

Tom peered up at him. "She's changed considerably since I knew her."

Ravenleigh appeared somber. "They all have, Tom. Adjusting to my way of life was much harder on them than I anticipated it would be. I fully expected Lauren to be more sympathetic with your present plight, but it appears she has her own plans to see to. Samantha might be willing to assist you in learning your way around a ballroom."

Only Tom didn't want Samantha helping him. He wanted Lauren, wanted an opportunity to get to know her again, to know the woman she'd become, wanted her to get to know him, the man he'd become. Wanted to see if he could change her mind about remaining in England—at least for a time.

"I haven't totally given up on Lauren helping me."

Ravenleigh nodded sagely as though he understood the undercurrent of emotion in Tom's voice. "It appears I may have not understood fully what it cost Lauren to move here."

"What it cost us both," Tom said quietly.

"Do you know what they're saying about Tom?" Samantha asked.

"That he's devilishly handsome, frightfully uncivilized, and incredibly wealthy," Lauren said, looking her gowns over, wondering why she cared so much what she wore to dinner, why she felt an almost uncontrollable need to make a favorable impression on Tom. Tom. The Earl of Sachse. She could hardly wrap her mind around that fact. "Lady Blythe and friends dropped by this afternoon to see what I could reveal about the new lord."

"Were they here when he arrived?"

"Yes."

"And?"

She glanced over her shoulder to look at Samantha, who was sitting on her bed with an expectant gleam in her eyes. "And what?"

"What happened?"

"What do you think happened? He was wearing trousers, which was enough to make Lady Blythe begin acting silly."

"Did Lady Cassandra demonstrate one of her infamous swoons?"

"No, thankfully."

"Is Lady Blythe going to set her sights on Tom, do you think?"

"I don't know. I didn't realize he was Sachse until after they left. Had she known that, I have little doubt that she would have made far more obvious advances than she did."

"How do you feel about that?"

"About what?"

"Oh, Lauren, don't be so difficult, echoing my every question. You can't deny that you've always held out a smidgen of hope that he'd come for you. You've turned away every lord who has asked for your hand. You either did that because you were waiting for Tom or because you had no wish to marry a lord."

A little bit of both, perhaps, Lauren thought as she moved away from the wardrobe and stretched out on the fainting couch near the foot of her bed. Her headache was returning with a vengeance. Perhaps she'd stay upstairs for the evening. She certainly had no desire to suffer through her sister's inquisition, and she had little doubt that once Samantha had taken a turn with her, Amy would be bounding in to ask questions. Or perhaps not. She seemed not to remember Texas nearly as well as her two older sisters.

"Do you love him?" Samantha asked.

She scowled at her sister. "I don't know him, not really. I see a man who was once a boy whom I liked, but that's hardly enough to make any sort of judgment regarding my feelings."

Samantha popped off the bed. "Let me know when you decide. He has all the qualifications I want in a husband, and if you're not interested . . ."

"What qualifications?"

"Good looks, charm, money, and a title."

"That's incredibly shallow. The looks will fade with the years, the money will diminish over time—"

"But the charm and the title will last forever."

Lauren stood. "You're baiting me. Surely you would want to know more than that about a man before you married him."

"Think what you will," Samantha said as she opened the door. "But unlike you, dear sister, I'm not opposed to marrying a lord."

Lauren watched her sister exit the room, her

parting words echoing around her. Was Samantha really taking an interest in Tom? And if she was, what did Lauren care?

Unfortunately, she was afraid that she might discover that she cared a great deal.

Lauren's mother had given Ravenleigh two daughters, Joy and Christine. Joy was nine, Christine six. Fair of complexion, they'd inherited their father's light blue eyes. They were too young to join the adults for dinner, but they'd come to the library to meet the new earl and had quite effectively charmed Tom. They already seemed like miniature adults. He imagined in a few years they'd be wrapping young men around their little fingers.

A short while later, after the girls had returned upstairs and when Ravenleigh excused himself in order to determine what was keeping the ladies from joining them, Tom took the opportunity to step out onto the veranda. Twilight was moving on, darkness was easing in, but with the help of the gaslights along the pebbled path, he could still make out the elaborate gardens. The lingering scent of roses wafted around him. He wondered if he'd be expected to learn the names of the various flowers and plants that seemed to fill every garden and park that he visited. These people seemed to love their gardens.

He shook his head. *These* people, whether it felt right or not, were *his* people.

Removing a cigar from the inside pocket of his jacket, he wondered if he wouldn't be better off excusing himself from dinner. He wasn't exactly dressed for a fancy feast, and the one thing he'd learned while enjoying meals with his father's second wife was that every meal was fancy, and a man was expected to be buttoned up good and proper. Tom wasn't wearing a waistcoat or an expensively tailored jacket—the tailor he'd hired had promised to make good on the delivery of those items within the next few days—and so Tom knew he didn't look like any English gentleman he'd met so far, and he was feeling out of his element. Lauren's mother would probably hold his inappropriate attire against him, and he found himself wondering why her opinion mattered to him so much.

Maybe because she'd successfully transformed herself into a proper English lady, while he had yet to become the proper English gentleman. Not that his assessment of her transformation was truly fair. His encounters with her years ago had always taken place when she was at her angriest, and, in retrospect, he didn't blame her for her reactions to his pitiful, inexperienced, and utterly inappropriate attempts at flirting with her oldest daughter.

Not that he'd behaved any better that afternoon. His reunion with Lauren might have gone more successfully if he'd paved the way with a bit more finesse and not brought up the debt, a silly reminder of their childhood that he didn't truly expect her to pay; but it served to keep her riled, and he'd always enjoyed watching the way a spark of anger could deepen the blue of her eyes. He'd often wondered if passion would do the same, but she'd left before he'd had the opportunity to find out.

He was still enjoying the flavor of his cigar when he heard the light footfalls, and instinctively knew to whom they belonged. He'd sensed her standing just beyond the shadows, watching him. He inhaled deeply, absorbing not only the rich aroma of the cigar but the fragrance of the flowery perfume wafting toward him. Underneath it all was the scent of *her*, like good whiskey, once experienced, never forgotten. He blew out the smoke he'd been holding in his lungs and waited, unmoving, until the feathery gray wisps disappeared into the night. Doing nothing more than extending the cigar slightly to the side, he asked, "Want to give it a try?"

"You always were a creature of bad habits, Tom."

"That's not an answer, Lauren. I've got a fresh one in my jacket pocket if you'd rather have it."

She sighed with obvious impatience. "Proper ladies don't smoke."

"Proper ladies don't drink or cuss. That never stopped you before."

"I was a child then," she said. "You were always

corrupting me, and I was silly enough to let you do it. I'm not a child any longer."

"That much is obvious, Lauren."

She moved up until he could see her profile out of the corner of his eye. Limned by the glow of the gaslights, she looked incredibly lovely. She had changed into a blue-gray dress, square at the neck, trimmed in lace. He thought with more light, it would enhance the shade of her eyes. She'd altered the style of her hair as well. With the curls and ribbons slightly different, her hair remained piled on top of her head as it had been earlier, leaving her long, slender neck exposed to his inspection—and he wished available to his mouth as well. The English went to a lot of trouble to prepare themselves simply to eat an ordinary evening meal.

"You had absolutely no idea that all this was over here waiting for you?" she finally asked quietly.

He took a slow drag on his cigar, released the smoke from his lungs. "Nope."

"It must have been rather a shock—"

"That's an understatement," he said.

"You said you don't remember any of it."

"I don't."

"Your mother must have loved you—"

"Or not loved me at all."

"Oh, Tom, don't think that."

"She left me, Lauren. What am I supposed to think?"

He considered pointing out that Lauren had left him, too, but he didn't see the point in harping on it. Besides, his mother was gone, Lauren wasn't. His mother had been given a choice. Lauren hadn't.

"I didn't know your father," she said, "but his cruelty was legendary. I think your mother wanted to spare you suffering what he was capable of inflicting."

"I can think of better ways to do it."

"She had no way of knowing you'd be orphaned, or that her letter explaining what she'd done would be left with someone who couldn't read. It took a great deal of courage for Lady Sachse to admit she was once illiterate . . . and it will take a great deal of courage for you to accept this burden that's been thrust upon you."

He shook his head. "It takes courage to face a cattle stampede. Coming here is just an inconvenience."

"In a few months, you might feel differently about what defines courage."

He couldn't see that it took much courage to attend balls, dinners, and operas. Of course, tonight's dinner would be the first one he would have with company other than the previous Lady Sachse, and her mind had been more centered on Archibald Warner than correcting Tom for his lack of proper manners. Not that he thought his manners were too atrocious. He'd had occasion to dine with businessmen and bankers and cattlemen. Working the cattle empire that was part of the Texas Lady Ventures had also exposed him to the sons of Englishmen. Their polished mannerisms had always appealed to him, and he'd worked hard to emulate them—to appear in control even when he wasn't. While he didn't think matters could get to the point that he'd have to show any sort of bravery, he didn't want to be uncomfortable in his new surroundings. It was evident that all the Texas ladies had worked hard to put away their Texas ways.

"I've got a proposition for you," he said, deciding he might be able to get what he wanted by sweetening the offer.

"I've had one of those from you before, Tom. I'm not interested."

"You haven't even heard it yet."

"You're wasting your breath."

"It's mine to waste. Teach me what I don't know, Lauren. I'll release you from the debt."

She released a taut self-deprecating laugh. "The debt? You can't possibly seriously think that I'm going to let you unbutton my bodice."

"Either that or give me back my two bits."

She scoffed. "Where do you think I'm going to find a quarter, in *this* country, after all these years?"

"That's your problem, darlin', but I aim to collect what you owe me, one way or another."

He could see her bristling over his daring declaration. Well, he'd done his own bristling over the years. And even though he knew hers was most likely one debt he'd never collect, he could still hold out hope.

"Surely by now, you've unbuttoned a bodice and had your curiosity satisfied," she said.

He'd unbuttoned his fair share, but he'd never found the experience completely satisfying. He took a puff on his cigar, deciding she didn't really want her question answered.

"Are you ignoring me?" she asked.

He turned then, facing her, holding her shadowy gaze, trying to figure out exactly what it was he was seeing: fear, disgust, disappointment? He'd had the unrealistic hope that his arrival would have brought her some measure of joy, that she'd share with him some satisfactory explanation for her silence all these years.

"I could never ignore you, Lauren."

"You did a good imitation for ten years."

"The hell you say!" His voice rumbled into the night, and he realized he'd tossed his cigar aside and taken a threatening step toward her only when she took a quick step back, her eyes widening and her breath coming in quick little hitches. A gentleman would have retreated, would have given her room, but he'd heard the rumors floating around, knew he was thought to be a savage, and at that moment he felt exactly like what they were claiming he was.

"I wrote you every night," he said, his rage controlled but seething. "Just like I promised. Every night the first two years you were gone. The third year, I wrote you every week. Then every month. I couldn't always mail them as soon as they were written because sometimes towns were few and far between when we were trailing cattle, but when I got near enough to a town I took them to the post office. I wrote you, Lauren."

She was shaking her head, shock evident in her eyes. "I never got them, Tom. Not a single one."

"I wrote them," he repeated, his anger dissipating as he began to realize the true reason behind her silence all these years.

"When did you stop writing them?" she asked.

"Never did stop completely. But I did stop mailing them." Lord, but he wanted to touch her.

"You're a thief, Tom. And you cuss. And you lie—"

Against his better judgment, he reached out, cupped her cheek, and pressed his thumb against her moist lips. "Never to you, Lauren. I never lied to you."

Tears welled in her eyes. "Why didn't I get them?"

He shook his head. "I don't know, darlin'."

"I looked every morning. It was years before I gave up. And even when I never heard from you, I kept hoping that you'd come for me. I hung on to that hope because sometimes it was the only thing that would get me through the day. You can't possibly begin to imagine how miserable I've been here, Tom, how much I missed the life we left behind."

Sometimes a man couldn't find any words powerful enough to take the tears from a woman's eyes. And so Tom didn't even bother to try.

He cradled her precious face between his hands, relishing the silkiness of her skin against his fingertips, doing what he'd wanted to do that afternoon, touch her with tenderness, experience again the softness that had all too often been denied him in his life. The path he'd trudged to this spot hadn't been an easy one, and he couldn't help but think that it wasn't going to get any easier, despite his earlier words of bravado. But for this moment he didn't want to think about all the challenges that awaited him.

He focused all his attention on Lauren.

The blue of her eyes lost in the shadows, the determined angle of her chin, her pert little nose. In some ways everything about her appearance was foreign to him, and in other ways it was achingly familiar.

As her eyes slowly slid closed, he lowered his mouth to hers. She tasted just as he remembered, and he knew a pang of regret so sharp that it took all his inner strength not to double over. The girl he'd longed for all these years had grown into a woman who could stir a man's passions with nothing more than her blue-eyed gaze focused on him. She smelled like flowers in the spring and was as warm as the sun-touched earth. He wanted to lift her into his arms and carry her farther out into the garden, where privacy could allow them to finish what they'd begun so long ago.

But it wasn't finishing that he truly wanted. It was starting again, and he didn't know where to begin. This lady with the occasional faint drawl, the perfect manners, the graceful walk, the poise, the charm, the knowledge to fit perfectly into this society was a direct contrast to Tom, who was still rough enough around the edges that he was in danger of damaging the reputation of any who came too close to him.

Once he'd loved her as much as a sixteen-year-old boy could love. He couldn't honestly say that he still loved her, if what he felt for her was true affection or merely phantom sensations stirred up from a time long past. The ground beneath his feet seemed as unsteady as it did when a stampede hit. He'd come there not knowing what to expect, and the only thing he knew for sure was that he felt more lost then he'd ever felt in his entire life. And, unfortunately, he'd only recently learned that all his life he'd been lost; he just hadn't realized it. Until the investigator had shown up at his door, Tom had never comprehended what a lie he'd been living. For all he knew, his time with Lauren had been false as well.

He'd thought of her every moment of every night of every year that they'd been separated. He'd taken her into his dreams, held on to her memory. As a fully grown woman—and she was fully grown now, no doubts there—she didn't look that much different than he'd expected she would. A little more round, a little more refined. She would have made a nice addition to the house he'd built—the house he'd built with her in mind on the acres of land that he'd bought near Fortune.

How ironic that she'd been waiting for him to come to take her back to Texas, and he'd been planning a homecoming for her. He'd always held out hope that somehow his letters hadn't gotten here or somehow hers to him had been lost. But he'd never given up on them completely . . . at least not yet. Not until destiny altered his path, changed his final destination.

Not until he tasted the sweet nectar of her mouth seasoned with the salt from her tears. She'd been miserable in England. What man would condemn the woman who'd once held his heart to a life of misery?

Chapter 5

Ten years earlier

Lauren could hardly believe that she was lying with a boy. Lying with Tom. On the cool, green grass beside the creek. In the dark. If it weren't for the full moon, she wouldn't be able to see him at all.

She was wearing her nightclothes, but she figured they covered her as much as her dress would. Tom, as always, was in his trousers and shirt. He'd started wearing a vest for carrying around his cigarette makings. She knew they were there, because she could see the bulge in his pocket, but he never smoked around her anymore.

He always came late at night, after her mama had gone to bed. He'd toss rocks at her window until she got up, clambered out the window from her upstairs bedroom, and climbed down the tree to meet him. Then they'd run to the creek and just lie there, talking about everything and nothing. She kept waiting for Tom to ask her to unbutton her buttons. But he never did.

It made her love him more for wanting to be with her while she was still all buttoned up.

"There," he suddenly said, pointing at the sky. "Did you see it?"

"Yeah." He was good at looking in the right spot and seeing them before they disappeared. "What do you think makes the stars fall like that?"

"I don't know. It's one of those things that can't be explained, I reckon."

"Where do you think they fall to?"

"I don't know. Maybe just another place in the sky, so folks down below can see 'em."

"Ma says if you make a wish when the star is falling, it'll come true."

"I don't believe in wishing."

She sat up and looked down on him. His hands were folded beneath his head, his long body stretched out over the ground. He'd only been working for the Texas Lady a little over a week, but he seemed so much bigger. She figured the work and the food were responsible. He wasn't living on stolen crackers anymore.

"That's sad, Tom, not to believe in wishing. A person ought to want some things."

"Didn't say I don't believe in *wanting*. I want plenty. I just don't believe wishing will get me the things that I want."

She drew her legs up to her chest, wrapped her arms around them, and pressed her chin to her knees. "But stealing will. Is that what you're saying? You won't wish for something, but you'll steal if you want it?"

"I ain't stole since I went to work. Told you stealing was bad if you did it when you got money. Now I got a bit of money, so I ain't stealing no more."

"I'm glad. I wouldn't want you to go to jail . . . or to hell."

"I ain't worried about hell. I been there already."

"You don't go to hell until you die, and only if you haven't been good."

"I was good, and I went to hell while I was alive."

Reaching out, she touched his elbow. She wanted to touch his chin where a few whiskers had started to grow, but she thought he might object to her actually touching skin, so she settled for the cloth that covered his arm. "On the orphan train?"

"With the family that took me in. Could never please the old man no matter how hard I worked. He'd lock me in a shed at night 'cuz he was afraid I'd run away."

"And you did."

"Yep."

"How'd you escape?" she asked.

"He started beating on me, for no good reason as far as I could tell. Wasn't the first time, but I'd gotten a little bigger and tired of it, too. So I hit back, knocked him down, and I took off running. I was a lot faster than he was. Just kept running till I got here."

"I'm glad you stopped here," she said.

"I wasn't planning to, least not for good. But then I got hired to work cattle." He shrugged. "No reason to move on when I got a full belly and a bed."

She was a little disappointed she wasn't the reason he'd decided to stay. It was wishful thinking, but unlike Tom she did believe in wishing. She looked out over the water of the creek.

He had such exciting adventures, had been everywhere, while she'd never set foot outside of Fortune. She considered telling him that when that star had fallen she'd wished that she'd get to travel to some exciting place, but her mama had also told her that wishes only came true if she kept them to herself; otherwise, she risked breaking the spell that would make them come true.

"You ever kissed a fella?" Tom asked quietly.

She didn't look at him, as she shook her head. "You ever kissed anyone?"

"No."

She heard the rustle of the grass as he sat up. "Been hankering to, though."

She peered over at him, fighting to hold back her smile. The thing about Tom was that he always pretty much said exactly what he was thinking. "Anybody I know?"

His slow lazy grin became visible in the moonlight. "I got something for you."

"What?" she asked, even though she figured she knew what he had for her: a kiss.

He reached behind her, took her braid, and draped it over her shoulder. She wondered why she could feel his touch of her hair clear down to her toes. She dug them into the grass, but it didn't stop them from tingling.

He brought something out of his vest pocket and dangled it in front of her. "A hair ribbon," he said.

"I can't tell the color in the dark."

"Same color as your eyes."

Her heart was pounding hard as he wrapped it around her braid and tied it into an awkward-looking bow.

"Did you steal it?" she asked.

"Nope, it's the first thing I bought with my hard-earned money."

She couldn't stop herself from smiling this time. "Truly?"

"Yep."

"What's the second thing you bought?"

"A penny's worth of licorice, but I don't have any of it left."

"I don't like licorice anyway," she said, fingering the bow. She'd never had a fella give her a present. Tom had to like her something fierce to give her a ribbon. Even the funny-talking Englishman who'd started visiting her mother of late had never given her mother a ribbon.

"Think you might want to try that kiss now?" he asked.

She lifted her gaze to his. "Is that why you bought me a ribbon? So I'd kiss you?"

"Nope. I saw it and thought of you. Even if you don't want to kiss—"

Quickly, she leaned forward, pressed her puckered lips to his, and jerked back. There, she'd done it. Before he could dare her to. He was always daring her: to smoke one of his cigarettes, to drink from not-quite-empty whiskey bottles he found outside the saloon, to meet him there by the creek. Things bound to get her into trouble if her mama ever found out. Kissing was surely the one that would get her a whupping.

She sat there, chewing her bottom lip, waiting for him to react, to say something. Anything.

"Well?" she finally demanded.

"That was like a star shooting across the heavens."

"Is that good or bad?"

"Just means it was quick, gone before I knew it was coming." He cupped her cheek, and she was acutely aware of how rough his skin felt against hers. His fingers and palm were callused in places. A workingman's hands. "Let's try this my way."

"Didn't think you had a way. Didn't think you'd ever done this before," she said.

"Doesn't mean I ain't been thinking about it."

"Who were you thinking—"

"Shh, gal, sometimes you talk too much."

Then his lips, warm and sure, yet gentle, were pressed against hers. And she thought she might love this boy until the day she died.

"Oh, Tom, it's awful! We're leaving!"

Tom stared at Lauren. She'd been in a panic ever since she'd clambered out her bedroom window, shinnied down the old, gnarled oak tree, grabbed his hand, holding on so tight it hurt, and pulled him into the copse of trees.

"Leaving?"

She nodded, the tears in her eyes capturing the moonlight. "That English fella asked Ma to marry him, and she said yes. We're moving to England."

The words stunned him, shook him clear down to his bootheels. She was the best part of living there.

Lunging at him, she wrapped her arms tightly around his neck. "Oh, Tom, I'm never going to see you again."

He wound his arms around her, holding her close, felt the tears on her cheeks, warm at first, cool against his neck. She couldn't be leaving. It was too soon. He didn't have anything to offer her.

She pulled back and looked at him as though she believed he had some sort of power to make everything right. "What are we gonna do?"

He swallowed hard, hating the truth of the words he was gonna have to say. "Lauren, I got nothing to offer you."

"I thought you loved me."

He glanced toward her house.

"I know you never said it, but I just thought—"

"I do," he said, cutting her off. That declaration was as close as he was going to come to stating his feelings on the matter.

"So what are we gonna do?" she asked again.

Hell if he knew. He thought about the fancy clothes that fella wore, the way he talked. As prissy as it sounded, there was an undercurrent of confidence to it, something about it that made a person listen and obey. Commanding, without yelling or beating it into you. He thought if the fella had taken him off the orphan train, Tom would have worked his heart out for him. Maybe that was the reason he was working so hard for the Texas Lady Ventures. Because he didn't want the man to be disappointed or to discover that he'd misjudged Tom's abilities. This Englishman would take good care of Lauren until Tom could come for her.

"I think you ought to go with them." He said it

like she had a choice, when he suspected that she really didn't. If her mama wanted her to go, she was going to be going.

Lauren stared at him, and he could see her struggling with the notion, the truth of his words.

"I'll come for you, Lauren, soon as I can. I promise it won't be long. I'll put all my money toward getting us a place."

In the nights that followed, he thought he'd die from the dread creeping into his gut whenever he thought about her leaving. By the creek, he had her describe what she wanted her house to look like, all the little things she wanted to have. Their last night together, they slept in each other's arms, fully clothed, bathed in moonlight.

At dawn, when he walked her back to the house, she whispered, "I'll miss you so much. Will you write to me?"

"Every day," he promised.

"And when you come for me, we'll be together, forever."

"Forever," he vowed.

Chapter 6

Tom's long-ago promises echoed through Lauren's mind. He'd kept the one, but fate would prevent him from keeping the other. Too many years had passed. What did she truly know about this man? What did he know about her?

Only that he had to stay, and she wanted to go.

Standing on the veranda, near the garden, she had no will to resist, but what woman in her right mind would *want* to resist the tenderness of his kiss. She almost thought she detected an apology. Perhaps it was simply a desire to distract her from her tears. She'd not even realized that they'd trailed down her face until he'd pressed his lips to hers, and the tears pooled and seeped between them, to be lapped up by his questing tongue.

His large hands, roughened from years of hard labor, cradled and stroked her cheeks. Englishmen didn't touch with bare hands. Tom possessed no such qualms, never had. But even in his youth, he'd possessed an undeniable respectfulness, urging her to the brink of scandalous behavior, but never forcing her to cross over.

She told herself that her affection for him was as her mother had always warned her: misguided, misplaced, misinterpreted. It was impossible for a girl to love a boy and for that love to remain steadfast as they each grew into adulthood.

Yet she couldn't deny that Tom still managed to stir her feelings. She thought she'd never grow tired of looking at him, never grow weary of listening to his voice, never seek an excuse not to be kissed or held by him. And even as she thought those things, she realized they were all the surface of the man. She didn't know the road he'd traveled to his success. She didn't know what other men thought of him. Had he earned their respect, their loyalty? Would they follow him wherever he led?

And what women had found their way into his heart over the years?

She'd entertained the notion of marrying Kimburton, had enjoyed his attentions. Surely at least one woman had gained Tom's favor. The pang of envy brought on by the thought was almost more than she could bear. To know his kiss, to know his touch, to know his body.

She'd once thought she'd be willing to trade her soul for the privilege. But trading her soul meant trading her dreams.

His place, his home was now and would forever be in England.

She broke off from the kiss, her knees so weak she could barely stand. His breaths were coming as rapid and harsh as hers. She was confused, lost, unsure of her feelings. She'd adopted anger at him to survive his not writing, and yet he'd written. She'd come to hate him, and now she realized the emotion was unjustified. And yet its remnants lingered, not entirely wiped away by the truth. How did she discard ten years of believing he'd abandoned her? Simply because he had not inflicted the wound didn't mean that it wasn't still there and scarred. Everything she'd believed, understood, accepted was suddenly unraveling just as he'd said his life was.

"Where does this new discovery leave us?" he asked quietly.

"I honestly don't know, Tom. What I've known all these years . . . what I've felt . . . I hardly know how to rearrange what I've understood to be the truth. I'm overwhelmed. I need time to sort through so very much."

He nodded, as though he'd known the answer before she'd spoken it. Or perhaps he simply understood better than she what it was to discover the truth of one's life had been a lie.

"I think it best if I don't stay for dinner," he said, his voice sounding like sand rubbed over rock. "Extend my regrets to your family. I'll show myself out."

Her heart urged her to call out to him, to stop him, but shattered promises kept her mute while the echo of his bootheels faded as her memories never had.

Long after Tom left, Lauren sat on the stone bench in the garden, surrounded by the roses that her mother loved to nurture. This small corner was her mother's one indulgence, her one reminder of the farm life she'd left behind—to work in the garden, rooting around in the soil where the roses grew. Gardeners tended the vast majority of the property, but this one perfect spot was her mother's realm. Lauren had spent many an hour sitting there, finding solace in the beauty her mother created, drawing comfort from the poignant fragrance surrounding her. She would miss this small corner of England when she left, but she still needed to leave and quickly, before she was trapped into once again staying.

Tears burned her eyes. She'd not expected to miss anything about the horrid place. She'd hated it before she'd ever arrived, because it had taken her away from everything that she loved, from so many people she cared about. It had taken her away from Tom. Tom who had promised to come for her . . .

And was there finally only because England had called him to come.

She couldn't deny that a part of her was glad to have seen him, to know he was safe and well. A part of her had even considered accepting his ludicrous proposition to teach him, not so much to get out of unbuttoning her bodice, but simply to have the opportunity to spend a bit of time with him. But she had to protect her heart. It was too vulnerable. She didn't want to place herself in the position of having to leave him again—and she quite simply didn't think she could stay there much longer without losing the final vestiges of herself.

Oh, she had adapted and adjusted and played the role of an aristocrat's stepdaughter, but she'd never felt that she'd shown her true self to these people. She'd wanted to be accepted, and so she'd changed. But then so had her mother and her sisters. They would gather in the quiet of the garden, practicing their enunciation. It was more than replacing the drawl. It was learning the proper words, inflections, style.

When her stepfather had stumbled across them one afternoon, exchanging words they'd heard, trying to decipher their meanings, attempting to use them correctly . . . a look of regret so incredibly profound had crossed his features that Lauren had been certain he would put them all on a ship and send them back to Texas. Instead, he'd hired a series of tutors to teach them diction, etiquette, walking, dancing, riding, dining, piano, singing, painting, and letter writing. No conceivable aspect of their behavior was left unschooled.

Tom wanted her to teach him what he needed to know. The man had no idea what all was involved. It would take months. Dear God, it could take years. He was brash and bold, a man of uncultured habits and wicked temptations.

And a part of her had no desire whatsoever to see him tamed.

Hearing the rustle of skirts, the quiet footsteps of a graceful stride, she wasn't at all surprised when a moment later her mother sat on the bench beside her, and said softly, "I've always enjoyed this section of the garden."

"Me too."

"As have I," her mother corrected gently.

"I'm not in the mood to play English tonight, Mama."

Her mother wrapped her hand around Lauren's where it rested in her lap. "Dinner is ready to be served."

"I'm not hungry."

"Samantha encountered Tom in the foyer. He offered his regrets, but apparently he remembered another pressing engagement and was unable to stay for dinner."

"Apparently."

"You spoke with him before he left?"

"Before he took his leave," she corrected out of habit, the same habit that had made her mother correct her only seconds earlier. Among the Texas ladies of the household, when it came to emulating those with whom Ravenleigh associated, they recognized no hierarchy, simply a heartfelt desire to help each of them fit in.

"Yes," Lauren continued. "I spoke with him."

"Did he say anything of interest?"

She couldn't quite identify the tone of her mother's voice. It was as though she'd expected him to reveal some horrible truth.

"He wants me to teach him to be a gentleman."

"He can hire someone to oversee that task."

"He was seeking to *hire* me. I refused, of course."

Her mother squeezed her hand. "I know it must be difficult to see him again after all these years . . ."

Lauren didn't realize until she reached up and wiped the cool dampness from her cheeks that the tears she'd felt earlier had continued to fall. She swallowed hard. "*Difficult* scarcely defines what I'm feeling. His place is here now, and I don't want mine to be."

She felt her mother's hand twitch.

Twisting around slightly, she studied her mother in the garden's yellowish light. Her transformation from a hardworking cotton farmer into a countess had happened so gradually that Lauren sometimes had difficulty remembering what her mother looked like before they'd left Texas. What she did remember was her mother's insistence that Lauren not spend time with that "incorrigible boy."

Lauren's heart kicked up its beat as realization began to dawn as slowly as the sun easing over the horizon. "Tom told me that he wrote me, Mama. All these years. He wrote me."

Her mother rose to her feet, took several steps forward, crossed her arms over her chest, and gazed out on the darkness.

"You kept his letters from me," Lauren said, with a boldness born of undeniable comprehension.

Her mother turned around. "You were so unhappy—"

"And you thought keeping his letters from me was a way to make me happier?" she asked incredulously, coming to her feet and fisting her hands at her sides, infuriated beyond reason.

"I thought it would make the transition to this new life easier if you didn't have the constant reminders of what was back in Texas."

"That's faulty reasoning if I ever heard it. You didn't keep Lydia's letters from me. Or Gina's." Gina had been one of her dearest friends in Texas. Now she was the Countess of Huntingdon, the wife of Ravenleigh's cousin, Devon Sheridan.

"That was different. I didn't think their letters would serve as continual reminders of what you'd left behind. You weren't sneaking out at night to meet with them."

"You had no right—"

"It's a mother's responsibility to protect her children."

"What did you think you were protecting me from?"

"Heartache. Lauren, I was trying to make the adjustment easier on you."

"Well, you failed miserably."

Even in the darkness, she thought she saw her mother flinch. She immediately regretted the harshness of her words, but she hardly knew what to do with the anger roiling through her. She'd never been so angry, so hurt. Never felt so betrayed. She'd often heard that the path to hell was paved with good intentions. She'd never truly understood what that meant, until that moment. Her mother had led her there—whether intentional or not. Maybe she'd never understood exactly what Tom had meant to Lauren, for surely she'd have not diverted his letters had she known.

"May I please have the letters now?" she asked, with resignation. The damage was done. Lashing out at her mother, whom she'd always respected and loved, wasn't going to undo it.

"I'm sorry, Lauren. I burned them."

Lauren felt as though she'd been struck. "He

says he wrote every day for two years," she said
quietly. "That's over seven hundred letters, Mama.
Did you ever read any of them?"

Her mother slowly shook her head. "No, that
seemed wrong."

"While taking and destroying them didn't seem
wrong to you?"

"It didn't seem *as* wrong because I had a good
reason for doing it."

"You had a reason, but I'm not convinced it was
a *good* one. Didn't you ever feel guilty?"

"Eventually. The boy's perseverance astounded
me, but by the time I discovered he wasn't one to
give up so easily, it was too late. If the letters suddenly started arriving, you might have questioned
what had happened to the others. I thought any
explanation I might have given would have been
inadequate."

"You mean you were afraid that I would hate
you for what you did."

"I was afraid you might have difficulty forgiving me, yes. But regardless of how many he sent,
my reason for taking them remained the same: to
protect you, to keep you from having false hope.
To give you a better life. It's too dark to show you
my hands—"

"I know your hands, Mama, as well as I know
my own. They've comforted me for as long as I
can remember." *And kept Tom's letters from me.*

"They're scarred, still rough and brown after all these years," her mother said, as though Lauren needed to be reminded. "Do you know the mortification I feel every time we dine with guests, ladies who have never had to bend with the strain of picking cotton, who have never lifted anything heavier than a fan? My ugly hands say more about me than *Burke's Peerage* says about them."

"They're not ugly, Mama. They speak to your strength, your determination. They're not something to be embarrassed by. Why would you be ashamed—"

"They're a constant reminder of what life was. I loved your father, Lauren, he was a good man. But the work was hard and the day was long and I was old while I was still young. Your father meant everything to me, and I sometimes wondered how I'd go on after he died. Then I met Christopher Montgomery and fell in love with him—when I never expected to fall in love again. He brought me to a world where my back never ached and my hands never bled. He pampered me and my girls, and I've grown to love the life he's offered me."

Grown to love? No, Lauren, unfortunately, had never experienced that emotion.

"I wanted my girls always to have this life," her mother continued. "I'd always hoped that you would grow to love it as well. Do you remember all the practicing we did, how often we'd laugh at our clumsy attempts to appear educated and refined, the list of elegant-sounding words we memorized—"

Fighting back tears, Lauren turned her head to the side, stared into the darkness that had so reflected her life. Looking away was easier than watching her mother wringing her hands, easier than remembering their loyalty and support for each other as they'd faced a new life.

"All I ever wanted was for you to be happy," her mother said quietly.

Lauren blinked away the tears and swallowed. "That's all I want as well, but I've been so lonely here. I don't belong. I never have. I never will."

"Your stepfather mentioned that you'd announced plans to return to Texas."

Lauren detected sadness in her mother's voice. "Yes." She took a deep breath, knowing the following revelation wasn't going to be well received. "I've been working in a shop, earning a wage, saving so I can pay for my passage back to Texas."

She'd sought the position shortly after Kimburton had delivered his proposal, when she'd realized that she couldn't bring herself to marry him. And if she couldn't marry him, as kind and generous as he was, she would never marry anyone—at least not anyone in England. Texas might be a different matter. She felt more at home there, had more in common with the people. She didn't have to put on airs, could be herself. Could find the happiness that had eluded her in England.

"When could you find time to work with all the volunteering you do at the mission, helping the poor?" her mother asked.

Lauren gave her mother a sad smile, which she wasn't certain she could see in the darkness. "I lied. I wasn't volunteering. It appears deception runs in the family."

Her mother took a step toward her. "You will resign your post tomorrow. Taking a job is beneath you and will cause your stepfather untold embarrassment if word gets out that his stepdaughter is working in a *shop*, of all places. What in the world were you thinking?"

"That I would wither and die if I had to stay here much longer. Ravenleigh is no longer responsible for me, Mama. And neither are you. I love you, but not the life you've given me. I'm going back to Texas; if it kills me to do so, I'm going back. So in a way, I guess you did me a favor. If you'd given me the letters, I might be married to Tom by now—then what choice would I have had except to be the dutiful wife of an earl?"

Having left Ravenleigh's more than an hour ago, Tom now sat in his fancy library, surrounded by objects that had belonged to those who'd come before him. The only things he'd contributed to the room were several bottles of whiskey he'd brought with him from Texas, the latest opened bottle held to his mouth as he gulped the brew.

Lauren's hair had darkened over the years to the rich sheen of golden honey. Tom had wanted to release it from the pins holding it in place and have it pour over his hands. He'd wanted to keep his mouth fastened to hers. He'd wanted to hold her in his arms and never release her.

But she had plans to return to Texas, and apparently it made little difference to her that he would no longer be there when she arrived. How could he compete with what Texas had to offer when he hadn't wanted to leave either?

He hadn't expected Lauren to be waiting for him, but it still disconcerted him to realize that a small part of him had held a measure of hope that she would be. Maybe from the beginning, he'd had unrealistic expectations where she was concerned, which was an odd thing for a man who had lived his life always being realistic about the possibilities and his options.

In the letters he'd written to her, he'd described his plans, his dreams, and Lauren had been part of them all. When she never wrote back, he should have hopped on a boat to find out why she was ignoring him. Not that he'd been in a financial position to go anywhere. He'd spent ten years working hard, saving money, and planning for the day when he could come for her.

He'd had everything in place, had actually been

planning his trip to England when the investigator had found him. And everything he'd been preparing had suddenly seemed to be for nothing. None of it mattered. None of it was going to accomplish anything. He was going to have to leave his cattle business in someone else's capable hands. The house he'd recently built had no one living in it.

His land, his house, his dreams . . . they all belonged to another man, the cowboy he'd thought he was. And now here Tom was, trying desperately to figure out exactly who he truly was, the place in this world that was his by right of birth.

The Earl of Sachse.

He figured he didn't look much like an earl. Didn't act like one either. Not that he was bothered by either of those things. He was used to a man being judged on his character, the strength of his handshake, the integrity of his word. Not his speech, his clothes, or his ability successfully to balance a teacup on his knee.

A man could reek to high heaven, but if he kept his word, he was worth his weight in gold. Dependability. Common sense. Integrity.

He lifted the bottle to his mouth and gulped the amber liquid, relishing it as it burned its way down his throat, warming him from the inside out. He wanted to pack up his things and catch the first steamship out. He couldn't blame Lauren for wanting to do the same.

It was close to being summer, but he had a fire

burning in the fireplace. A chill and dampness saturated the night. He wondered if he'd ever get warm living there, wondered if he'd ever come to love it the way he loved Texas.

Sometimes he thought the cruelest thing his mother had done was to give him a glimpse of a life that he couldn't hold on to forever. He'd reached for dreams not knowing that he'd have to betray them for the duty that was predetermined from the moment he was conceived.

He didn't *need* any of this, but it needed him. They thought the barbaric American didn't understand, but he understood it all too well. He was British by birth, American by upbringing. Something within these walls called out to him. Something beyond them touched him.

He couldn't explain it. To be part of two countries, to love one and to want to love the other. To want to belong and to know that, deep down where it mattered, he didn't. And he probably never would.

Chapter 7

Lauren sat beside her bedroom window, the curtain drawn aside just enough that she could look out onto the fog-shrouded street, see the dim glow of the gas streetlamps. A kerosene lamp—the flame low—on a table beside her bed provided the only light flickering in the room and served well her melancholy. All these years she'd felt abandoned. All these years, Tom had kept his promise.

Would receiving his letters have made any difference at all? Would reading his words have eased her loneliness? Was her unhappiness rooted in leaving Texas or only in leaving him?

She remembered crying herself to sleep so many

nights, missing him so dreadfully; but when his letters never came, she'd begun to shift her thoughts to Texas, to all the things there that she missed. It was a lot easier to yearn for something that could never betray her than continually to risk being hurt by longing for someone who already had.

Only he hadn't. That was the irony behind the entire situation. She had lived the past ten years through the prism of deception.

Looking inward more than outward, she suddenly realized that she was listening intently for the pop of rocks against her windowpane. Tom had always come at night, long after everyone was in bed, and Lauren would crawl out the window and climb down the old gnarled tree . . .

When she'd first come to England, she'd chosen her bedroom in the London residence based on its easy access to a large tree outside, as though she thought some night Tom would be standing outside trying to get her attention, surrounded by shadows and moonbeams, inviting her to join him. She wasn't certain when she'd given up on his coming for her. It was as though one moment she suddenly realized that the hope had vanished, leaving behind a gaping hole of loneliness that she'd despaired of ever being able to fill.

She couldn't help but believe that he'd experienced the same loss. A promise broken not by their hand but another's. It hadn't been fair to either of them.

The click against the windowpane nearly caused her heart to stop. She peered into the street. And there he was. Her cowboy, with his black duster reaching his calves and his hat in his hand. A cowboy in the streets of London.

She parted the curtains a bit more, so he could see that he had her attention, gave a quick wave, extended a finger—that she wasn't certain would be visible to him—to signify that she would be down shortly, closed the curtains, and hurried to her wardrobe where she found a simple dress that required no confining corset. Its loose fit and buttons in the front freed her from needing assistance in putting it on. It was something she'd purchased when she still had the hope that he'd come for her, something she wanted to have on hand so she'd always be set to go the moment he appeared. She'd taken such pains always to be ready, and yet nothing had truly prepared her for his arrival.

She unbraided her hair, brushed it out, then pulled it back, using a broad silk ribbon to hold it in place. She certainly didn't look elegant, but she couldn't help but notice that she did appear as though she was anticipating *something*. Being with Tom. At a scandalous time of night. After so many years. For just a moment to be a young girl without cares.

Opening the door, she peered into the hallway decorated with portraits, plants, and small tables adorned with enough items to keep the maids dusting for the better part of each morning. No one was about though. She rushed quietly along the corridor, down the stairs, grateful to discover that the butler was not standing watch in the entry hallway. Her heart pounding with anticipation, she crossed over to the heavy mahogany door, opened it, stepped outside, and closed it behind her. She tiptoed down the front steps, along the walk, until she reached Tom.

"What are you doing here?" she whispered.

"I was sitting in my stuffy library, drinking my whiskey, and it occurred to me that I could give you a little bit of Texas tonight."

"And just how in the world—Oh!"

Quickly sliding an arm beneath her knees and one at her back, he'd swung her up into his arms.

"Shh!" he ordered, holding her close.

She couldn't stop herself from smiling as she wound her arms securely around his neck and pressed her head to his shoulder. Lord, but he'd gotten considerably stronger over the years. She didn't want to be impressed or flattered by his attentions, but she couldn't seem to help herself.

"What on earth do you think you're doing?" she asked.

"Escorting you to my carriage."

"This isn't the proper way to do it," she chastised, as his long strides ate up the distance.

"I'll let you demonstrate the proper way later. I want to get us on our way before anyone comes out to stop us."

A footman dressed in Sachse livery opened the carriage door as they neared. With a smoothness that made her wonder who he might have practiced this maneuver with, he had her inside the carriage, climbing in behind her as she took her seat. He sat across from her, lost in the shadows, but she could feel his gaze fastened on her. The carriage sprang forward.

"How did you know which room was mine?" she asked, to shatter the silence weaving around them.

"I paid a servant handsomely to tell me."

"It had best have been handsomely. If my stepfather finds out, the poor man will get sacked."

"If it was a man."

He sounded so diabolically clever and pleased with himself.

"Do you have a destination in mind?" she asked.

"Yes."

"Are you going to tell me?"

"I'd rather it be a surprise."

She glanced out the window. "I spoke with my mother after you left. She admitted to taking your letters."

"I'd pretty much figured out that she had."

"She burned them."

She thought she heard him grunt, maybe with regret over the loss of his words that could never be recovered.

"Did you get the letters I wrote you?" It occurred to her that she'd been so stunned to learn that he'd written that she hadn't thought to ask.

"No."

She sighed wistfully. "I guess she took those as well. I used to leave them in a silver bowl in the entryway so a footman could see that they were sent out in the morning mail. It never occurred to me that . . ." She let her voice trail off.

He leaned forward, took her hands. His were rough, callused, not the hands of a gentleman. Would Tom be as embarrassed by what his hands revealed about him as her mother was?

"It doesn't matter, Lauren."

Only it did matter. His words were irretrievably lost to her.

He said nothing further. Maybe he didn't need to. Simply being with her was enough for the moment.

Christopher Montgomery watched his wife's misery with an aching in his heart.

"Come away from the window, Elizabeth."

"You could have stopped her from leaving."

"She's twenty-four, old enough to make her own decisions."

She spun around, tears in her eyes. "You had more than enough time to go down there and confront him."

He smiled slightly. "I believe he was wearing a pistol."

She failed to appreciate his poor attempt at humor. He crossed over to her, wrapped his arms around her, and held her close.

It hurt his heart to see her suffering so. She'd shared her three daughters with him and then blessed him with two more. Unlike most aristocrats, he'd never wanted a son. His twin brother should have been the Earl of Ravenleigh, but that secret was known only to the two of them. With a clear conscience, Christopher would pass the title on to his nephew. But for now, he cared only about comforting the woman he loved beyond all reason.

"If we forbid them to see each other, they will find a way, no matter how badly you wish they wouldn't."

She tilted back her head. "He doesn't understand the rules here. He's going to ruin her."

He wiped a tear from her cheek. "Or he might prove capable of giving her what we never could: happiness."

"But at what cost?"

"Sometimes all we can do is be there to help our children stand back up if they fall."

"And if we're responsible for the fall?"

More tears had gathered in her eyes, far more than he could possibly wipe away.

"Elizabeth—"

"Oh, Christopher, I did something horrible, and I don't know how to make it right."

He drew her against his chest. "Just tell me, love, and we'll make it right together."

* * *

It was so quiet on the bank of the Thames, just outside of London. The ground was cool beneath Lauren's back, in spite of the fact that she was lying on Tom's duster, inhaling the scent of him as she stared up at the sky.

"It's never as clear as a Texas sky. I've never seen a falling star here."

"If you did, what would you wish for?" Tom asked, trailing his finger lazily up and down her arm.

She turned her head to look at him. He was braced on an elbow, gazing down on her. She'd thought he'd do more than hold her hands in the carriage, but he hadn't. And perhaps that was the reason her heart had tightened, then swelled, because he was with her not for an unbuttoned bodice, but for something more. A piece of what they'd left behind in Texas, left behind in their youth.

"I don't know. I'm not even sure I would wish."

"Did you stop believing in wishes coming true?" he asked.

She released a small laugh. "No, I still believe they come true, but unfortunately, when mine have it hasn't always been in a way that I expected or had in mind."

"What did you wish for that you didn't want?"

"It was one of the nights when we were down by the creek. I found myself envying the life you'd led; it took you so many places, gave you so many experiences. I was feeling dull and boring. I wished on a falling star, I wished that I would travel. I just didn't think I would go so far, or be gone so long."

"I always liked that about you. That you believed in wishing."

"I was concerned you thought I was just being silly."

"No, Lauren. Just because I couldn't believe didn't mean that I didn't appreciate that you could. I hate knowing you don't wish anymore. I think you ought to take up the practice again. You might be surprised how your wishes might turn out."

"If I were wishing, I think I'd wish for your letters back. Whatever did you say in all those letters?"

"Well, let me see if I can recall." He turned his head up toward the sky as though he would see the words written on the stars.

"Dear Lauren. I ran across three stray calves today. They had no brand so I branded them and added them to the herd. Yours, Tom."

She laughed. "How frightfully romantic."

He turned his attention back to her, and she could see his grin. "It gets better. Dear Lauren. I worked to get an ornery steer out of a muddy bog today. Almost broke my back doing it. I really missed you. If you'd been here, you could have done the pushing while I did the pulling. Yours, Tom."

Laughing harder, she shoved his shoulder. "That is *not* what you wrote to me."

He chuckled low. "Pretty much. I'm not much of a letter writer. Most of them weren't long. Just a sentence or two, just enough, so I could keep my promise to write every day."

Reaching out, she cradled his cheek, rubbed her thumb over the mustache that she was coming to adore. It suited him. "And to think, all this time, I never knew." How could her mother have destroyed his letters? "If you wrote as often as you said, you must have written over a thousand letters."

"You doubt my claim?"

"No. But I doubt all you wrote about was cattle."

He turned his head, and she wondered what he was looking at in the distance.

"After a few months passed, and you didn't write back, I thought maybe you were as bored by my letters as I was, so I tried to write about something other than cattle. I wrote about how lonely I was."

Her heart tightened into a painful ache for the loneliness they'd both experienced over the years.

Taking her hand, he began running his thumb in a circle around her palm. "Do you remember what you wrote in the letters I never got?"

"Not exactly, but close enough for you to get the gist of it. Dear Tom. All the girls I meet are lady something or other. I don't know how to be a lady. Yours, Lauren."

"You are a lady, Lauren. You always have been."

"A lady wouldn't have offered to let a boy un-button her bodice, so that ten years later he's still demanding that he be allowed to do it."

"You can't blame me for wanting to. Hell, dar-lin', what if I gave you a present all wrapped up and all I did was let you untie the string. You can't tell me that ten years later you wouldn't still want to see what was inside the package."

Oh, he made her want to laugh again. She combed her fingers through his thick hair. "Oh, Tom, you see things in such simple terms when so much more complicated issues are at hand."

"Those buttons on your dress look pretty plain and simple to me. I don't think unbuttoning them would be that complicated or any great hard-ship."

"Ah, but it could turn out to be both. What if you looked but couldn't resist the temptation to touch?"

He lowered his head slightly, his voice a low rumble. "I think you're afraid that you might de-cide you didn't *want* me to resist the temptation."

Oh, she could very well decide that, and per-haps that was her fear, that loosening her buttons might be enough for him, but certainly not enough for her. If his stroking her arm, stroking her hand warmed her so much, what in the world would happen if he stroked more?

She needed to distract him, distract herself from

this potentially dangerous direction. She swallowed hard, determined that their behavior tonight would remain above reproach. "I wrote other letters."

"Did you now?"

She heard amusement in his voice, as though he knew exactly why she'd turned the topic back to letters, that he was fully aware that he did tempt her in ways that he shouldn't.

"Dear Tom. All the boys I meet are lord something or other. I don't like them very much. Yours, Lauren."

He chuckled low. "Glad you didn't fancy any of the fellas you met over here."

She thought about telling him about Kimburton, but what was the point? That aspect of her life was over.

"I think I wrote a couple of lengthy letters about my clothes," she said instead, "especially after my first trip to Paris for a Worth gown. In Texas, I put on a dress in the morning and took it off before I went to bed at night. Here, I change my clothing three or four times a day, depending on the activity or where I'm going or who I'm going to visit. Sometimes I feel guilty for not being happy when I've been given so much, and there are others with nothing."

"You've really been that unhappy over here?"

She slowly shook her head. "I can't explain it, Tom. Everything I missed. The smells inside the general store when we went into town on Saturday. The open friendliness of people, everyone greeting you regardless of who you were or who your parents might be. As long as I sirred or ma'amed my elders, I didn't get into trouble for addressing someone inappropriately." She peered over at him. "Here, they have rules for who can sit beside whom during dinner. Introductions are so formal. Even when you run into someone you know, you have to adhere to the proper way of greeting him . . . or her. It's tedious."

"So tell me, darlin', how are you getting back to Texas?"

"On a ship."

He laughed, a full-throated sound. "You know I figured that much out on my own. But passage on a ship costs money. Is Ravenleigh paying for it?"

"I wouldn't presume to ask. He's been a wonderful father, and I don't wish to place him in an awkward position. Mother desperately wants me to remain here. She thinks life is too hard in Texas, that I've forgotten what it's really like."

"It is hard, Lauren."

"It's a different kind of hardship here, Tom, but it's still hard. Don't think it isn't."

"I wouldn't do that. But you still haven't answered my question. How are you paying for passage?"

"It's terribly scandalous, and you have to promise not to tell anyone."

"Who would I tell?"

"I've taken a position at a shop."

"A shop? What kind of things does it sell to be scandalous?"

"The scandal has nothing to do with the shop itself, but what my working there represents. My stepfather is a peer. For it to be known that I'm working would cause him embarrassment. I went to great pains to locate a shop in an area of London that isn't likely to be visited by anyone of importance."

"Ravenleigh seemed surprised that you were planning to return to Texas."

"I'd told him and Mother that I was spending my days doing charity work."

"You lied?"

"I didn't see that I had a choice if I wanted to accomplish my goal of returning to Fortune. Why even tonight Mother ordered me to resign my post."

"Will you?"

"How can I when it limits my opportunities, forces me to remain here?" Sighing, she shook her head. "I'll think about it all tomorrow. Right now, I'm weary of talking about me. Tell me about you. What have you done all these years?"

"I've been a cowboy all these years," he said. "Nothing extraordinary in that."

She couldn't stop herself from reaching out, cupping his chin, rubbing her thumb over the thick hair on his face again. "Why did you decide to grow a mustache?"

"You don't like it?"

"I like it just fine," she said, pleased that her opinion mattered to him. "I'm simply trying to figure out some of the things you've thought over the years, to understand some of the decisions you've made."

"Second year out on the cattle drive, they made me trail boss. I was all of seventeen, giving orders to men a lot older than me, so I thought if I grew some hair over my lip, I might look a little older, a little tougher so they'd take me more seriously."

"Oh, my gosh, Tom, you must have been the youngest one ever."

"There were younger ones during the war. It's not that hard."

When had Thomas Warner become so modest? She had to continually remind herself that a good deal about Tom had changed, just as a lot about her had changed. They weren't the same people any longer. She was torn between wanting to know him better and fearing that particular path would lead only to more heartache.

"It's a lot of responsibility," she told him.

"It meant I got paid more, meant I could get the things I wanted quicker."

"And what did you want?"

"My own ranch. A cowboy who works for an outfit has little chance of ever having a family, and no chance whatsoever of providing for them the way he'd want to."

"Do you have your ranch now?"

"I sure do. I just finished building the house. I pounded a lot of the nails in myself, wanted it to have my mark on it. I've always wanted something permanent, something sturdy that would outlast me. I find it ironic that all this time, I had estates over here that I never knew about."

"It doesn't diminish what you did in Texas. What did you name your ranch?"

"Lonesome Heart."

Her chest tightened, a knot formed in her throat. There was nothing she could say to that, nothing he could say either. The name of his ranch said it all for both of them. The silence eased in around them, comforting, familiar.

"What's your earliest memory?" he asked, with so much solemnity that she wondered where the silence had taken him.

"Seeing you behind the general store."

"Not of me," he said quietly. "The memory that goes the farthest back in your mind, before you ever met me."

"Oh, gosh." She closed her eyes, thought for a moment, opened them. "It would have to be of my father, dressed in gray, kneeling before me, telling me that he loved me, promising me that he'd come home." With startling clarity, she realized she'd had a lot of broken promises in her life. "It was a promise he wasn't able to keep."

"If I'm doing the calculation right, you were only four."

She nodded, even though he probably couldn't distinguish her movements in the shadows. "Close to that. I'm not sure how long the war had been going on before he went to fight."

"I was a little older when my mother took me away from here, and I have no memories of any of it, Lauren. I don't remember saying good-bye to anyone. I don't remember any hugs or tears. I don't remember if I was scared or excited. I don't know if I thought we were going on an adventure. When I look back, my memories begin in New York."

"What if they made a mistake, Tom? What if you aren't Sachse?"

"Have you ever been to the Sachse residence in London?" he asked, obviously not interested in pursuing her question.

Was he like other men she'd known—so enamored of the title that he didn't want to contemplate that it wasn't his? Wouldn't entertain the notion of giving it up? She couldn't help but feel slightly disappointed in his unwillingness to pursue the possibility that he wasn't Sachse.

"I've seen it from the outside, of course, but I've never been inside," she finally admitted. "I don't remember Lady Sachse ever hosting a ball, and if she gave a dinner, I wasn't invited."

Suddenly he sat up. "I want to share something with you, but it's at the house."

"Tom—"

"I know it's not proper for you to be in a gentleman's house without a chaperone, but what we're doing here isn't exactly proper either. The only one who will be awake at this time of night is the butler, and Matthews isn't going to tell anyone. Since I've been here, I've learned that servants keep what goes on between the walls to themselves."

"Unless someone pays them handsomely," she reminded him.

"No one's going to know, Lauren. Come to the house with me."

"It's after midnight," she said, not entirely comfortable with the notion of going into his home that late, which was silly really. Nothing could take place inside his residence that couldn't take place there by the Thames.

"It won't take long," he said. "I'll have you home before the sun is up and anyone has realized you're gone."

Her curiosity overrode her hesitation. Besides, she wasn't quite ready to give up her time with Tom. "All right."

Chapter 8

Lauren stared at the portrait of the last Earl of Sachse. She shifted her gaze over to the man standing next to it. The resemblance was uncanny. "You have kinder eyes."

Tom glanced back over his shoulder at his father's striking image. Even if it hadn't been the largest framed portrait in the gallery that surrounded the balcony overlooking the entry hallway, it still would have commanded attention. The pose, the expression of the man rendered in oils demanded it. "He was a handsome devil," Tom admitted.

She laughed. "Like father, like son."

"God, I hope not."

Her laughter abruptly died as she recognized the burden of his father's legacy mirrored in Tom's somber eyes. He stepped away from the wall, crossed his arms over his powerful chest, and leaned back against the balcony railing. He'd removed his duster when they'd arrived, and she could easily see the bulge in his arms that came by way of hard, honest work. While most of the gentlemen had their clothes custom tailored, she suspected Tom's tailor would find himself challenged, because he'd probably seldom been required to make clothing for such a fine physical specimen.

"I've been in London only a few days," Tom said, snatching her attention away from his muscles to the seriousness of his expression. "I've visited a gentleman's club, my solicitor, a business manager, the bank, and your family." Holding her gaze, he shook his head slowly. "Not a single person I've met regretted my father's passing. No kind words are ever associated with his name. The same held true while I was at my ancestral home. Everyone looks at me as though they're waiting for a fatal blow to be delivered. This afternoon in your drawing room was the first time that I've felt any sort of welcome from anyone I wasn't related to. The only family I've met is Archibald Warner. He's a fine gentleman, but his blood is far enough removed from my father's that his every action wasn't scrutinized with suspicion."

"Tom, I'm sure you're misreading people's reactions."

"Do you know why I'm so wealthy?"

The question was asked matter-of-factly, without any boasting, as though the extent of his wealth was simply something achieved without fanfare. Still, she couldn't help but think it an odd question. What in the world did one have to do with the other? She shook her head, raised a shoulder in helplessness, and stated the obvious truth, "Because you raised and sold cattle." What was the price on beef these days?

He gave her a small smile that indicated he thought she was innocent and naive. "If it was that easy, everyone in Texas would be wealthy."

"Then what was your secret?"

"I can look at a man and accurately judge his honesty, his trustworthiness, his dependability. I can close a deal with a businessman with nothing more than a handshake, knowing he'll do right by me and leaving him knowing I'll do right by him. I can look straight in a man's eyes and know his opinion of me. When I meet the gazes of people here, I see them wondering how close the acorn fell from the tree."

She couldn't help herself. Her gaze went back to the portrait, and she shivered. Something about the man was chilling. It was more than arrogance. An air of entitlement wreathed him, as though he thought he stood well above anyone else.

"I've got two things going against me—my father and my upbringing."

She looked back at Tom, waiting. Obviously, he'd given considerable thought to everything he was telling her. She remembered the ladies in her drawing room, referring to his barbaric ways—

"I know they consider me a savage, Lauren," Tom said, as though reading her thoughts. "I look enough like my father that people can't overlook my roots. They expect me to behave like him. People know I was raised in a fairly untamed land, and they're looking at me like I'm some trick pony, and they're waiting for me to perform. The way I see it, I've got only *one* thing going in my favor."

She waited for him to reveal what he thought his advantage might be, but he did nothing more than hold her gaze. Finally, she asked, "And what is that, Tom?"

"You."

She felt as though the balcony had crumbled beneath her feet. "How do you figure that?"

"Because you know these people, you know how to meet their expectations, and while you may not have liked it, as Ravenleigh said this afternoon, you adapted. I've attended meetings, had dinner, and engaged in business dealings with cattle barons. Hell, I'm a cattle baron, if you want the truth of it. I want—I need—to show these people that I can hold my own here." He lowered his gaze, studied his boots, then lifted his gaze back up to hers, and for the first time she saw his vulnerabilities. "Maybe I need to show myself, too."

Her heart tightened painfully at his quietly delivered confession. She saw the pride in his stance, and what it had cost him to reveal his insecurities. She remembered the confident way he'd strode into the drawing room. She remembered how uncomfortable he'd appeared in the library explaining his change of fortune. He was a complex man, and she barely knew him. In spite of the fact that no one expected him to know how important everything was, he did comprehend the extent of all he'd inherited.

She didn't know how to respond, didn't know exactly what he was asking.

"But to accomplish what I need to do, I need some help, darlin'. You want to go back to Texas? I have four thousand acres of good Texas ranch land, house and cattle included. It's yours. Just help me be the lord that my father wasn't."

When he delivered such a heartfelt plea, gazed at her with such earnestness, without bravado, without daring or challenging her, but simply asking . . . Had Thomas Warner ever asked for help in his entire life?

"Tom, there is so much—"

"I'm not asking for forever, Lauren. Just the Season." He gave a quick nod. "And yep, I know what the Season is."

"Lords don't say 'yep.' "

One side of his mustache twitched. "Some habits are going to be hard to break. Will you help me break them?"

Break them and in the process possibly break him? He'd had years to let the wildness in him run free, but English society would seek to hold him to its rules, mores, and etiquette. It would slowly destroy everything about him that had once appealed to her. Make a civilized man out of one who had never known restraint. Perhaps that was the reason she'd refused earlier to teach him. She didn't want to be responsible for turning him into the type of man that she could never love. Didn't want to see him change, because he would change. It was inevitable.

She knew what it was to resist, and she knew what it was finally to accept a new life, even though she abhorred it. It was the reason she'd decided to leave, the reason she couldn't stay now that he was here. Because he had no choice in the matter. He had to stay. He was a lord.

And in the staying, he would cease to be her Tom.

"I know I'm asking a lot—"

She held up her hands; he fell silent. Asking a lot? He had no idea. She felt the last remnants of hope that she might have meant something powerful to him wither away. If he'd ever considered that they might again have what they'd had in their youth, surely he wouldn't have offered to provide her with the means to leave, to support herself, to be an independent woman away from him. Swallowing hard, she nodded. "Passage back to Texas. That's all I want, Tom."

So she wouldn't have to stay and witness what she was about to create.

He gave a brusque nod, again without arrogance, as though he'd feared she'd turn his offer aside, and was greatly relieved that she hadn't.

"I'll have my lawyers draw up the paperwork."

"No need. You said you handled deals with a handshake." She took a deep breath, stepped forward, and extended her hand.

He wrapped his long fingers around hers, but instead of shaking her hand, he drew her closer. "I do it a little differently when I close a business deal with a woman," he said, using his free hand to cup her cheek, his thumb stroking the corner of her mouth. Even though it seemed innocent enough, it burned right into the heart of her womanhood.

"Do you?" she asked, sounding as though she had no breath in her body, possibly because she didn't. How could he steal away her breath with nothing more than a light touch?

He lowered his mouth to hers, and as inappropriate as it was, she welcomed the kiss, parting her lips slightly when his tongue insisted she do so. With a deep groan that shivered between them, he deepened the kiss, the hunger there but restrained as he leisurely took his fill. She didn't remember moving forward, but she was suddenly aware of her breasts flattened against his chest, the fingers of her free hand tangled in the hair at the nape of his neck as heat and desire swirled through her.

He'd taken her to the river so they could get reacquainted, to remember happier times. He'd brought her here, so she could understand what it was he was facing. And now he was giving her a sampling of what *she'd* be facing: day in, day out, in the presence of a man who could turn her knees into porridge. Ah, Lord, she didn't know whether to be afraid or giddy.

He drew back, desire evident in his gaze as it swept over her face. The weakness in her knees spread through her entire body, and she wondered how in the world she was going to manage to walk down the stairs. "So how many women have you closed business deals with?" she asked, needing anger, jealousy, disappointment—something, anything—to get her body to quit reacting as though his lips were still pressed to hers.

A slow, sensual smile flashed across his darkly handsome face. "This was the first, darlin'."

She couldn't help herself. She laughed at his audacity, laughed because if she didn't, she might weep for what they could possibly have had. "We might need to establish rules—"

"Darlin', I have enough rules to learn. I don't

need you adding to them. I'll behave." His grin broadened. "Within reason."

Keeping his earlier promise, he delivered her home long before the sun came up. After they arrived, he helped her out of the carriage and walked with her up the steps to the door.

"I've started taking an early-morning ride in Hyde Park," he said.

"So I've heard. Lady Priscilla apparently saw you there."

"I'm probably doing it all wrong. Go with me in the morning and teach me how to do it proper."

She narrowed her eyes at him. "You're riding a horse, Tom. I'm sure you know how to do it properly."

"Riding isn't the problem. It's knowing which people I can talk to and which I can't."

"All right. I'll meet you along Rotten Row at the fashionable hour of eleven."

"Good night, Lauren."

He turned to go and she called out to him. "Tom?"

When he faced her, she smiled. "In the morning? Leave your gun at home."

Chapter 9

"**T**om is the Earl of Sachse."

Sitting within her cousin's parlor, Lauren let the words she'd just announced expand to fill the space separating them. She'd awoken early, following only a few hours of sleep, after a fitful night of dreams in which the ship she was traveling on was continually tossed back onto English shores by incredibly large waves. At one point, she'd tried swimming the Atlantic, only once again to find herself back where she started. Upon awakening, she'd actually been exhausted by her tribulations.

She'd needed to talk with someone she trusted, someone who would understand. So as soon as her maid, Molly, had helped her dress for the day, Lauren had sent for a carriage, even though the hour was unfashionably early. Thankfully, her relationship with Lydia went beyond mere blood to include devoted friendship, and it wasn't governed by the movement of the hands on a clock.

"*Your* Tom?" Lydia asked, yawning, sitting in a nearby chair, her bare feet tucked beneath her. She tugged on the sash of her emerald green satin robe as though she needed to do something to prevent herself from falling back to sleep.

Resisting the urge to crack her knuckles— because ladies did not allow their bodies to make unseemly noises—Lauren glared at Lydia for being so blasé about this whole situation. Of course, the fact that she was barely awake might have some bearing on her reaction.

"He's not *my* Tom. But, yes, *that* Tom, the one we both knew in Texas."

"That's incredible. How did this come about?"

"He's the son—"

"I understand that part, and I've heard all the stories about the lost lord, but my word, Lauren, he's a man we know. I danced with him in Texas at my birthday party when I turned eighteen."

She was surprised by the flare of jealousy that remark ignited. "You never mentioned that."

"I knew you were pining for him—"

"I wasn't pining for him."

"Yes, you were, but that's neither here nor there

now. Tom is Lord Sachse." Lydia shook her head. "I'm not sure London is ready for a lord accustomed to doing things his way."

"I can pretty much assure you that it's not, which brings me to my visit. I need your help."

"Of course. Whatever do you need?"

Lauren came to her feet and began pacing in front of the fireplace where a low fire worked to ward off the chill of the morning. She was grateful that Lydia's husband, Rhys Rhodes, the Duke of Harrington, had possessed the decency to make a tactful retreat after Lauren assured them that nothing was horribly wrong.

"My help," Lydia prodded.

"I've agreed to teach Tom what he needs to know to survive here." She stopped pacing and faced her cousin. "I know it's rather short notice, but I thought my first lesson would involve dining, and I was hoping you might see your way clear to host a small dinner party this evening."

"How small?"

"The four of us, plus Gina and Devon."

"Consider it done."

Lauren returned to the gold brocade chair. "Thank you. I thought if we kept the dinner intimate it might help Tom feel not quite so self-conscious if he makes a mistake."

"I can't imagine the Tom I knew in Texas being self-conscious about anything."

"There's a lot to learn."

Lydia studied her for a moment. "But that's not what's troubling you. What else did you want to tell me?"

Lauren felt the tears sting her eyes. "All these years Tom wrote me. Mother destroyed his letters before I had a chance to see them, destroyed the ones I wrote him before they were mailed."

"I can't believe Aunt Elizabeth would do something so underhanded. Why would she do such a thing?"

"She thought it would make it easier for me to adjust to life over here if I didn't have reminders of life back there."

"But she gave you my letters."

"Exactly. I think she was more afraid that I'd run away to be with Tom."

Lydia smiled softly. "Are you going to do that now that he's here?"

"I sneaked out of the house to be with him last night."

Lydia raised an eyebrow. "And?"

"We rode through the streets of London in his carriage, watched the stars for a bit, and struck a bargain for me to teach him. At the end of the Season, he'll provide me with passage to Texas."

"Who's idea was that?"

"He made the offer, and I accepted."

"Your acceptance surprises me. You've always wanted to go back to Texas, but I suspected Tom was the reason—if not in whole, then at least in part. Now that he's in England, I assumed—"

"That I would give up my dream of returning to Texas? No, Lydia. I've never felt comfortable here. I've never felt as though I belonged."

"You hid it well, Lauren. My goodness, you guided me through the maze of English etiquette. I don't know what I would have done if you hadn't held my hand."

"You would have done just fine. You published a blasted book on the subject."

"Etiquette that I gleaned from all the letters you wrote me over the years."

Lauren sighed. "Don't you ever feel like you're living in a little box over here? That if you try to break out of it, they'll just nail it shut?"

Lydia visibly shuddered. "You're describing a coffin. Don't be so maudlin."

"I don't mean to be. I just never really expected to spend the remainder of my life over here."

"I don't understand why you find such fault with it."

A servant appeared in the doorway, quietly entered the room, and set a tea service on the table beside Lydia. "Thank you," Lydia said.

Lauren held her silence while the servant left, and Lydia began preparing a cup of tea for her guest. Despite the early hour and the fact that she'd been roused from slumber, her cousin looked incredibly content.

"You truly do love it here, don't you?" Lauren asked.

Lydia peered over at her and smiled softly. "I truly do. If you'll forgive my boldness, I think the difference between us is that I have someone here whom I love with all my heart. I think you've had a difficult time of it because you left your heart in Texas."

"You think I left my heart with Tom?"

Lydia gave her a pointed look. "Didn't you?"

"That was so long ago, we were such different people. I came to understand that more clearly when I was with Tom last night. When he kissed me, it wasn't the kiss of his youth."

The teacup rattled as Lydia set it on the tray, scooted up in the chair, and leaned toward Lauren. "What? You completely overlooked revealing that juicy tidbit. When did he kiss you?"

"In the garden, then later to seal our bargain. And I owe him a debt that I feel certain he's going to expect me to pay before I leave for Texas."

"What debt?"

Only to Lydia could she dare confess the not-quite-proper behaviors of her youth and Tom's daring proposition. "Before I left Texas, Tom paid me a quarter to unbutton my bodice, and I never carried through on my part of the bargain."

"Are you telling me that he's expecting you to unbutton your bodice?" Lydia was smiling brightly.

"It's not amusing," Lauren said pointedly.

"I'm not saying that it is, but you were fourteen. I've always thought Tom was an intelligent man, but this is downright silly."

"Apparently he doesn't think so.

" 'Why are you here, Tom?' I asked.

" 'I've come to collect a debt,' he had the audacity to announce for all the world to hear."

"Perhaps it was a debt that Ravenleigh owed him."

"No, if you'd been there to see the intensity of his gaze, you would have had no doubt what debt he was referring to."

"Your mother always considered him to be a bad influence. I'm beginning to see why. Although perhaps she'll find him more acceptable now that he's titled."

"Ironic, isn't it? She'll find him more acceptable while I'll find him less."

"Why would you find him less?"

"His life is about to become all the things I've never liked."

"You like balls, parties, and entertaining."

"Where a woman can't speak her mind, politics, or religion. Where a woman is ushered out of the room so men have an opportunity to engage in manly endeavors, such as smoking and drinking. Where all behavior is watched and commented on."

"And what if you discover you still have a place in his heart?"

"Highly unlikely. He's provided me with the means to leave. Why would he do that if he wanted me to stay?"

"Oh, Lauren, don't you see the truth of it? He's a man, and if he's anything like Rhys, he finds it incredibly difficult to express his true feelings. Perhaps he feared rejection if he asked you to stay."

"And so he gave me the means to leave?"

Lydia shrugged. "Who can decipher a man's logic?"

"And what of this silly debt he thinks I owe him?"

A wicked gleam came into Lydia's eyes. "Tell him if he behaves himself, you might just pay it."

Having missed dinner the night before, Lauren was incredibly hungry. After returning from Lydia's, she went to the small dining room, where breakfast was always served with an elaborate assortment of offerings spread over the side table. She had to admit that she would no doubt miss the varieties available to her at Ravenleigh's homes, always laid out for casual enjoyment.

On her plate, she placed buttered eggs with tomatoes, kippered salmon, and toast with marmalade. Much more was offered, but she decided those would suffice for the morning. A footman pulled out a chair for her, and Lauren took her place. She was rather surprised that her parents weren't there yet. Her stepfather's pressed newspaper was still set beside his place setting, so she knew he had yet to come down for breakfast. She wondered if her mother had as difficult a time sleeping as Lauren had. If so, she suspected her stepfather had as well.

She stared at her plate, suddenly once again without an appetite. Surely Lydia had only been teasing about Lauren fulfilling her promise to Tom, although the notion was certainly intriguing. And why not carry through on her promise? Once she left England, her life would begin anew, just as it had before when she left Texas. She didn't know why a tinge of sadness crept in with the thought of beginning over.

Lydia had identified correctly that Lauren really didn't know Tom, at least not the Tom who had appeared the previous day. Even if he had come for her, she couldn't honestly say she would have left with him. Lady Blythe had also spoken true. Who knew what sort of influences he'd had over the years?

She knew her stepfather's brother and his friends had played some role in the man that Tom had become. That couldn't be helped. After all, he'd been working for them. But so had a whole host of other men. It was childish to think that she had any idea of the kind of man Tom had become.

Glancing up at the click of footfalls, she watched as her mother and stepfather walked into the room. Neither looked well rested. Neither went to the side table. Her mother sat in the chair beside Lauren's, her stepfather took the chair on the other side of her mother, providing as he always did an air of solidarity. During all the years they'd been there, Lauren couldn't recall a single moment when he hadn't given her mother his full support when it came to the manner in which she'd disciplined her daughters. Lauren wondered if he'd approved of her mother's thievery regarding the letters written between two young lovers.

"You're up early," her mother said, as though she needed something to break the tension that had been left between them the night before.

"I had some matters that needed to be taken care of."

Her mother nodded as though she knew exactly what those matters were when in truth, she couldn't have even a hint of an idea. Lauren's days of sharing her worries, concerns, and plans with her mother were over.

Her mother sighed. "I owe you an apology. Ten years' worth as a matter of fact. I thought I was doing what was best."

"Mother, I'm sure a day will come when I'll forgive you, but unfortunately, that day isn't today."

"I don't expect it to be today, Lauren. If I had it to do over . . ." Her voice trailed off.

Ravenleigh placed his hand over her mother's fist where it rested on the table. Lauren could tell that he'd squeezed it gently, could see the love for her and for her mother reflected in his kind eyes. Her mother nodded as though Ravenleigh had communicated his thoughts to her.

"Before we left Texas," her mother began, "I sold the farm and placed the money in a trust your stepfather has guarded like a hawk over the years. It was my intention to give you your portion on the day that you married, a final gift from your father. I've decided to give it to you early, so you'll have the means to provide for yourself—at least for a while—after you return to Texas. Your stepfather has offered to purchase your ticket for passage. He thinks we could manage to have everything settled so that you could leave within a week."

Lauren felt the tears sting her eyes. It hurt to see how much it cost her mother to let her go. Her chest tightened painfully with the evidence not only of her mother's love, but her stepfather's as well. He'd always been so good to her, and she had little doubt that it was his influence more than her angry words flung at her mother that had turned the tide. Using her linen napkin, she wiped her tears, hardly able to find the words needed to express her gratitude. She held Ravenleigh's gaze when she rasped, "I can't tell you how much your generosity means to me, how much it's always meant to me. My share of my father's legacy will be well taken care of, and as generous as your offer is to pay for my passage, I've made other arrangements—"

"It's not necessary for you to work at that shop," her mother interrupted.

"I know. I'm planning to give notice of my leaving this morning. I've made arrangements with Tom. He's going to provide for my passage in exchange for which I'll teach him what he needs to know."

Her mother looked stunned, Ravenleigh didn't look quite so surprised, and she wondered what, if anything, he and Tom may have talked about while alone in the library.

"I see," her mother finally said. "Well . . ."

"Yes, well," Lauren responded. "As soon as I've been to the shop, I plan to meet Tom at the park. Tonight we'll be dining at Lydia's. I'll instruct him to call for me here, if you have no objections."

"No objections whatsoever," her stepfather said, before her mother could respond. He stood, clapped his hands together. "Now that's all settled I'm famished."

He headed for the side table.

Her mother looked at her scarred hands. "I do appreciate that you didn't risk your neck and try to climb out of your window when he came for you last night. I assume this won't become a nightly ritual."

"Mama, you have to let me live my life, make my own mistakes."

"So you recognize that he's a mistake."

How could her mother offer independence with the one hand, yet chains with the other?

"I recognize that I'll never know if you continually clip my wings."

Her mother looked at a loss for words, but Lauren had nothing else she wanted to say on the matter.

An overpowering fragrance of roses wafted into the room. Lauren turned her head to see the butler striding in, two footmen in his wake carrying enormous bouquets of roses, one white, the other yellow.

"My lady," Simpson said, with a slight bow, "these were delivered with instructions that the white were for the lady of the house, the yellow for her eldest daughter."

As the flowers were extended to Lauren and her mother, he also handed them each an envelope. Inside hers, Lauren found a note that simply read, "A little bit of Texas." Burying her nose in the fragrant bouquet that had to be comprised of at least two dozen roses, she peered over at her mother. "What does your note say?"

"No hard feelings."

How Texan and to the point.

"For what it's worth, he said he only wrote a sentence or two in each letter," Lauren said.

Her mother cleared her throat and stood. "Well, if his words were as honestly delivered as these, that might be all he needed. I need to see about getting these roses into water."

She walked out of the room, and Lauren looked to the end of the table where her stepfather had quietly taken his place, although it looked as though he had yet to begin eating. "She meant well all these years," he said quietly.

"I know." With the bouquet still cradled in the crook of her arm, she rose and walked to his end of the table. Leaning down, she kissed his cheek. "I love you, Papa."

Twice Tom had managed to give her a little bit of Texas. She strolled out of the room wondering if little bits of Texas had been there all along, and she'd simply failed to notice them.

"My lord?"

Tom glanced over at the butler he'd not heard enter the dining room. He still found it unnerving that the servants moved through the house so unobtrusively and silently, like phantoms. It was enough to make a man jumpy. One of the reasons Tom had stopped wearing his gun before Lauren's edict. His valet had startled him yesterday morning, and Tom had drawn it on the man, who had immediately crumpled to the floor in a faint.

Tom turned his attention to the butler and the silver tray he extended. On it rested an elegant embossed card. Tom read the name. Obviously word was spreading that he was in town.

"Show them in."

The butler bowed slightly. "As you wish, my lord."

Using the linen napkin, Tom wiped his mouth and hands, tossed the cloth onto the table, shoved his chair back, and stood. He wasn't wearing a jacket—which was improper when receiving guests, but he figured these guests might be forgiving.

A woman more elegant than he remembered her to be, bestowing on him a smile that rivaled the sun in brilliance, waltzed gracefully into the room, a dark-haired gentleman dressed much as Tom knew he *should* be dressed following in her wake.

"Thomas Warner, look at you," Lydia said, reaching out, taking his hands in her gloved ones, and squeezing. "Why didn't you let us know you were in town?"

He felt his face heat up at her chastisement. "I only got here a couple of days ago. I haven't quite figured out this practice of calling on people yet."

He was surprised to notice that she seemed to be inordinately pleased by his response.

"I want to introduce you to my husband," she said, stepping back slightly, an incredible amount of love and pride reflected in her eyes. "Rhys Rhodes, the Duke of Harrington. Thomas Warner, the Earl of Sachse."

Tom liked what he saw in Harrington. His silvery gray eyes reflected a forthrightness that Tom related to and respected. He was a man Tom could take into his confidence, a man he could trust to keep his word with nothing more than a handshake.

"Sachse," Harrington said, in a deep refined rumble.

"Harrington." Tom shook his head. "Have to admit I find it odd, this practice of not calling a man by his name."

"Trust me, using titles will come naturally to you in no time. Does my stepfather know about your good fortune?" Lydia asked.

Her stepfather, Grayson Rhodes, was another of the Englishmen who'd arrived in Texas following the Civil War. Tom had visited with Rhodes when the man had returned from his visit to England with his family a year earlier, so Tom knew Lydia's husband was the man's half brother, the legitimate heir to the dukedom, while Rhodes had been the duke's bastard. Older, firstborn in fact, but not legitimate, so he'd not inherited what his father had left behind. Sometimes the family connections got so complicated that Tom thought they needed to devise a chart to sort it all out. And here he was in England, adding to the complications.

Tom shook his head. "I didn't tell anyone before I left Fortune. I didn't see the point. I kept thinking once I got here, I'd discover it was all a mistake."

"This is absolutely incredible."

"I couldn't agree more."

"You had no idea?"

"None." Tom glanced at the table, glanced at them, didn't know if it was proper but offered anyway. "You're welcome to join me for breakfast."

"I would be delighted," Harrington said. "The

moment Lydia realized she knew you, she wouldn't be content until we were on our way over here. My stomach has been protesting ever since."

"Help yourself," Tom offered.

When plates were filled and everyone was sitting at the table, Lydia gave him a pointed look, and demanded, "So what are your plans regarding Lauren?"

Tom nearly choked on his deviled sausage. He swallowed hard, wiped his mouth, held Lydia's gaze, and responded honestly, "I haven't quite decided."

Although that wasn't exactly true. He had her for the Season . . . then, well, he'd worry about that when that time came.

"Is she the reason you knew I was here?" he asked.

Lydia nodded.

"Did you know she's making plans to return to Texas?"

Lydia seemed to hesitate, as though she wasn't quite sure how much to reveal. "In the early years," she finally said, "after she came here, she often wrote me. The letters were always tear-stained. She had a difficult time adjusting, but she seems self-assured now, never complained . . . honestly, I only recently realized that she still dreamed of returning to Texas."

Tom nodded.

"I do know that she's going to help you through

the Season. During that time, perhaps you could convince her to stay," Lydia suggested.

Tom held her gaze, keeping his words honest. "I don't know that I want to."

Not only because it seemed cruel to hold her if she didn't want to be there, but because he was no longer sure of his feelings where she was concerned.

Ten years. They'd both changed. He didn't know if what they'd had once could thrive in England, and he knew for damned sure that it couldn't if she wasn't where she wanted to be.

"Why has he not yet arrived?"

"Surely he will be here at any moment."

"Perhaps we've missed him."

"He was riding quite early yesterday morning."

"You might have said something sooner."

While Rotten Row was favored by the ladies for spirited riding, the four ladies who had been in her stepfather's parlor the previous afternoon seemed hesitant to be off. They'd been waiting at the entrance when Lauren had arrived. One did not have to be a genius to determine for whom they waited.

"I can't believe you took up a post outside his residence and watched for him," Lady Cassandra said.

"I was fairly certain the man at Ravenleigh's was Sachse. How many men dressed as cowboys are roaming around the streets of London? I simply wanted to confirm it for myself."

Lady Blythe followed her statement with a stern look at Lauren, whose heart had begun beating erratically with the knowledge that the woman might have been hiding in the bushes when Tom had escorted Lauren into his home.

"You might have confirmed that I'd identified him correctly. It would have saved me hours of sitting in front of his residence," Lady Blythe admonished.

"Quite honestly, I didn't realize he was Sachse until later," Lauren said, trying desperately to sound contrite, when in truth she wanted to pepper Lady Blythe with questions regarding her spying.

"Did he see you?" Lady Priscilla asked.

"No. I was well hidden inside my coach. Darkness had settled in by the time he arrived home. Although quite honestly, I'd been prepared to wait longer. He must have left your residence immediately following dinner."

"He did leave quite early," Lauren offered, not certain why it bothered her so much that the ladies were so interested in Tom. She'd expected their curiosity, of course. She simply hadn't expected how much she disliked their prying into his affairs, especially when those affairs involved her traipsing about with him in the middle of the night.

"Oh my word, is that he?" Lady Cassandra asked. All eyes turned in the direction she was looking.

"It must be," Lady Blythe announced. "But he's not wearing his greatcoat this morning."

"It's a duster," Lauren explained impatiently.

"Is he wearing a pistol?" Lady Cassandra said.

"I can't tell," Lady Priscilla said. "But it doesn't appear so."

"Do you suppose he has ever fired it?"

"Do you think he's ever killed a man?" Lady Blythe asked.

"It would be inappropriate to ask," Lady Cassandra said.

"I find Americans fascinating," Lady Anne said. "Unfortunately, Richard has no patience for them." Blushing, she darted her gaze to Lauren. "My apologies. I meant no offense."

"I assure you, none taken." Lauren had always found Lady Anne to be the most sincere and kindest of the group. She turned a bright smile Tom's way. "Good morning, my lord."

With a broad grin, Tom swept his hat from his head in an extremely gallant gesture. "Ladies."

Lady Blythe began rapidly blinking as though a gnat had flown into her eye, and she was attempting to dislodge it; Lady Cassandra began patting her chest; Lady Priscilla giggled, Lady Anne smiled. Honestly, Lauren would think they had never before seen a man if she didn't know better. Yes, Tom was novel, different, unlike what they were accustomed to, but did they have to carry on so? It was beginning to grate on her nerves. On the other hand, if they were so enamored, perhaps others would be as well, and Tom's entrance into society wouldn't be nearly as bumpy as he'd feared.

"My lord," Lady Blythe said, laughing lightly. "How terribly naughty of you not to confirm who you were when I correctly guessed while we were all gathered in Miss Fairfield's drawing room."

"My apologies, darlin'. I'm still not used to being a lord. And since Ravenleigh and his family didn't yet know . . . well, I wanted to tell them in private."

"I daresay I shall only forgive you if you allow me to ride alongside you."

"Well, now, I did promise Miss Fairfield that I'd join her this morning, so I'm obliged to keep that promise." He winked. "But it would be my pleasure to offer you my other side."

Lauren couldn't help but think how smoothly he'd handled what could have become an awkward moment, and she found herself wondering how many women in Texas he may have practiced his flirtation skills on. He'd certainly developed them beyond what they'd been outside the general store.

"And my pleasure to take it," Lady Blythe gushed.

Lauren wasn't certain when Lady Blythe had

become such an irritant, but she couldn't deny that she found her to be exactly that as she nudged her horse near Tom's right side, while Lady Blythe guided her horse around to his other side, where she promptly began to engage Tom in conversation, hoarding his attention like a miser accumulated gold. Lady Cassandra, much to Lauren's surprise, urged her horse up alongside hers.

"You know," Lady Cassandra whispered, "I'm not at all certain it will be as difficult as we'd first surmised for him to find a suitable wife."

"I'm not certain he's looking for a wife," Lauren said, again surprised by the flare of jealousy that the thought sparked. Of course, Tom would find a wife. He needed an heir, an easing of loneliness, and someone to help him manage his households. She couldn't fault any lady for wanting to fill the position.

"Why wouldn't he be?" Lady Cassandra asked. "He needs an heir after all."

Maybe it was only that Lauren didn't want to contemplate that he *might* be looking. "He has to grow accustomed to life over here."

"It appears he's already adjusted fairly well. Except for the clothing of course."

"I rather like his clothing," Lady Priscilla said, in a conspiratorial whisper from the other side of Lady Cassandra. "I find it quite roguish."

Yes, it did seem quite roguish, his shirt molding against his body with no jacket to hide the ripple of his muscles with each of his movements. Lauren dropped her gaze to his bare hands, roughened by hard labor, where they held the reins with ease. She fought not to envision those long, sturdy fingers slipping her buttons free of their moorings, peeling back the cotton . . . would they tremble now as they had when he was younger? Would she shiver with desire? Would his knuckles graze against the inside swells of her breasts, breasts she'd barely had when he'd made his daring proposition? Would his gaze heat with yearning for what the bargain would deny him—the touch of her flesh?

She tore her gaze from his hands, wondering when the day had grown so unseasonably warm, when drawing in a breath had become so difficult, as though all air had disappeared.

Lady Blythe's delighted laughter echoed through the park, more irritating than her voice. A lady was supposed to laugh with utmost decorum.

"That's not fair," Lady Priscilla said. "We can't hear what they're saying." She called out, "Lady Blythe, what's so humorous? Do tell."

Lady Blythe leaned forward, gazing around Tom's firm body. "His lordship was explaining that he's wearing a ten-gallon hat. Hats in Texas are sized by how much water they hold. Can you imagine?"

"Why would you put water in your hat?" Lady

Priscilla asked, but Lady Blythe had already turned her attention back to Tom.

"They use it as a basin for washing up or watering a horse," Lauren explained.

"It's a strange life they live over there. It *is* dreadfully uncivilized," Lady Cassandra said.

"Frightfully so apparently," Lady Priscilla said. "It's hardly fair that Lady Blythe is getting all his attention." She leaned forward. "My lord, do you enjoy being a cowboy?"

Grinning, Tom turned his gaze away from Lady Blythe, and Lauren was again struck by how handsome he was. Roguish, yes, but more than that, extremely masculine. He appeared strong and capable. No one looking at him now would suspect he had any doubts about his place in this society. She was suddenly feeling quite humbled that he'd chosen to trust her with his insecurities.

"Indeed, I do," he told Lady Priscilla, "but I'm more than a cowboy. I'm a rancher. I've got my own land and cattle and men who work for me."

"Is that how you became so fabulously wealthy?" Lady Priscilla asked.

Tom's deep laughter rang out, the raspy sound shivering along Lauren's spine and all her nerve endings, wrapping itself around her heart. He didn't seem at all offended that Lady Priscilla had made an entirely inappropriate inquiry. "Now, darlin', whose been spreading nasty rumors about me?"

"There's nothing nasty about being wealthy."

"Speaking about it is nasty, though," Lady Cassandra affirmed.

"I was only curious as to how a man might acquire wealth. My father inherited all of his, so I've never given any thought to what a man must do if he hasn't any money."

He has to work, hard and long, Lauren thought, working his muscles until they were like bands of steel, remaining beneath the sun until his skin was browned.

"Cattle got me my start," Tom acknowledged. "I did a little investing and got lucky."

Lauren thought she could see the barest hint of a blush appear beneath his chin, or perhaps it was a reflection of the red bandanna he wore around his neck. She supposed some habits were difficult to break. She contemplated telling him that he was unlikely to encounter any dust storms in London, but then it occurred to her that perhaps he wore the bandanna to hide evidence of his discomfiture.

She wondered if he were embarrassed speaking of his success. If he was painting a modest portrait of his endeavors. It seemed contradictory for a man who sat so tall and proud in the saddle to show any hint of embarrassment, but then the Tom she'd known had always been short on words. Perhaps he was simply uncomfortable with the inquisition regarding his accomplishments.

"What do you think of London?" Lady Anne asked.

"A bit more crowded than I'm used to," he said.

Lauren thought she could detect his blush fading. How intriguing.

"Other than the crowds," Lady Blythe began, "what do you think of it?"

"Haven't seen enough of it to really form an opinion. I was at Sachse Hall until a couple days ago."

And he'd almost immediately shown up at her door. She couldn't help but feel a bit flattered that he'd come to see her family so quickly, and while his original intention might not have been to reacquaint himself with her, she couldn't deny that he'd strolled into her drawing room long before going to her stepfather's study.

They'd reached the end of their journey. As they all brought their horses to a halt, Lauren couldn't help but think that Lady Blythe looked as though she was anticipating something more.

"I thought to walk for a bit if you'd care to join me, my lord," Lady Blythe said.

"I'd love to, darlin'," Tom said, "but I promised Ravenleigh I'd escort Miss Fairfield home."

"Oh, yes, of course," Lady Blythe murmured. "Perhaps another time."

Tom tipped his hat to the ladies before turning his attention to Lauren. "Ready, darlin'?"

Oh, she was more than ready, as she urged her horse forward to fall into step alongside his. He rode with such ease, such command as he sat in a Western saddle rather than an English one, his legs long, his thighs thick.

He swung his head around, his intense gaze roaming over her face as though he were seeking to familiarize himself with every line, as though he were searching for something she might have hidden. "You're awfully quiet this morning. Did you not sleep well?"

"What has one got to do with the other?" she asked.

One side of his mustache twitched. "I just thought maybe you were tired, and that's the reason you haven't said anything."

"I haven't said anything because I didn't have anything to say. Unlike Lady Blythe, I don't believe in mindless banter."

"You're not jealous that I was giving her attention."

"Of course not." Irritation was not jealousy, and she had every right to be annoyed that Lady Blythe's intrusion had prevented Lauren from giving Tom a proper lesson. She thought her reasoning sounded quite reasonable.

He chuckled low, actually had the audacity to wink, reach out, and chuck her under the chin with his bare finger. "Lydia sends her regards."

If it weren't for his finger supporting her jaw, it would have dropped open. "You saw Lydia?"

"Yep, bright and early this morning. Not as

early as you did apparently. She and her husband joined me for breakfast. I like Harrington."

She lifted her chin slightly to get it away from the unsettling touch of his finger. The way rumors flew around London, she could only imagine what part of her person they'd have him touching by nightfall. "I'm not at all surprised that you two hit it off. He was quite the scoundrel before Lydia reformed him."

"Do you think I'm a scoundrel?"

"You can't deny that you had your moments, but you seem to have put away your rapscallion ways, at least where these ladies are concerned. You handled yourself very well."

"I would have preferred just riding with you," Tom said, knowing the words he spoke were truer than any he'd shared with Lady Blythe. She was pleasant enough, but there was a fake quality to her that Lauren never exhibited.

She wore a dark blue riding suit, buttoned clear to her throat, where a light blue cravat completed the picture of maidenly virtue. A gauze veil of the same light blue shade was wound around her dark blue hat. Her hair was piled up beneath it. She looked elegant, composed, not at all as casual as she had the night before, while lying with him beside the Thames.

He couldn't claim to prefer one aspect of her over the other. He found all facets of her just as intriguing as he had in his youth. Truthfully, more so. At sixteen what he'd felt for her, he was coming to realize, was as strong as a boy could feel. What a man felt could be much more intense, run more deeply, and he was beginning to think that he might have barely touched the surface regarding what he was capable of feeling for her. He had a powerful hunger where she was concerned, and he wasn't certain he could do anything to alleviate it.

"It was a nice touch, sending my mother flowers this morning," she said.

Tom felt the heat of embarrassment warm his neck. "I'm trying to get on her good side."

"Why?" Lauren asked.

"She's been mad at me since the moment our paths crossed, and with you helping me, I figure we're bound to run into each other." He shrugged. "So I sent her some flowers to pave the way for a bit more compassion."

"If you decide that you'd rather not run into her, she and Ravenleigh have made it possible for me to return to Texas without your assistance."

Tom felt his gut clench so hard he was in danger of tumbling from his saddle. "We made a bargain you and me."

He fought back the grimace because his voice came out sounding rougher than he'd intended.

"I'm aware of that, and I plan to see it through to the end of the Season. But I wanted you to know that if you wanted to hire someone else—"

"I don't."

She smiled. "Tom, in the light of day, your offer is far too generous—"

"I'm content with it."

She nodded. "All right. We're having dinner at Lydia's this evening."

"She mentioned that."

"We'll part company here," she said. "Bring your carriage around for me at seven."

He furrowed his brow. "Lydia said dinner was *at* seven."

Lauren's smile grew. "Well, yes, of course. But one must always arrive fashionably late. I'll see you this evening."

She set her horse into a canter. Tom was tempted to follow, but instead he drew his horse to a halt and simply watched her ride away. He wondered if a time would ever come when it wouldn't hurt to see her increasing the distance that separated them.

Chapter 10

"I can't believe you're going out this evening with a gentleman, without a chaperone. Papa will no doubt be waiting in the entry hallway with a dueling pistol—"

"No, he won't," Lauren said, cutting off Amy's diatribe, critically studying her reflection in the cheval glass. Her dress was white with a modest neckline, the skirt following the line of her legs, pleated in the back with a short train. Pink satin trim added a bit of color.

It was the third dress she'd changed into. Molly had begun to lose patience with her, so Lauren had given her leave to go, but now she wondered if the neckline was too low or not low enough. No buttons in the front. That was a blessing. At least Tom wouldn't have his attention on buttons and, therefore, would be able to concentrate on the lessons she planned to deliver. And perhaps her mind wouldn't wander to the possibilities of what might happen if he went beyond unfastening buttons to unlace her corset or loosen the ribbon on her chemise. She did wish he hadn't reminded her that something remained unfinished between them.

"Mama might—"

"She won't," Lauren interrupted irritatingly. She suddenly felt as though her corset had been laced too tightly, and why in God's name were they having such a hot summer?

"Are you blushing?"

"No, I'm simply warm. And I've already spoken to Mama and Papa so we will have no misunderstandings regarding tonight."

She'd asked them to make themselves scarce, because she didn't want Tom to begin the night feeling uncomfortable. Most households would welcome a lord with pleasure, but she knew her mother had her prejudices against Tom, prejudices that she doubted a bouquet of flowers would have the power to erase.

Amy scrunched up her mouth. "Are you certain you don't want me to accompany you?"

"I'm sure."

"It's scandalous behavior, Lauren."

"I'm going to be with Tom, Amy. And we'll be at Lydia's."

"That's my point. I know you trust him, but he *is* a man, and ladies younger than thirty do not travel alone in the company of a man who is not their father or brother. It's simply not done."

"It sounds as though you're quoting from an etiquette manual."

"I had to memorize the blasted thing. Might as well put it to some use even if that use is merely repeating it. Anyway, I'm serious about going with you. For propriety's sake."

"If we'd never left Texas, we would have grown up without chaperones. Do you know that it's not unheard of, especially in the areas where the people are really scarce, for a woman to travel all day and night with a man who isn't her husband or brother, just so they can attend a dance? No one thinks anything of it. Here everyone is so damned suspicious."

"You swore."

"So I did." Had she spoken a single swear word aloud since arriving in England? Tom could corrupt her with apparently no difficulty simply by being in her company for a short time where his bad habits could rub off on her.

She turned to face Amy, who was lying on her stomach on Lauren's bed. Her hands were folded beneath her chin, her blue eyes intent. All her sisters had blue eyes, but those fathered by a Texan

had eyes of a dark blue, while the two youngest—
fathered by Ravenleigh—had inherited his pale
blue eyes.

"Here it's as though everyone expects no one to
be able to resist engaging in improper behavior
and so they guard well against it with chaperones
and rules," Lauren said. "In Texas, men are so respectful of women and hold them in such high
regard that chaperones aren't needed, rules aren't
required. Common sense prevails. The men aren't
going to take advantage of a woman. So for tonight, I'm pretending that I live in Texas."

"A bit of flawed thinking there. Tom may have
lived in Texas, but his bloodline is English, and
Lady Angelina heard from Lady Caroline who
heard from Lady Deborah that the afternoon
when he first came to this house he swept you into
his arms in an inappropriate manner that had
Lady Blythe practically swooning."

Lauren rolled her eyes. The gossips of this town
were incredible. "I'm surprised the rumors going
about have me still wearing my clothes by the
time he left the room with Papa."

Amy grimaced. "Actually, I've heard one where
you weren't."

Lauren scoffed. "With an audience of ladies
looking on, he removed my clothes?"

"It does sound rather preposterous, but it does
make for a more interesting tale." Amy sat up. "So
did he sweep you into his arms?"

"No. He did nothing more than say hello." And remind her of a debt owed.

"He loves you, you know?"

"Papa?"

"Well, he does, of course. But I was talking about Tom."

"You should call him Sachse."

"He doesn't look like a Sachse, he looks like a Tom."

Lauren went to her vanity, picked up a crystal bottle, and dabbed a few droplets of expensive French perfume behind her ears, and, hoping her sister wasn't watching too closely, between her breasts. The gown wasn't low enough to offer more than the barest hint of her upper swells, but its close fit left no doubt that she was no longer flat as a plank of wood. Curiosity getting the better of her, she asked, "Why do you say he loves me?"

"Because of the way he looks at you. His gaze seldom strayed from you in the library yesterday, and it's so intense—it's almost as if he's trying to memorize every aspect of your appearance as though he suddenly expects you to disappear."

Because she would disappear. At the end of the Season. She supposed she should warn her sisters, so they could begin adjusting to her imminent departure.

The door suddenly burst open to reveal Samantha breathing heavily. "He's just arrived. Oh my God, Lauren, are you certain you'll be safe with him?"

"Of course I'm certain. Why wouldn't I be?"

"Well, because he cleaned up rather nicely. I believe even Mother is shocked."

Panic shot through Lauren. "Mother's downstairs?"

She and her stepfather were supposed to remain in their chambers or the library. They weren't to greet Tom.

"She and Papa," Samantha said.

"Oh, Lord, I thought they understood that I didn't want them about," she said, as she swept out of her room and dashed down the stairs.

"Well, it is their residence," Amy pointed out, following in her wake.

"I know, and it's becoming so terribly inconvenient."

"Only because you think our previous life was more appealing than this one."

"It was."

Lauren hurried down the steps.

"But—"

"Forget it, please. I don't wish to have one of our all-too-familiar arguments now. I have more pressing matters—"

She nearly stumbled when she caught sight of Tom. Or at least she thought it was Tom. Surely it was. Yes, most definitely it was. The eyes at least would forever give him away and the manner in which his gaze always met and held hers, as though he could see clear into her soul, her heart, her very being.

Was it that gaze that made Amy think he loved Lauren? He'd looked at her like that from the moment she'd first seen him behind the general store.

"My word, he did clean up nicely," Amy murmured.

"Shut up," Lauren demanded.

She'd seen nothing wrong in his appearance before. Dressed as a cowboy, he'd been handsome, overpowering. But tonight . . .

No evidence of the cowboy was in sight. Tom wore a double-breasted dove gray tailcoat and trousers, with a single-breasted burgundy waistcoat. A black silk bow adorned his pale gray pleated shirt. His boots had been replaced by black shoes, polished to such a high sheen that she imagined if he looked down he'd be able to see his reflection. And in his left white-gloved hand, he held a black top hat.

His ebony hair was combed backed, tamed. His dark eyes were shining as he gave her one of his slow, sensual smiles. It was the only part of him that still reminded her of a brazen cowboy.

She didn't remember walking the rest of the way down the stairs, but she must have because her slippered feet finally landed on the marble floor of the entryway.

"Hello, darlin'," he said, his voice echoing between the walls.

"You look . . ."—she laughed lightly—"very proper."

"Despite the rumors, I'm not a total heathen."

"Speaking of rumors," her mother began. "If you insist upon going out without a chaperone—"

"Mother," Lauren said, cutting her off. "We've already discussed this matter. The only people who will know that I went out this evening, much less that I went out without a chaperone, are the people in this house and those in Lydia's. If rumors start, I'll know exactly where to look, and I shall be none too happy."

Her mother glared at Tom. "If you take advantage—"

"I'll hand you the horsewhip myself," he said.

Her mother jerked her head back slightly, blinked, as though at that moment she was seeing something about Tom that she'd never before noticed. She lowered her chin somewhat, relaxed her pursed lips. "I actually came in to thank you for sending the flowers. It was a lovely gesture."

"My pleasure, dar—ma'am."

Lauren bit back her smile, thought perhaps her mother was doing the same. "Don't wait up," she announced, as she headed for the door.

The butler opened it, and Lauren walked through, waiting until Tom joined her.

"That could have gone worse I suppose," she said. She looked at Tom and smiled. "I'd planned to have Harrington discuss various wardrobes with you, but it seems you picked that little tip up on your own."

"Lady Sachse had taken me to a tailor. It just took him a while to get my clothing made. You approve of the job he did?"

She couldn't decide if he was searching for compliments or reassurances that he would fit in this evening. "He did a splendid job. You look incredibly handsome."

"I wanted to be deserving of having the most beautiful woman in London at my side."

"Dangerous talk, Tom. Keep that up and I won't be able to resist and may find myself wishing I did have a chaperone."

They'd reached the carriage. He took her hand, to help her up the steps, but something in the slight pressure of his fingers over hers caused her to still and look at him.

"Would that be so bad?" he asked, quietly. "To be unable to resist?"

"It might upset our bargain."

"Again. Would that be so bad?"

She dropped her gaze from his eyes to his lips, felt her mouth go dry. "Our agreement was that I would teach you, not be seduced by you." She lifted her gaze back to his, regretfully realizing that her words had served only to further incite his desires. He'd always welcomed a challenge. "You really must learn not to be quite so open in displaying your . . . thoughts."

"You know what I'm thinking?"

She nodded quickly. "I believe I do, yes."

"And you're bothered by the direction they're headed?"

"Flattered," she admitted. "But wary. A gentleman wouldn't seek to make a woman feel uncomfortable, and we are in the midst of a lesson regarding what is proper and what isn't."

She thought she saw disappointment wash over his handsome features before he assisted her into the carriage. Taking her seat, she was surprised to notice a large bouquet of pink roses resting on the seat opposite her, the fragrance filling the carriage.

"Who are those for?" she asked, as Tom sat opposite her.

"Our hostess."

"That's very thoughtful," she said.

"It seemed the least I could do."

She wished she hadn't advised him to hide his emotions. He'd managed to master the technique perfectly. Sitting there, she had the uncomfortable realization that she hadn't a clue as to what he was thinking. She gazed out the window already deeply regretting the bargain that she'd struck: to turn him into the sort of man she could never love.

While the well-sprung carriage rumbled toward their destination, Tom pretended to listen while Lauren prattled on about forks, spoons, and knives, how various dishes would be served, when was the proper time to begin eating—as soon as the food was set before you, no need to wait until everyone had been served; when to stop—do not wipe your plate clean and do not ask for an additional serving; what to expect—seven or eight courses; what would be expected of him— pleasant conversation. She was giving him exactly what he'd asked for: the boring mundane rules of polite society.

Strange that what he'd asked for wasn't truly what he wanted. Oh, he wanted to prove himself to these people, but he was beginning to realize that he wanted to prove himself to her more. The approval in her eyes when she'd come down the stairs and first caught sight of him had caused his chest to swell with such satisfaction that he'd almost popped the pearl buttons right off his shirt. He'd seen desire in her eyes, desire that mirrored his own, but that was obviously an emotion not to be displayed. A shame. How was a woman to know that a man wanted her if he had to keep the passion leashed?

As she continued on with hardly a breath in between, he was beginning to realize why she'd numbered them.

"Is that number thirty-five?" he asked, interrupting her lengthy soliloquy.

She stared at him. "Pardon?"

"One of your sisters mentioned you numbering the rules. I lost count of where we were."

"I told you that you would have a lot to remember." She looked out the window as though suddenly embarrassed by everything that she'd said. Or perhaps hurt by the gruffness in his voice. Whenever he was with her, the longer he was with her, the deeper his voice seemed to sink.

"You don't have to teach me everything in one sitting. You should enjoy the evening a bit."

"You're not paying me to enjoy the evening." She turned her attention back to him. "You're paying me handsomely to see that you're turned out properly."

It was beginning to irritate him that she was taking the terms of their arrangement to heart. He wanted her help. He couldn't deny that, but he'd also welcomed the opportunity to spend some time with her.

"So who all will be there tonight?" he asked.

"You remember Gina?"

"Pierce?"

She nodded. "She's married to the Earl of Huntingdon now. They'll be there. Just the six of us. I thought to keep it small so that if you do fumble, you won't be quite as self-conscious. Lydia and Gina were both where you are at one point, and their husbands understand that it takes a while to learn everything. So everyone will be circumspect if you blunder and no one outside those walls will ever hear of any mistakes."

He pretended he was playing poker, careful not

to reveal the cards he was holding, because he didn't want her to know that it disappointed him to realize that she *expected* him to blunder. Perhaps that was his fault, based on previous conversations, based on his request for her help. But he was a little more refined than she seemed willing to give him credit for.

Perhaps the evening would be a learning experience for them both.

The more Tom came to know the Duke of Harrington, the more he liked him. Perhaps because, like Tom, the man had found himself unexpectedly titled. Well, not completely like Tom and not totally unexpectedly. He was the second legitimate son and had grown up knowing he always had a small chance of becoming duke, unlike Tom, who'd never had any inkling of what awaited him.

The man was without pretense, earning a glare from Lauren when he told Tom to call him Rhys.

"Tom is supposed to be learning how to address people properly," she'd chided.

"I'll purchase him one of Lydia's books," Rhys had promised.

Tom had also taken an instant liking to Huntingdon, perhaps because when he'd removed his gloves before dinner, it was evident that he had the hands of a farmer, and from what Tom had gleaned so far, aristocrats weren't supposed to engage in manual labor. But apparently times were changing.

Dinner had actually been enjoyable, with pleasant conversation and no one judging his actions. There was a method to the madness of so much silverware, utensils to be taken from the outside in. Mastering eating with his fork in his left hand had taken some time, since he was accustomed to using his right, but as Lauren explained to him it was a sign of good breeding to use only his left hand. The right was for the knife, which he mentioned he might use to slit his throat.

He'd noticed Rhys fighting not to smile at that comment, while Lydia and Lauren had seen fit to chastise him profusely for uttering such a vulgar remark. Getting Lydia riled was almost as much fun as doing the same to Lauren.

Sitting beside him, she tried gently guiding him through the meal, with quiet whispers and slight nudges, only a few times losing patience with him and snapping at him because he wasn't trying. He honest to God didn't see the point. If holding a fork in his right hand caused someone to think less of him, he wasn't altogether convinced that he was going to put any stock in the person's opinion anyway.

The seating arrangement hadn't been quite up to what it should have been had the dinner not been a practice. Tom hadn't minded. Lauren sitting beside him so he could smell her perfume, feel the warmth radiating from her body, was a hell of a lot more pleasant than having her sitting across from him.

"Thank God, that's over," Rhys said, as soon as the ladies quit the room. "I can barely tolerate these formal dinners."

Dinner had come to an end after eight courses. The ladies had retired to the drawing room, while the gentlemen remained at the table for some brandy and supposedly *manly* conversation. Tom didn't want to seem ungrateful, but he'd rather have had the ladies present. He didn't think they were appreciated enough there. He didn't see a need to chase any away so he could talk to a man, but Lauren had insisted.

"Formal? Good God, man, formal is when a hundred are in attendance. This affair was simply a pleasant evening," Huntingdon said.

Rhys looked at Tom, nodded toward Huntingdon. "Unlike you and I, he's never had the luxury of knowing anything other than a nobleman's life."

"When was the last time you harvested wheat?" Huntingdon asked.

"I have to confess that the closest I've come is loading ships, and that, my friend, is backbreaking work."

Chuckling, Tom gained the attention of both men. "I thought peers were supposed to pretend never to lift a finger."

"Quite so," Huntingdon said. "Sorry for the slip."

"So how are my brother and his family?" Rhys asked, as the footman poured him some brandy.

"They were doing well, the last I saw them," Tom said. "Building a new house, doing a little traveling."

"I'm glad to hear it. Grayson had a difficult life growing up here, not being legitimate and all that. It's terribly frowned upon, and my older brother Quentin was not the kindest of brothers."

"Is cruelty common among the aristocracy?" Tom asked. "Because I've heard a few bad things about my father, as well."

"Not really. For the most part, the aristocracy is made up of good men and women who take their duties and position quite seriously and with a great deal of honor and nobility. But like all aspects of society, exceptions abound, and we have our bad apples." Rhys took a sip of brandy. "I believe this is the part of the evening where I'm supposed to instruct you on after-dinner manners. Lauren whispered in my ear before leaving the room that you possessed—in her words, not mine—the nasty habit of smoking. Therefore, here are the rules as I know them. If you decide to enjoy a cigar or cigarette, you can't rejoin the ladies. It's not polite to be around them with your clothing smelling of smoke. Of course, if your host has a smoking room and can offer you a

smoking jacket, then it's allowed. I have neither."

"A shame. I have some fine cigars in my jacket
pocket."

"Truly? Of all my vices, I've yet to add smoking
to the list. Do you think stepping out on the veranda would serve to keep the smoke from getting into our clothes?"

Tom grinned. "It's my place of choice."

Rhys had the glasses filled with more brandy,
before escorting Tom and Huntingdon to the veranda. Before long, each was puffing on a cigar
and enjoying the brandy.

"I believe this may be the start of a bad habit for
me," Rhys said.

"I can think of worse habits. Have even engaged
in a few," Tom said.

"As have I, although marriage has curtailed my
number of bad habits considerably."

"So I understand that you knew Gina in Texas,"
Huntingdon said to Tom.

Tom nodded. "Not as well as I knew Lydia,
since Gina's family left Texas. Does she ever talk
about wanting to go back?"

"No, I think she's quite happy here."

Leaning against the pillar, Tom wondered what
it would take to make Lauren happy here. "So tell
me. How important is all this stuff that Lauren
thinks is so damned important?"

"You mean the Season?" Rhys asked.

"The Season, the manners, the etiquette, the making of a good impression. Any of it. All of it."

Studying Tom, Rhys took a puff on the cigar. "Actually, it's terribly important. It broadens or limits your options, depending upon how well you . . . *perform*. Believe it or not, your most pressing task is to get married and produce an heir to inherit your titles."

Tom couldn't help himself. He laughed. "You're not serious."

"Unfortunately, I am. If I understand your financial situation, based upon the rumors circulating, you have no problems there. You need to oversee your estates, of course, but much of that is simply delegating, then following up to make sure the work is done properly.

"However, a good deal of effort goes into finding a suitable wife, and that, my new friend, is the true purpose of the Season. Each ball is a marriage market. You look the offerings over, make your selection, charm her, so that by Season's end she is wearing your ring rather than someone else's."

"So if I'm not looking for a wife, I could skip all this nonsense."

"I thought Lauren was planning to return to Texas."

"She is." That didn't mean Tom had given up on her completely. He took another puff on his cigar. "I know she's unhappy here."

"I can't speak to that. I only met her last Season. Before that, I was somewhat of an . . . outcast."

Tom narrowed his eyes at Rhys, studied him. "How does one become an outcast?"

"A bit of family scandal, which to my way of thinking, doesn't make me the ideal choice for instructing you in proper behavior. However, supposedly all is forgiven, and I've regained my good standing, but only because Lydia made it so."

"She's happy here."

"Incredibly."

"How did you make that happen?"

"Don't think I really had much to do with it. She simply thrives on all the ceremony that I find tedious."

"If you find it tedious, then why are you in London?"

"Because she loves it so, and I love her. Besides, I must begin laying the groundwork so that our children, when they come along, will be accepted and loved by all who know them."

Tom grimaced. "I'm used to a man being judged on his own merits."

"A man can rise above his family's scandals. A man's scandals can also bring his family down. Improper behavior is not tolerated well, especially by the older ranks. As much as I wish it were otherwise, I would advise you to take Lauren's lessons seriously. A soiled reputation is not easily washed clean."

"Lauren says it takes courage to thrive here."

"Indeed, and probably of a sort you're not accustomed to. I suspect the dangers you faced in Texas were exceedingly clear, visible, without question. Here, they are not always so blatantly obvious."

"I'd been thinking that if I could figure out what was really making Lauren unhappy, I could fix it so she might decide to stay."

"Ah, then you wouldn't have to wife hunt."

Tom looked out at the darkness. If Lauren left . . . "How can you marry someone you don't love?"

"My father did. He and my mother spent a good deal of their lives miserable, and it rained down on their children so they, too, were miserable."

"Yeah," Tom said quietly. "I could see where it could make a lot of people unhappy."

"Speaking from experience," Huntingdon said, "a marriage of convenience need not always be miserable. I married for money and was fortunate enough to gain love as well."

"Still, you must admit that among the aristocracy, marrying for reasons other than love is usually the case," Rhys said. "Politics, prestige, money . . . they are more often sought after than love. I suppose that's the reason so many take lovers."

"I can't imagine marrying for any of those reasons," Tom said.

"Are you telling me that love is the only reason that people marry in Texas?"

Tom finished off his brandy, shook his head. "No. Men need helpmates, women need security. Sometimes it's to fight the loneliness. I guess it just seems that our reasons are more honest than yours."

Rhys chuckled. "You're going to have to stop thinking of yourself as not one of us. That won't sit well among your peers."

"And you think that's something I need to worry over? What sits well with my peers?"

"If you do one day take a wife, if you do one day have children, then yes, you'd better give a damn that your peers think well of you. That's not to say that you can't be your own man. You simply do it within the confines of our society."

Tom was beginning to understand why Lauren was miserable there. It wasn't a place where a girl would let a boy unbutton her bodice. It wasn't a place where a boy would even presume to ask. With their chaperones and strict behaviors, it was a wonder a man could figure out who he might enjoy spending the rest of his days with, let alone who he might love.

Three dark-haired lords had sat at the table during dinner. Observing them, based on their behavior, Lauren had been unable to distinguish the two who had been raised in England from the one who hadn't. Only when Tom spoke did evidence surface that he'd journeyed a serpentine path to his destination.

Yet even when he spoke his drawl was not quite as pronounced as usual, as though he was working to keep his differences at a minimum. She'd been sitting beside him so she could quietly comment on his manners when appropriate—and had spent most of the meal uttering few words, other than insisting he keep his fork in his left hand.

"I thought dinner went smashingly well," Lydia said, as the ladies sat in the drawing room, drinking tea while the men drank brandy in the dining room. "Don't you agree, Lauren?"

"What? Oh, yes," Lauren said, trying to focus her attention on the conversation rather than her thoughts during dinner. She knew Lydia and Gina would probably disagree, but she'd thought Tom had been the most handsome of the three, and watching him had certainly been no hardship.

"Tom seemed to be very comfortable in our company during dinner," Gina said. "I still break out in hives when Devon even mentions attending some sort of large affair."

Lauren thought it interesting that the two ladies she trusted most of all had such different views on etiquette: Gina abhorred anything to do with it, while Lydia thrived on it.

"You worry about it too much," Lydia said.

"Strange words from someone who thought it

was important enough to write a book about," Gina responded.

The one thing they both had in common was that neither was shy about expressing her opinion.

"Lauren, you seem miles away," Lydia said.

Lauren looked at her cousin, looked at her friend, shook her head. "I'm surprised, that's all."

"By what?" Gina asked.

"I'm afraid I'm as guilty as the ladies of London in thinking that Tom is going to behave like a barbarian."

"There's not a lot that one can get wrong during a dinner," Lydia said.

"Not a gentleman, anyway," Gina said. "The arrangement of the seating, the courses to be served, everything of any importance is left to women. Men just have to sit where they're told and eat what's placed before them."

"Yes, I suppose that's true enough." Still, something bothered Lauren about tonight. "He seemed so sure of himself."

"Why wouldn't he? He was among friends," Lydia said.

"You didn't give him a lesson when you went to visit him this morning?"

"Of course not. I only wanted to make him feel welcome."

"What does it matter if he's getting lessons elsewhere?" Gina asked.

"It doesn't, except I could be on my way to Texas if not for my promise to teach him."

"I can't believe that you'd want to miss the Season," Lydia said.

"Only because you love it so," Gina said.

Lauren shook her head. "After turning down Kimburton, my Season will be most boring. I suspect I'll have very few dances."

"You're an heiress, Lauren," Gina reminded her. "You'll have dances and plenty of them. His friends may feel sympathy for Kimburton, but there isn't a lord in London who wasn't glad to know he might have an opportunity to fill up the family coffers with what marriage to you will provide. Trust me, I know all about how desperately some want to fill the coffers."

It was filling the Huntingdon coffers that had led to her marriage to Devon. A marriage of convenience that had unexpectedly turned into a marriage of love. Whereas if Lauren had married Tom long ago, their marriage of love would have become a marriage of convenience. Although she couldn't help but wonder how different her experiences in England might have been if she'd had him at her side, exuding confidence even when he wasn't sure of himself. To constantly have his kisses, his touch—

"So what are your plans regarding Tom?" Lydia asked.

Swallowing hard, Lauren stared at her cousin. "Pardon?"

"Tom. What other lessons do you plan to teach him?"

"Oh, lessons, yes. Umm . . . well, there's your ball next week, of course. We'll need to review the protocol there."

"Did you want me to have a small ball, so you might practice?" Lydia asked.

Lauren laughed. "No, that won't be necessary. I can explain what he needs to know. He wants to be seen as not being a barbarian. I suppose an outing to the theater might suffice."

"Are you really going back to Texas?" Gina asked, effectively altering the direction of the conversation, before Lauren could completely compile a list of lessons.

She smiled warmly. "Indeed I am. Does it make you jealous?"

"Strangely, no. Going to Texas would mean leaving Devon. I can't imagine my life without him in it. You loved Tom once—"

"I was a child. We've both changed considerably."

"What if while spending time with him, you fall in love with him again?" Lydia asked.

Ignoring her cousin's question, Lauren got up, walked to the window, and looked out on the garden. "It looks as though the gentlemen have gone outside to smoke cigars."

"Should we join them?" Gina asked. "I've always thought separating the sexes after dinner was silly."

"You think everything is silly," Lydia said.

"Because most of it is."

"What do you think they talk about when they banish us from their presence?" Lauren asked quietly.

"Rhys assures me that it's nothing of any importance," Lydia said.

"We could always sneak up on them and eavesdrop," Gina said.

"That would be highly improper," Lauren reminded them.

"We're Texas ladies," Gina said. "We've earned the right to be improper."

Lauren spun around, smiling. "Earned the right?"

Gina shrugged. "Maybe *earned* isn't the right word. Whatever the word is, however, is unimportant. If we want to know what they're saying, we should just go listen."

"I'm trying to teach Tom proper behavior."

"Boring behavior if you ask me."

"I didn't ask you," Lauren snapped. "And do you think I want to watch him change, do you think I want to be the one responsible for caging up everything about him that I once loved?" She buried her face in her hands, fighting back the tears.

"Lauren?"

She felt both her friends at her side. Sniffing inelegantly, she dropped her hands to her side. "I'm sorry. He doesn't want to embarrass himself, and I promised to teach him, and I know it's silly, but I miss the boy he was."

"That would be the case even if you weren't teaching him," Lydia said. "He stopped being the boy you knew a long time ago. Maybe it's time you took a good, hard look at the man."

"That was much more enjoyable than I thought it would be," Tom said, as the carriage traveled through the quiet streets.

He sat across from Lauren but she could smell the faint scent of a richly aromatic cigar and the barest hint of the brandy he'd sipped and the incredibly, wonderful masculine fragrance that was him. He took up so much space inside the carriage, not because he was huge, but because she was simply so aware of his long legs and hard muscles and broad chest and wide shoulders. Take a good, hard look at the man her cousin had suggested. As though Lauren had any choice. As though every aspect of his appearance didn't draw her eye, wasn't pleasing. As though she wasn't aware of each breath he took. As though she couldn't make out the outline of his hands in the dark resting on his thighs, couldn't clearly envision them reaching for her buttons—

"What are you thinking?" he asked.

"Lydia"—she cleared her throat hoping to make her voice stop sounding like a hinge in need of oiling—"will be hosting the first ball of the Season next week. I was simply making a mental list of everything we need to address before then." Liar, liar. "I suppose we should make arrangements for dance lessons—"

"I know how to dance."

She laughed lightly. "The dancing here is a bit different than what you're used to, Tom."

"I know how they dance over here. Lydia's stepfather gave a bunch of us cowboys a few lessons right before her eighteenth birthday. I think that was part of his birthday gift to her: making sure she didn't get her toes stepped on."

"Oh, yes, she'd mentioned that you'd danced, she just hadn't indicated that you were very good at it."

"I don't know why she would."

Because it was a part of him that Lauren wanted to know about. She was greedy for any little tidbit of information. Glancing out the window at the night, she didn't know why it bothered her to think of her cousin dancing with Tom, being held in his arms, feeling the warmth from his body . . . of dancing with him when Lauren never had. Surely she wasn't jealous. No, of course not. She was simply mystified that there were so many aspects of Tom with which she was unfamiliar, things that he had experienced that she had no idea about.

Picking at the fabric of her skirt, she considered all that she didn't know. Finally, she said, "Before coming here, you could have asked Grayson Rhodes to teach you what you wanted to know."

"I didn't have time, except to get on a steamship and try to figure out what all this mess was about. Besides, I wasn't sure I wouldn't get over here and discover it was all a mistake. Then wouldn't I look like a fool, going around telling people I was an earl when in fact I wasn't?"

She'd never realized before how much he worried about the impression he made on people, and she wondered what aspects of his life were responsible for that.

"So you feel you can handle a ball quite satisfactorily?" she asked.

"I think so."

"Then I'll arrange a few other outings between now and then. It's important to be seen, and if Lydia and Rhys accompany us, you should be able to have a few introductions before the ball so you won't feel as though you're walking among strangers."

"I like Rhys," he said, as though he'd grown bored of talking etiquette. She'd tried to warn him.

"Lydia loves him so much."

"I think the feeling is mutual."

"Last Season he tried to send her away, but she refused to go. She stood by him when no one else would."

"For a town that has so many rules about proper behavior, there sure seems to be a lot of scandal going on."

"Imagine how much more we'd have if we had no rules."

"Maybe it's having all the rules that causes all the problems. Some people just feel a need to break rules, or at least to see how far they can bend them."

"Is that what you do, Tom? See how far you can bend them?"

"Don't you know me well enough, Lauren, to know I'm not content with bending? I much prefer to break them."

"What if someone gets hurt?"

"I don't see how using a fork in my right hand is going to hurt someone."

"Are there rules you wouldn't break?"

"Of course there are."

"I should tell my mother that. It might put her mind at ease."

"I doubt it."

A dangerous undercurrent shimmered through his voice, warned her that she needed to change the course of the conversation. "Did you know that here ladies are expected to swoon? Lady Blythe once had a swoon party where all the girls—this was a while ago—had to practice swooning and gave each other advice on how to make it look more convincing."

Tom chuckled. "I can't see you swooning."

"I never have. I think it's silly, to appear helpless when you're not."

"Maybe the ladies swoon because they think it makes the men feel strong, like they're protecting them.'"

"It's still silly. Would you want to marry a woman who was completely helpless?"

"No. I want a woman who could stand up to me, who could take my teasing and tease back. A woman who would put me in my place if I got out of line."

"Maybe I'll write a book like Lydia's, but I'll call it *A Lady's Guide to Taming a Cowboy*. It should sell quite well as long as you're not married and every lady in London thinks she has a chance at capturing your heart."

"Rhys said they don't necessarily marry for love here."

"That doesn't mean they don't try to capture hearts. It's part of the game. And you will need to marry, Tom. You'll need to provide an heir."

"Ravenleigh hasn't. Is he worried about it?"

"It seems contradictory, but he never has pressured Mother to give him a son. At least not that I'm aware of. As a matter of fact, he seems quite content to pass everything on to his nephew." She yawned. "All in all you did very well tonight."

"I didn't want to embarrass you."

"That was the beauty of having dinner with Lydia. No one would have cared."

"I think I could consider Rhys a friend."

"Yes, you probably could, considering you both have a bit of wickedness in you."

"I think you like wickedness."

"Don't tempt me into proving you wrong, Tom."

"I think you're afraid you'll prove me right."

He moved across the carriage until he was sitting beside her.

"A gentleman isn't supposed to sit beside a lady—"

"I know." He touched his finger to her lips. No gloves. When had he removed his gloves?

"Don't you get tired of spouting rules?" he asked.

"It's what you're paying me to do."

"When it's just you and me, I don't give a damn about the rules."

Before she could even contemplate objecting, his mouth was covering her, his tongue delving deeply, hungrily. She could taste the brandy he drank earlier, could taste the unique flavor that was him. She should shove him aside, insist that he stop . . . and she would in a few more seconds. She would allow one more sweep of his tongue, one more groan, one more whimper, one more—

The carriage rolled to a stop, and they broke apart. She could see his satisfied grin in the shadowy confines of the conveyance.

"You didn't prove anything," she said.

His grin simply grew. She knew she was protesting too much. Where he was concerned she seemed to have no will to resist.

The door opened, and the footman helped Lauren alight. Tom followed and escorted her up the steps. At the top, she placed her hand on the door handle.

"So what's next?" he asked, as though he realized that she planned to disappear before he could kiss her again.

"I'll talk with Lydia, see when she's available and send word to you."

He trailed his finger along the side of her neck and desire raced down to the soles of her slippers. "It was just a kiss," he said quietly.

Just a kiss? That was like saying the Crown jewels were just jewelry or Big Ben was just a bell.

"Moments like that will simply make it more difficult when the time comes for me to leave."

"So you'd rather have no memories to take with you?"

She looked over her shoulder. "I'd rather we stick to the bargain we made."

"All right." He took her hand, very slowly peeled off her glove, and pressed a kiss against her knuckles. "Just remember that we've made two bargains, and they both need to be kept."

Before she could comment that the bargain they'd made as children would never be kept, he'd turned and hurried down the steps. She wouldn't keep it. He was being silly to even think that she would.

As she walked into the house, she decided that come morning she would have Molly discard any dresses or gowns that Lauren had with buttons in the front. Not that she thought Tom would take advantage without permission, but because the truth was, he'd guessed right. She was afraid he was a temptation she couldn't resist.

Within his carriage Tom stroked the glove, pulled it between his fingers, wondered when Lauren would realize that he hadn't given it back to her. Every moment spent with her was pure torment, to be near and not touch, to give in to temptation and kiss, but not possess.

He wasn't exactly certain when his plans regarding her had changed, when he'd decided that he didn't want her to teach him as much as he wanted to demonstrate to her the passion and fire that could exist between them.

He didn't want her leaving with anything left unexplored between them. And that meant doing all in his power to break through her reserved facade. To undo her years of training.

To make her want him as desperately as he wanted her.

Chapter 11

"**I** inquired. He's been invited."

"Then surely he will show."

"One can only hope."

"He might not realize the importance of this affair."

"It's the first ball of the Season. Of course he realizes its importance. He's been here long enough to learn to appreciate a few of our customs."

"I do hope you have no plans to seize all of his attentions this evening, as you apparently have since his arrival."

Standing with the four ladies who had been in her stepfather's drawing room the afternoon Tom had arrived, Lauren couldn't seem to stop herself from blushing as Lady Blythe directed her last statement Lauren's way with obvious disapproval. Her glare was hard, her lips pursed, and her brow arched. The dancing had yet to begin, and the ladies were engaged in their customary gossiping session. The fact that it was indeed the first ball of the Season—hosted by the Duchess of Harrington no less—also meant that many of those in attendance had a good deal of catching up to do, and a few other ladies were nudging up against their circle, striving to determine what juicy tidbits they might have missed.

"During the time I've spent with him, his attention has been focused more on learning your rituals than on me," Lauren explained, resenting that she felt any need at all to explain her actions or her time with Tom. Over the past week, accompanied by Lydia and Rhys, she and Tom had attended a performance at Albert Hall, browsed through the National Portrait Gallery, visited the Crystal Palace, and strolled through the zoological gardens. Everywhere they went, Lydia was quick to introduce the new earl to anyone of importance, which was the advantage of going through London accompanied by a duke and his duchess: There were few people they couldn't impose upon for introductions.

Tom was always charming, dazzling the ladies with his roguish smile. Even his slow drawl didn't seem to grate on anyone's nerves as hers had. Lady

Blythe had spoken truly that first afternoon: When one was wealthy and titled a good many faults were easily overlooked. As a matter of fact, Tom was handling himself so well that Lauren was really beginning to wonder if she had any true purpose other than to provide him with a decoration for his arm and occasional conversation. Not that either was any hardship, but he was much less untutored than she'd realized.

Oh, some of the minute details would throw him from time to time: the practice of tipping the street sweepers who cleared the streets ahead of them so they could cross without stepping in horse dung, sitting in a shop so items could be shown to him—he'd purchased fans for all the ladies in Ravenleigh's household. Small things. Things he could have easily learned through observation. He was extremely generous—

"He sent me flowers, you know," Lady Blythe said. "After we rode through the park last week. Pink roses."

Too generous perhaps, Lauren thought, suddenly unreasonably irritated that he was showering attention—

"The ones he sent me were white," Lady Cassandra said.

"Mine were red." Lady Priscilla giggled.

All eyes turned to Lady Anne. She blushed. "Mine were an assortment of red, pink, and white. 'I appreciate the warm welcome,' was written on the note that accompanied them. I thought that was extremely sweet of him."

But none had been sent yellow roses, Lauren couldn't help but notice, taking delight in the realization that those had been reserved for her and her alone. A little bit of Texas.

The ladies nodded, murmuring that Sachse had expressed the same sentiments to them. Very tactful on his part, not to single one of them out for more attention while at the same time making each feel special. Very tactful and very clever.

"And the color of your flowers?" Lady Blythe asked Lauren, a bit of snideness in her voice that Lauren didn't appreciate.

"I didn't receive flowers after we rode in the park," she said, not inclined to reveal that hers had come before. They knew enough about her public moments with Tom. The private ones she intended to hold to herself—not that they'd had many private moments, but still . . .

"Do you think he'll come dressed as a cowboy tonight?" Lady Cassandra asked.

"I daresay that would be scandalous," Lady Blythe announced.

"He wasn't wearing gloves when he appeared at Ravenleigh's or the morning when we rode together in the park." Waving her fan frantically in front of her face, Lady Cassandra appeared on the verge of a swoon. "I've never touched a man's bare hand before. I do hope he shall ask me to dance."

"What if he doesn't know how to dance?" Lady Priscilla asked.

"Oh, he knows," Lauren assured them.

"Did you teach him?" Lady Priscilla asked.

"No, he picked that up in Texas, all on his—"

"Oh, my word, I think that's him," Lady Blythe interrupted breathlessly.

"I believe you're right," Lady Cassandra said. "I daresay it is quite a quandary whether I prefer him dressed as a cowboy or a gentleman. Although I must confess that I don't recall him looking quite so extraordinarily handsome."

"He does still look exceedingly dangerous, though. A wolf in sheep's clothing. I can scarcely breathe," Lady Blythe said.

Perhaps your corset is laced too tightly, Lauren considered murmuring, but held the words back, because she, too, was having difficulty breathing.

Tom was quite simply gorgeous. Every ounce of English blood he possessed was on display. Oh, he still possessed a slight swagger, but his mien radiated confidence and self-assurance. His black swallow-tailed double-breasted jacket, open to reveal his white silk waistcoat, did little to hide the breadth of his chest and shoulders. A white silk tie adorned his white shirt, and brought out the swarthiness of his deeply tanned complexion. The darkness of his skin was a stark contrast to the paler complexions of many of the other men in attendance. Yet so much more about him caused every head to turn toward him. It was the manner in which he strode through the room, dark and feral, sleek, like some ferocious beast that might be captured but never tamed. Not a wolf, but something more regal: a lion perhaps, a tiger, a panther. A creature that prowled through the night.

In spite of her recent tutoring and instructions, she'd failed to tame him, and that knowledge pleased her immensely. She had yet to destroy that which made him magnificent. And he was magnificent, as he cut a swath through the other men as though they hardly existed—with only a brief acknowledgment here and there—his gaze boring into her as though no other lady inhabited the room. With all these people gathered around, how had he managed to find her so easily?

Before he reached her, the music began signaling that the first dance of the evening—a waltz—was soon to begin. Lauren's dance card was almost completely filled, but she'd deliberately left the first dance open. Only now did she realize why.

Tom came to a stop before her, his gaze roaming over her, his eyes filling with an appreciation that caused her heart to speed up, her skin to grow warm.

"Good evening, darlin'," he said in that low rumble that sent shimmers of pleasure cascading through her.

"Hello, Tom." She shook her head, curtsied slightly. "Hello, my lord."

He grinned, his mustache shifting up to accommodate the width of his smile. "No need to be so formal, Lauren."

Before she could comment, he'd turned to the others. "Good evening, ladies. I can't recall ever seeing so much beauty in one place."

Lauren heard the tiniest of squeals and a wistful sigh.

"I hope I haven't arrived too late to reserve a dance with each of you."

Lady Blythe giggled annoyingly and held up her wrist, dangling her dance card in front of him. "I believe dance five is available. It's a waltz."

Tom took the pencil she offered and scrawled his name on her card. Then he looked at Lady Cassandra. "What about you, darlin'? Do you have a dance for me?"

Lady Cassandra began frantically waving her fan, and Lauren feared she was on the cusp of demonstrating one of her infamous swoons.

"Number eight," she fairly squealed, as though her corset was also laced up too tightly.

Lauren was feeling quite nasty; she didn't want to acknowledge that it might stem from the fact that they had such a keen interest in Tom or that he might be the slightest bit interested in them. She didn't like seeing him flirting with them, even though she knew it was his nature to flirt harmlessly with anything that wore skirts.

Tom signed Lady Cassandra's dance card, then

Lady Anne's and Lady Priscilla's. And as a few of the other ladies who'd been gathered nearby pressed in on him, he signed their cards as well. Then he winked, somehow managing to take in the entire assemblage. "Now if you ladies will excuse me, I promised my first dance to Miss Fairfield."

Tom reached for Lauren's hand, but before he could grab it she placed her hand on his arm.

"You offer a lady your arm," she said quietly.

He grimaced, and she thought she could see a blush beneath his collar. He wore no bandanna that might reflect any sort of red coloring onto his skin. How interesting that he was so easily embarrassed, that he did actually blush.

"Thanks," he said, as he escorted her onto the dance floor, where he smoothly took her within the circle of his arms.

"I must say that you are certainly charming the London ladies," she said.

"I'm trying. Harrington explained that my most important task is to find a wife."

She lost her footing—

"Whoa," he said. "Are you all right?"

—but his hold on her was sturdy enough that they managed to avoid any embarrassing mishap.

"Yes." She laughed self-consciously. Of course, he would marry. She knew that. She simply hadn't accepted it. "I didn't realize you'd already begun the wife hunt."

"The 'hunt' part makes it sound a little barbaric."

"Yes, I suppose it does, but still I didn't realize that you were searching for a wife already."

"Not seriously pursuing one at the moment. I'm simply keeping my options open." His gaze roamed over her bare shoulders. "I sure do appreciate your dress."

"I believe Charles Worth would shudder if he heard you call it a dress. It's an evening gown."

"It suits you."

"Worth has an uncanny ability to know the style and color that will most flatter a woman. His gowns are considered works of art, and I daresay that he charges enough that they could be framed and hung on walls as such."

Tom laughed. "Still a bit of country in you, isn't there, Lauren?"

"I sometimes fear there's more than a bit."

"Why does that frighten you?"

"That was simply an expression. I actually hope I've retained some of the country. I worry a bit that I won't fit in when I return to Texas. Wouldn't that be ironic, to find that I've changed so much that I might feel as out of place there as I once felt here?"

"I think if you set your mind to it, you can fit in wherever you want."

"I can at least give the appearance of fitting in," she admitted. "Speaking of fitting in, you certainly have adapted well. I don't think you're going to need me at all tonight."

"Oh, darlin', I need you. Don't doubt that for a second."

There was an undercurrent to his words, something more than the idle banter. She wanted to touch his cheek, brush back his hair that had fallen forward. As he continued to swirl her around the room, she became lost in the heat of his dark gaze. She didn't want to think of him looking at anyone else in quite the same manner as he looked at her: as though she was still his.

The music drifted into silence and quiet murmurs began to take up the space left behind as people started to seek out their next partner. Lauren had never had a chance to dance with Tom in Texas. She was glad that at least she'd leave England having had one dance with him.

He leaned near, bending his head slightly. "It was my pleasure to dance with you, darlin'. I hope you've saved at least one more dance for me."

Her heart fluttered with the seductive rasp of his voice, the wafting of his breath just below her ear. She nodded, barely able to push out the words. "The last one."

"I'll be counting the minutes."

As he escorted her off the dance floor, she realized that she would be as well.

Tom had never had occasion to experience jealousy, but at the moment it was sure rearing its ugly head. Lauren was without a doubt the most beautiful woman in the room, and one of the most sought after. Her dance card was obviously filled because she had yet to sit out a dance. Tom seldom took his eyes off her, which made dancing with any other lady a dangerous undertaking.

"Stop watching her."

Tom shifted his gaze to Lydia. It seemed that they'd both improved since they'd danced in her family's barn on her birthday. "I can't say I think much of this two-dance rule you have over here," he said.

She gave him an impish grin. "If we didn't, she wouldn't have much of a chance to dance with anyone else, now would she?"

Not if he had anything to say about it. Not that he thought he would. During the past week, during each of their outings, she'd been polite and reserved while rattling off instructions, explanations, and examples of what was considered proper and what wasn't. He couldn't deny that he'd learned a lot or that she was doing exactly as he'd asked: teaching him to project the polished veneer of a civilized man. But they'd seldom had a moment alone, to truly talk, to explore possibilities.

It had taken every bit of restraint he could muster not to go out every night and toss rocks at her window to get her attention.

"Oh, someone's brooding," Lydia said.

He dropped his gaze to Lydia's. "My apologies.

I was just thinking about everything we've done in the past week, and it doesn't seem like we've really had any time to just . . ." He let his voice trail off. To just what? To get to know each other again?

"The Season is known for being a whirlwind of activities."

"And you love it."

"I do. And I'll warn you that it's about to get much more hectic, now that the first ball has taken place."

More hectic? He couldn't imagine. He wanted to embrace this life, but he found himself longing for the quiet of a star-filled night.

"If some other lady catches your fancy, and you'd like an introduction, do be sure to let me know, and I'll arrange one," Lydia offered.

"I appreciate the kindness."

The final strains of the music fell into the silence. To his surprise, Lydia rose up on her toes and whispered, "I have it on good authority that *she* is in the habit of always taking a turn about the garden during dances twelve and thirteen."

Tom grinned down on her. "Now I appreciate that bit of information even more than an introduction."

She smiled warmly. "I thought you might."

The promise of a rendezvous echoed through Tom's mind as he danced with Lady Blythe, maybe the second-prettiest gal in the room. She was flirtatious, and he couldn't deny that he enjoyed the way she smiled whenever he called her darlin'. But she couldn't hold his attention. It seemed the only woman with that power was Lauren.

Lauren to whom he'd promised to purchase passage to Texas at the end of the Season. He couldn't have made a more unsatisfying bargain if he'd made his deal with the devil.

He slipped outside during the eleventh dance and stood in the shadows, watching as others— some discreetly, some not as much—made their way along the gas-lit path that led into the gardens. Some moved about almost guiltily, and he wondered if they had plans to leave the path, to go where they couldn't be seen, to be a little daring, a little bold, to cast propriety aside for a little bit of fun.

That's what he was missing: good old-fashioned fun. He couldn't explain why he wasn't having a good time. He enjoyed the company, and he was certainly engaged in a variety of activities, but he couldn't truly identify the purpose behind any of them—unless it was simply to be seen and in the being seen to make an impression on London.

He wondered how long he'd feel this need to impress, how long before he'd feel that he'd succeeded at putting his father to rest.

Hearing the music waft into silence, he turned his attention to the French doors, envisioning Lauren's latest dance partner escorting her back to her circle of friends, wondering how long she'd wait to make her escape. Not long at all.

A grin crept up his face as she appeared in the doorway, disappearing so quickly into the shadows, that if he hadn't been waiting for her, he might have missed her. He stepped forward, and she released a startled gasp.

"Oh, what are you doing here?" she asked.

He chuckled low. "Do you have any idea how many times you've asked me that since I got to London?"

"Obviously it bears asking when you continually show up so unexpectedly."

"You didn't ask Lydia to tell me that you'd be out here walking?"

"No. My cousin seems to be involved in a bit of mischief. I didn't realize she was so acutely aware of my habits."

Her voice contained no censure, maybe a spark of teasing, as though she wasn't completely upset that Lydia had shared her little ritual with Tom.

"Why do you always stroll in the garden during these particular dances?"

"I simply need some time away from the madness, and planning always to sit out the same dances worked well."

"So do you mind if I join you?"

"Not as long as you behave."

"You take away all the fun." Still, he extended his arm, and she placed her hand on it.

"You seem to be enjoying the ball," she said, after they'd taken a few steps and settled into an easy stride.

How could he explain? He was in favor of having a good time, couldn't deny that he found pleasure in holding a woman in his arms and whirling her over a dance floor, and yet—

"There are so many rules that it diminishes the fun a bit."

She smiled up at him. "I've never quite been able to put my finger on exactly what it was that bothered me. Perhaps that's it. I can't deny that I enjoy dancing, and the gentlemen are always pleasant—"

"Maybe too pleasant."

Before Lauren realized what he intended, he'd snaked an arm around her waist and guided her off the path and into the shadowy darkness behind a trellis of roses. She found her back up against a wall, Tom so near, not touching, but close enough that she could feel the warmth of his body seeping into hers.

"Admit it, Lauren. What you don't like is that they're too refined over here, that they don't tempt you to do the forbidden."

He grazed his bare finger along her cheek. When had he removed his glove? Did he always have to remove it before he touched her?

"They're proper," he said.

He boldly trailed his finger down to her collarbone, stealing her ability to speak as it passed along her throat.

"They're tamed," he continued, as his touch dipped slightly lower, hovering just above the swell of her breast, causing her nipples to harden in anticipation, her knees to weaken.

"And, darlin', you've always had too much wildness to settle for the tamed."

Hungrily, he blanketed her mouth with his, his hand moving up to stroke her cheek, the underside of her chin, her throat . . . improperly in a proper sort of way. He certainly could have been more bold, and she was so far lost in the passion elicited by his questing tongue that she wouldn't have objected. He could have peeled back her bodice, exposed her to his dark gaze, and she'd have not cared.

He took only what he was certain she was willing to give, and she was beyond thinking clearly so that she might urge him to take more. Instead, she simply returned his kiss with equal fervor, raking her hands up into his hair, holding him tightly in place, at once wanting him near and fearing that without his support she would simply collapse to the ground because her legs had somehow lost the strength to hold her up without powerful assistance, and he was beyond any doubt powerful.

His arms came around her like banded steel, pressing her close as he changed the angle of the kiss so he could increase the intimacy. Heat and desire almost overwhelmed her. She'd managed over the past week to keep both at bay, to think of Tom as a project, someone to be taught, but not touched, someone to expose to London life without wondering what it might be like to live with him. She fought to remain aloof, to build up her walls, to refrain from wondering how different it all might be if he were still in Texas waiting for her.

She thought he'd become properly civilized.

Instead, his kiss was clearly demonstrating the error in her thinking. He was still as untamed as the land that had once brought them together.

And so was she.

To want as badly as she did to have his mouth devouring hers, to need his arms around her as much as she did. Want and need, bouncing back and forth, like a ball across a tennis lawn. Want. Need. Need. Want.

His mouth was suddenly gone, and she found her cheek pressed into the crook of his shoulder, where she could hear the hammering of his heart, each harsh rapid breath, his and hers, filling up the night, drowning out every other sound.

How long had they been there? How many dances had passed? Had they been missed?

She felt something tickle faintly over her shoulder, went to brush it away, and realized it was her hair. Panicked, she pushed away from Tom, reached up to touch her coiffure, and realized that a good deal of it was no longer in place. She could hardly return to the ballroom with swollen, tingling lips and mussed hair. And she had a feeling he might look equally untidy. After all, she recalled her fingers scraping along his scalp. She didn't know why she didn't recall his doing the same.

"There's a side door that leads into the servant area that will at least get us back into the house, hopefully undetected so we can put ourselves back to rights," she told him.

She felt him tugging on loosened strands of her hair, could see the flash of his grin in the faint light provided by the gaslights.

"I like the way you look now," he said.

"You can't see me clearly in the dark."

"Clear enough."

She wished the deep rumble of his voice didn't make her want to latch her mouth on to his again. Wild indeed. She made a move to edge past him, and he grabbed her arm, effectively stilling her movement.

"Don't go get straightened up," he said. "Let's just leave."

"Leave and do what? I think this little foray behind the roses has clearly demonstrated that neither of us is as civilized as we should be."

"It also demonstrated that we're not as wild as we could be. You're still dressed."

Completely and absolutely, which she considered somewhat of a miracle since her body had grown as warm as Texas in August.

"Tom, it's completely inappropriate for me to leave with you."

"Even if we're not seen?"

"My parents will be looking for me, as well as the gentlemen to whom I've promised dances. No, I'm sorry. I can't risk ruining my reputation."

"You're leaving, Lauren. In Texas, your reputation will be whatever you damned well want it to be."

"But I'm not there yet, and I have my family to consider. I won't have any embarrassment visited upon them, because you and I haven't the strength to behave civilized."

She freed her arm of his grip, pressed a kiss to her fingertips, and touched them to his warm lips. "Last dance. I'll see you then."

She peered out from behind the trellis, saw no one about, and hurried to the side of the house, grateful that she knew her cousin's house as well as her own and could make it safely inside where she could quickly put her hair back into place and hope no one noticed that it didn't look quite as it originally had.

Get back inside where it might be easier to resist the temptations offered by Thomas Warner, who not only tempted her to leave with him, but tempted her to stay as well.

* * *

Tom wasn't enjoying his second dance with Lady Blythe as much as he had the first, mostly because he was viewing it as simply a way to pass the time until the final dance, when he would again hold Lauren in his arms. A shame he wouldn't be able to do more than that, at least not in a gaily lit ballroom. He wondered if she might be willing to take another walk in the garden.

Out of the corner of his eye, he caught sight of Lauren coming back into the ballroom, no outward appearances that she'd almost been ravished behind the roses. How could she look so calm and unaffected, when he was still carrying the scent of her on his skin?

"My lord," Lady Blythe began.

Tom tilted his head slightly, wondering what she was waiting for. "Yes, darlin'?"

She released her short breathless giggle. "I do so love when you call me that." She gnawed on her lower lip, did a quick glance around, before locking her gaze on his. "My lord, I couldn't help but notice that you seem to give quite a bit of attention to Miss Fairfield."

Tom fought not to clench his jaw or tell her that to whom he gave attention was none of her business. He was proud of the smile that he gave Lady Blythe and the flat tone of his voice. "Yes, as it happens, I do."

"I hope you won't consider me too presumptuous, and as a rule, I'm not one to speak ill of anyone, can't tolerate gossip and the hurt that it has the potential to cause, but as you are only recently arrived in London, you might be unaware that Miss Fairfield has gained a reputation as a lady who lures a man in only to humiliate him. The poor Duke of Kimburton sought her favor last Season, and she granted it, unwaveringly, until he was assured that he held her heart. When he asked for her hand in marriage, she humiliated him by declining."

Tom lost the battle not to clench his jaw. "Maybe he misunderstood—"

"Oh, no. You can ask anyone here. She flirted with him shamelessly. A lady shouldn't encourage a man for whom she feels nothing. It's quite simply not done. The result is disastrous, to his heart, to his confidence. All were convinced that she favored him. No one was surprised when he proposed marriage, but all were stunned, shocked, actually, when she rejected the offer without explanation or any inkling as to the reason."

"Is Kimburton here tonight?"

He wanted to see the man, get his side of the story.

"Oh, my word, no. He was mortified. He's chosen not to come to London this Season, and I, for one, can hardly blame him. I tell you this only as a precaution. I have always liked Miss Fairfield and still consider her a friend, but even as a friend I cannot approve of her blatant disregard for the duke's honor, and I fear she may lead you down a similar unhappy path."

She blinked, smiled, blinked again. Tom usually wasn't at a loss for words, but he hardly knew what to say, mostly because his mind was reeling with the knowledge that another man had asked for Lauren's hand; that Lauren had actually encouraged him, that she might have even been seriously considering the offer.

"I would never encourage a man whom I did not wish to wed," Lady Blythe said, as though she'd grown tired of waiting for Tom to come up with some sort of response, to fill up the silence stretching between them. "It seems rather cruel to me."

"I don't guess it's possible that he misinterpreted her actions—"

"Oh, no. On occasion she rather boldly sought him out, and everyone simply attributed her forthrightness to her American upbringing, but now one must wonder if she perhaps had an ulterior motive, although one can only guess what it might have been. And as I don't have a propensity toward unkind behavior, I must sadly confess to being at a complete loss regarding what she might have been thinking."

The music drifted into silence. Lady Blythe placed her gloved hand on his arm, her eyes filled with concern. "I beg of you, do take care where she is concerned. It is obvious you are vulnerable to her wiles. And as I said, it would pain me greatly to see you hurt. While I have only been in your company a short time, I have grown rather fond of you."

"I appreciate your concern."

The lie rolled off his tongue with ease, when in truth he wanted to lash out at her for the things she'd told him. His muscles were tense, his jaw aching as he escorted her off the dance floor and returned her to a group of young ladies who were tittering and giggling. Suddenly he was irritated with everything.

He left them to their gossip, and he had no doubt they would begin to gossip—about him, about Lauren.

He wondered why she'd never mentioned Kimburton, wondered exactly what her feelings toward the man had been. It seemed he and Lauren had a hell of a lot more to discuss. He wanted to find her and—

"—believe she had the audacity to attend this ball."

"The Duchess of Harrington is her cousin. She could hardly not come."

"On the contrary, I believe she should have had the decency not to show regardless of any relationship she may have with the hostess."

"I daresay she seems to have caught Sachse's attention."

"Poor blighter has no idea regarding the humiliation she's capable of inflicting."

"Perhaps we should seek an introduction, so we

can explain the truth of the matter and save him the misfortune of making a complete fool of himself where Miss Fairfield is concerned."

"No introduction needed," Tom said to the backs of the three men standing at the edge of the dance floor. If he hadn't been in a dangerously foul mood after Lady Blythe's revelations—before hearing their pompous words—he might have laughed at the way they all jerked and spun around as though they were puppets dangling on strings.

"I say, Sachse, I don't believe we've been formally introduced," the taller and lankier of the trio said.

Tom, unkindly, could envision him serving as a scarecrow in a field of corn. As a matter of fact, he wouldn't mind hanging him on the poles himself.

"Allow me to do the honors," the man continued as Tom held his silence. "I'm the Earl of Whithaven and my cohorts"—chuckle, chuckle—"are the Marquess of Kingston and Viscount Reynolds."

The other two gentlemen mumbled greetings.

"You were gossiping about Miss Fairfield," Tom said pointedly.

"Oh, no, no, no, dear fellow," Whithaven said. "Women gossip. We were merely . . . conversing, exchanging concerns, speculating on the inevitability of a Season gone awry. We couldn't help but notice that you seemed quite smitten by Miss Fairfield—"

"I don't see that it's any of your business."

"Perhaps not, but we felt that we should warn you that she treated one of our friends rather badly last Season. A very likable chap, Kimburton, and that is not even taking into consideration the prestige of his title, for which she showed blatant disregard."

"Because she said no?"

"Because, old chap, she gave every indication that she would say yes. I lost a fortune on the wagers. Hardly sporting of her to dupe us all."

"Hardly *sporting of you* to wager on the outcome." He'd made his delivery in a perfect British accent that had all three men bugging their eyes.

Tom took a step toward the man who appeared to be the leader of the bunch. "If I were you, I'd stop talking about Miss Fairfield, or I'll be making a wager on whether or not you're fast enough to duck my fist."

"You wouldn't dare."

Tom gave his head a shake, turned to go, couldn't do it—

His fist was flying into Whithaven's face before he realized it. The man would have lost the wager had he made it. He wasn't fast enough to duck. He stumbled back into a dancing couple before landing on the floor with a thud.

Someone screamed, Tom heard a few gasps, a squeal, the music suddenly stopped, Reynolds was sputtering.

"See here!" Kingston said. "That was uncalled for."

Tom felt a hand on his arm, looked over to see Lauren staring at him, her brow deeply furrowed, horror at his actions clearly etched in her eyes. "Tom, what on earth do you think you're doing?"

"Being a barbaric Texan."

"Is there a problem?" Harrington asked.

Tom turned to the man he'd thought he might be able to develop a friendship with. "I'm sorry for disrupting your party. I should have taken this outside."

"Perhaps you should come to the library—"

"No, thank you, I think it would be best if I left." He looked over at Whithaven. A woman with blond hair and green eyes was kneeling beside him, while Kingston and Reynolds were muttering and trying to get the man's nose to stop bleeding.

Then Tom was storming out of the room before he did more damage. So much for proving he wasn't his father.

Chapter 12

～∾∾～

Tom was so angry that he could have chewed nails. Angry at himself for losing control, angry at Whithaven for daring to dare him, angry at Lauren for showing interest in another man, even if that interest had ended.

Angry at himself for storming out. Angry at Lauren for not following, not that he'd invited her to, but still he'd thought she might come after him. Angry because he wore the veneer of civilization, but that's all it was. A veneer that looked good on the outside, but the shining surface hid from view the rotting wood beneath. He wished they'd never come searching for him. He wished his father's blood didn't race through his veins.

He was angry about that most of all.

That he couldn't be the man he'd become.

He sat in a heavy, brocaded chair in the sitting area of his bedchamber, a fire burning in the fireplace because he couldn't get used to the chill of the night or the cold of the house. Even the whiskey he was downing straight from the bottle seemed unable to warm him.

He heard the door open, close. Damned valet. The man seemed to think he was in charge of more than Tom's clothes; he was in charge of his life. "Thought I told you to go on to bed, that I could undress myself tonight."

"Actually, I don't recall your saying that to me."

Lauren.

Tom came up out of the chair so fast, turning so quickly, that his head spun, and he thought he might bring up the whiskey he'd already downed.

Standing just inside the room, she wore a simple dress, not a single flounce, ribbon, or bow on it. Something she could have put on without any help at all, something like what she'd worn that first night when they'd gone down to the river. Her hair was piled on her head, and he cursed himself for longing to see it released, draped around her shoulders, flowing down her back. Where she was concerned, he seemed unable to stop himself from longing for a lot of things.

He couldn't take his eyes off her as she crossed the short distance separating them, moving around a small table until she was near and nothing separated them except the memories that joined them.

Her eyes reflected a sadness that made him want to reach out, take her in his arms, and comfort her, assure her that everything would be all right. But he'd never been a man to make promises he couldn't keep.

"I'm here to make good on the debt I owe you," she said quietly.

His gut clenched so tightly that he almost dropped to his knees. Her words were the last he'd expected to hear.

"And when the debt is paid, I want to be released from the bargain we made."

He could hardly blame her for that request. He had no doubt that his earlier actions had brought her shame. He nodded. "Agreed."

"Do you remember the conditions of the debt, Tom? The conditions that apply to you?"

He swallowed hard. "Look, but don't touch."

"I want your word that you'll keep your end of the bargain."

His word? Not to touch what he so desperately wanted to hold? To walk away from what he so desperately wanted to claim? Did she know what she was asking of him and what it would cost him to follow through on his end of the bargain?

His hands were already shaking so badly that he figured they'd be here all night while he struggled to make them work. "I won't touch you, but you'll have to do the unbuttoning."

She gave a brisk nod. "And with that little change in the arrangement, you'll consider the debt paid in full?"

Nodding, he took a step back. "Pay up, Lauren."

Pay up so he could release her from both bargains. Pay up and he'd purchase her passage back to Texas within a day. Pay up and she'd never have to spend another minute with the savage who couldn't bring his best behavior to a ballroom, who'd acted as though he were in a saloon. He didn't deserve her. He never had. He wanted her running from him as fast as her legs would take her.

She dropped her gaze to the floor, licked her lips, took a deep breath . . .

And just stood there.

"I'm not going to consider the debt paid until those buttons are undone," he said.

"How many?"

"Clear down to your waist."

He thought she flinched, watched as her cheeks turned as red as a summer strawberry, thought about calling the debt paid, but when this was no longer between them, they would have nothing. "Come on now—"

"Stop rushing me! I've never done this before."

He knew it was wrong to let her spark of anger so please him. But it did. She had the ability to stand up to him, the ability to give back as good as she got. She deserved a man who would give her the best, and that wasn't him.

"You've never unbuttoned a bodice?" he asked.

"Not in front of a man."

"It's no different."

"Of course it's different. How would you like it if I insisted you unbutton your trousers?"

He couldn't stop the slow smile from spreading across his face. "I'll be happy to oblige if it'll make you feel more comfortable."

A corner of her mouth twitched. "You're always corrupting me, Tom."

"Keep taunting me, Lauren, and I'll decide that I need to do the unbuttoning."

"Don't rush me, Tom."

"Don't rush you? Hell, woman, I've waited ten years! Now do it!"

Before he did lose what little patience remained to him. The impatience seeped right out of him when she raised her hands to that first button just below her throat and he saw how badly they were shaking—almost as badly as his would be if they were about to do the same task.

"Lauren?"

Lauren lifted her gaze back to his. The tenderness in his voice, in his eyes was almost her undoing.

"Just take your time," he said quietly, without the anger or the impatience that had marked his earlier words.

It was an odd thing to be in the reality of a moment she'd fantasized about over the years. She was taunting him, deliberately, making him wait for what he wanted, just as she'd had to wait all these years. Wait for him to come for her until she'd given up on him, until she'd almost given herself over to another man's promise.

She wasn't afraid of Tom. She never had been. Not from the first moment she'd laid eyes on him. But he did call out to the wildness in her, to the part of her that wanted to be wicked, to do things that she knew were wrong. To be the uncivilized hellion that London's ladies whispered about with meanness. To be everything she had shoved aside.

She sometimes felt as though she'd been suffocated, shaped and molded into what her mother thought she should be, what society thought she should be, rather than the woman she truly was. Only with Tom did she ever feel that she had a chance to be herself.

Which was the very reason that she was there. Because there was a wicked part of her that did want to unbutton her bodice for him . . . a terrified part that feared he'd be disappointed with what he saw.

He'd not spoken a single word about love. He was interested in her for a debt owed, a bargain to be kept. And it was time she kept it. Released them both from the past.

He wasn't going to touch her. He wasn't going to

see much more than was revealed by her most immodest of evening gowns. It was just the idea . . . that she would slowly reveal what was presently hidden. And slowly was exactly how she intended to do it. Make him wait a little longer.

She pressed her fingers against her palms to stop their shaking and took a deep breath to try to stop her body's trembling. The tremors cascading through her were distracting, and she was afraid that he could see them, traveling over her skin, that he would know how nervous she was.

She reached for the first button, not certain if it was her fingers or the ivory that was so terribly cold. That she managed to loosen it so easily was encouraging, for surely, then, her nervousness didn't show. With the second button, she'd expected his gaze to dip, but it didn't. It remained steadfastly fixed on hers. With the fourth button, he bunched his hands into fists at his side. With the fifth he reached out with one hand and grabbed the mantel, his fingers digging into it until his knuckles turned white, and she was surprised that the black marble didn't crumble within his grasp.

A light sheen of dew appeared on his forehead, and she wasn't even certain that he continued to breathe. When she loosened the final button, she eased her fingers between the parted material and brought it back to reveal the white cotton of her chemise and while she was still modestly covered, she felt as though she were completely naked.

He lowered his gaze then, and what she saw in his eyes was almost her undoing. Raw, feral desire, a yearning so great as to be painful.

He turned away from her, grabbing the mantel with his other hand, bowing his head, staring at the flames dancing in the fire.

"The debt's paid," he rasped. "You can go."

It was what she wanted, to be free of the debt, to have nothing between them that could separate them. She took a step toward him—

"Get out of here, Lauren," he growled through clenched teeth without looking at her, "before I do something we'll both regret. I proved tonight that I'm not far removed from being a barbarian."

And that, too, was the reason she was there. Because she'd seen his face after he hit Whithaven, had seen the shame and mortification he felt before he'd quickly masked it. She'd seen a man who wanted to prove he was different from the man who had come before him, different from his father, and in the eyes of those surrounding him, had seen that he was thought to be the same.

"A barbarian would have me on the bed already," she said quietly.

He looked at her then—and in his eyes, she saw not the boy he'd once been, but the man he'd become, a man who was barely holding on to his passions. "I'm warning you. You'd better go."

"Barbarians don't warn." She took a step closer.

"Why *did* you hit Whithaven? Did he say something—"

"He said a lot."

"About you?"

She watched as the muscles in his jaw jumped.

"About me," she said softly. "What exactly did he say?"

"That you had someone. I'm busting my back in Texas and you're favoring some fella—"

"I never got your letters," she said calmly. "Ten years. You can't possibly believe in all that time that some gentleman didn't give me attention or that I didn't give attention to him. You can't tell me that you never had a woman—"

"Mine were all paid for. Not a one of them ever thought she meant something to me, Lauren, not a one ever expected a marriage proposal, not a one ever thought I'd give her the honor of taking my name. Not one stood a chance of taking your place in my heart."

In his heart. She'd held a place in his heart. Did she still?

She moved nearer. "It's different over here, Tom, different for a woman. A woman's value is based upon what she brings to a marriage. From the time she has her coming out, her only acceptable goal is to get married. She is constantly on display, no matter where she goes: for a stroll in the park, to a concert, a ball, a dinner. The way she is dressed is commented on, the way she behaves is the subject of conversations. Every damned aspect of her life is scrutinized: Does she have the proper friends? Did she dance the proper number of dances?

"So, yes, when Kimburton singled me out for attention, I reciprocated. It was so damned wonderful to feel that I had to please but one man instead of a hundred. And he was so incredibly nice, and for a while I wasn't lonely. For a while, I didn't go to bed every night thinking about you."

"Why did you turn him down?"

Her throat burned with the effort to hold her tears at bay, but they escaped, spilling over onto her cheeks. "Because I realized that if I married him, I would have to live here forever, and I couldn't promise him forever. That's when I went to work, when I started making my plans to return to Texas, because I had to know if you'd forgotten me."

"Ah, darlin'." Then he was there, holding her near with one arm while with the knuckles of his other hand he tenderly gathered up her tears. "I could never forget you, Lauren. Sweet Lord, girl, how could you ever think that I would?"

He lowered his head and brushed his lips over hers as lightly as a breeze wafted over the first blossoms of spring. Yearning so intense nearly caused her knees to buckle, and she thought if he wasn't supporting her with one strong arm, she might have fallen.

He slanted his mouth across hers and settled in

as though he had plans to take up permanent residence. Somewhere in the far recesses of her mind, she thought she should object, but her heart was winning this battle, begging her to stay, to finish what they'd started so very long ago, when they were both too young to care about anything or anyone other than themselves and their wants. Before society stifled them with rules, before earlier promises gave way to later ones.

He nibbled on her lips, then glided his tongue over her mouth as though to heal what he might have hurt, but his actions caused no pain, except to her heart, which had been without him for too long and could no longer be with him forever. Still, she relished his touch, his attentions, and when she parted her lips in welcome, he took full advantage, using his tongue to explore, to taunt, to tease. No other man had ever kissed her as Tom did, and she realized with startling clarity that she'd never wanted another man to be so intimate with her. Kissing Tom, pressing her body against his, recognizing the feel of his burgeoning desire, was as natural as breathing.

There was no shame in these feelings, no dishonor in this closeness. She wanted to do more than unbutton her bodice. She wanted to remove all her clothes, unbutton his trousers, and remove all his clothes.

Tom deepened the kiss, relishing the feel of her arms winding around his neck, her body flattened against his. The willowy girl who had climbed out her bedroom window to meet with him had grown into a woman that a man's arms ached to hold. She fit perfectly, and it was all he could do to restrain himself, not to discover how perfectly he might fit within her.

With a groan, he tore his mouth from hers, lifted her into his arms, and carried her the short distance to the bed. Gently, he laid her down before following and stretching out beside her. Her gaze was riveted on his face, as she watched him, but he saw no fear. He saw only desire that rivaled his and something that ran much deeper.

He kissed her chin, her jaw, and trailed his mouth along the column of her throat, so silky smooth, so soft. A sloping pathway to more softness.

He raised himself on an elbow and, with his forefinger and thumb, he grabbed the end of the bow that kept her chemise closed. Such a flimsy piece of satin for such an important job.

He slid his gaze up to hers, taking in the creamy texture of her skin, the slight blush that marred it where his roughened jaw had journeyed, and he cursed himself for not shaving after he got home, but he'd had no way of knowing she'd come to him. Or maybe it was his mustache that had caused the damage. For her, if she asked, he'd shave it off as well.

He kept his eyes on hers, his breathing ragged, waiting for her to react to his veiled request, and her answer came as he'd hoped, with nothing more than a lowering of her lashes that struck him deep in the gut.

When she'd been unbuttoning her bodice, he'd never wanted anything in his life more than he'd wanted to cross over to her and finish the task, brush his knuckles against the inside swells that she was so slowly revealing. He'd always known he was a man of determination, but until that moment he'd never known how much control he had over himself. Only a man encased in steel could have looked at her and not taken.

He swallowed hard, his mouth suddenly dry, his breaths coming in harsh gasps. He tugged on the ribbon, watched as the bow ceased to exist. Fighting to hold his fingers steady, he pulled the ribbon loose of its moorings, watching as the material parted to reveal her flesh.

With the side of his hand and the gentlest touch, he moved the material farther aside to reveal her breasts, in full, the pale pink nipples, the light blue veins. His gut and groin tightened so much that it was almost painful. "You are so beautiful."

"I'm not really very fully growed," she whispered.

With effort, he shifted his gaze up to hers. Her cheeks were a bright reddish hue. "Not like Lady Blythe or Lady—"

He touched his finger to her lips. "You're perfect."

"I'm small." Her breath wafted over his hand.

"You're perfect." He lowered his mouth and kissed her while he moved his hand down, his fingers curling over her perfection.

Lauren was beginning to wonder if the fire had jumped out of the hearth and was blazing around them. She'd never felt so hot and flushed in her entire life. Tom's kiss was as feral, possessive as his hand laying claim to that which he wanted. She couldn't envision any of the gentlemen of London behaving as Tom did, ravishing her to within an inch of her life. For surely she would die from the sensations that he was creating with each sweep of his tongue, each stroke of his fingers.

This time when he trailed his mouth along her throat, he didn't stop at its base, other than briefly to dip the tip of his tongue into its hollow, then he continued on, kissing the inside swell of her breasts, before journeying on to kiss and plunder that which he'd brazenly paid to see. She combed her fingers up into his hair, still too long, still so thick, still dark and beautiful, with the firelight glistening over it.

And then it was as though whatever he'd held leashed, he released. With a deep groan, he returned for another kiss, this one more intense, more possessive than any that had come before it. It was a prelude to a promise she wasn't certain she could keep.

They were suddenly hands, mouths, tongues,

touching, kissing, stroking, pressing. His body was weighing down on hers. A pleasant weight. She would have thought that his height, the breadth of his shoulders would have made her feel as though she were suffocating, but instead she only felt the increase of passion, the desire to have him closer, as close as possible.

She was barely cognizant of a subtle shifting of his weight and then his hand was beneath her skirt, gliding up her thigh . . . rough skin against smooth flesh, hands that had tamed horses, trailed cattle, branded, roped, fought stampedes were working to tame her, and in the taming, he was unleashing the wildness in her.

She pushed her hands against his shoulders. Breathing heavily, he stilled, holding her gaze. The intensity with which he looked at her sent desire, hot and burning swirling through her.

"I unbuttoned my buttons for you," she rasped, surprised by the harsh sound of her own voice. "The least you can do is unbutton yours for me."

"If I do that, Lauren, your clothes are coming all the way off."

She nodded.

He pushed himself up until he was sitting on the edge of the bed, looking down on her, his hands working the buttons free with such haste that she almost laughed. Instead, she sat up, too, reached out, and took hold of his cuff, slipping the button through its loop. She did the same with the other.

Then she sat back and watched as he pulled his shirt over his head, to reveal his magnificent chest.

Reaching out, she touched an old scar that ran across his ribs. "How did you get this?" When he didn't answer, she looked up at him, into his eyes, saw the haunting look of memories best left behind. "Was it when the old man who took you off the orphan train beat you?"

Slowly he shook his head and rasped, "No."

"How did you get it?"

"My father," he said through clenched teeth.

His father? The horror of that statement must have shown on her face, because he continued. "I'm remembering things, Lauren, and I'm wishing to God that I didn't. I wish I hadn't hit Whithaven—"

She pressed her fingers to his lips. "I know. But we can fix that. We can, Tom." She lowered her head and pressed her lips to the puckered flesh.

His breath caught and she felt him go absolutely still. "Lauren?"

She looked at him, watched as his throat worked while he swallowed.

"I don't want to remember the past tonight," he finally managed to say, as though dredging the words up out of a bottomless well. Then he hitched up the corner of his mouth in the all-too-familiar grin, the smile that she'd loved from the moment he first bestowed it on her. "Are you going to unbutton my trousers?"

She felt the heat cascade through her with a scalding intensity. She wanted to be bold, brave, wanton . . . a Texas girl not an English miss . . . but in the end she disappointed herself and probably him by shaking her head.

If he was disappointed he showed no signs of it as he placed his hands on the button at his waist. Watching it pop free, parting the material, she began easing her dress and chemise off her shoulders. She'd wiggled out of her clothing, by the time he finished with his buttons and was shoving his trousers down to reveal the full measure of his manhood.

She swallowed hard, smiled, met his gaze. "My goodness, Tom, you're fully growed."

Laughing, he dove onto the bed, onto her, kissing her madly, touching her passionately. Hungrily, greedily, tasting, stroking, exploring . . . all aspects of her body. He removed the pins from her hair, fanning it out over the pillow only to fist his hand in the strands and bury his face in the abundance of it, inhaling deeply as he did so, as though to take her very essence deep within him.

She skimmed her hands over his back, his shoulders, along his sides, her fingers now and then noting a trail of puckered flesh and she cursed the life that had delivered the hurt even as she recognized that the journey he'd taken had brought him to her. Had his mother never taken him away, never left him to be raised by others, she doubted that he would have become the kind of man she could have loved this deeply, this intensely. And she did love him, had always loved him.

She could give herself all the reasons in the world for why she'd turned down Kimburton's offer, but the truth of the matter was, when it came right down to it, he simply wasn't Tom. Wasn't her cowboy. Wasn't the boy who had stolen her heart beneath a vast star-filled Texas night sky.

Her mama had always called Tom a thief, but how could a person truly steal what he already owned?

Tom nestled himself between her thighs, and she felt the first urgent pressing of his body against hers, hard to soft. She was ready for him, she knew she was, but there was discomfort and she stiffened.

"Damn, but you're tight."

"I'm sorry," she said, barely breathing.

He chuckled low. "Don't apologize, darlin'. That's a good thing. At least for me."

"Should we be talking right now?"

He raised up on his elbows, cradled her face between his work-worn hands. "When it comes to this, Lauren, there aren't any rules, or any dos or don'ts, except to make sure that it doesn't hurt and that it feels good. I don't know how to stop it from hurting you, darlin'. The first time, anyway. After that, it's supposed to be better. Or so I hear."

"I'll hold you to that promise of making it not hurt the second time."

"I'll keep that promise."

He lowered his mouth to hers, his tongue sweeping through, teasing, cajoling, almost distracting her . . .

He swallowed her cry as he joined his body to hers. She held him tightly, to hold him still, could feel the quivering of his muscles as he fought for control. He kissed away a tear that rolled from the corner of her eye.

"I'm sorry, darlin'."

"It wasn't that bad, Tom. It's just . . ."

He lifted his head, held her gaze, a question in his eyes . . . doubt, worry, concern. Emotions he seldom showed the world, that he only revealed with her. Her rough cowboy, who could melt her with a kiss, who wore a gun strapped to his thigh, her tough cowboy had a soft heart.

"I've wanted this for so long, imagined you this . . . close," she whispered.

He blanketed her mouth with his as he began to rock his hips against hers, shallow and deep, long and short, slow and quick, until they found their rhythm. She felt the pleasure begin to build, intensify, until she was digging her fingers into his backside, urging him on. He carried her higher, farther . . .

Until the pleasure streaked through her, and she cried out for him, for her, for them. His guttural groan mingled with her cries as he arched his back, delivering a final thrust, and she felt the heat of his seed pouring into her.

Breathing heavily, he collapsed on top of her, both their bodies covered in a fine sheen of moisture.

"That was like a falling star," she murmured.

He chuckled low. "So quick, you almost missed it?"

She wrapped her arms around him, squeezed him tightly. "No, Tom. So beautiful, it was worth searching for."

Chapter 13

Tom awoke to find her sitting on the floor in front of the fire, a blanket draped around her, her clothes still strewn on the floor beside his. He thought about telling her that he loved her, that he'd always loved her, but it seemed a cruel thing to do, as cruel as taking her to his bed when he had no plans to hold on to her.

He got out of bed, picked up his trousers, drew them on, and buttoned them up. If she heard him, she gave no indication, just sat there staring into the fire that was close to going out completely. He wondered if she had regrets.

He wouldn't trade these moments with her for anything, but he wasn't sure she could say the same. She wanted Texas, and he could offer her only a little bit of it. Probably not enough for a woman who had taken to working in a shop so she could get herself back to the place that she loved.

He sat beside her, one leg raised, resting his wrist on his knee, gazing at her because he didn't know how much longer he'd have before she wasn't there anymore.

"What are you thinking?" he asked.

"How funny life is. You think you have it all planned out, that you know what you want, then just like that"—she snapped her fingers—"you don't know anymore."

He took strands of her loose hair, rubbing them between his roughened fingers, memorizing the texture for when the day would come that he couldn't touch it.

"What don't you know, darlin'?"

She looked at him then, such sadness in her eyes, that he thought he'd do anything in the world to take the sadness away. "I don't know what I'm going to do, Tom. If I go back to Texas, you won't be there."

"I will be sometimes. I've got my businesses. I can't just let them go."

She scooted up against him, laid her head against his shoulder, her arm around his stomach. He held her.

"Will you come see me when you come to Texas?"

His chest tightened with her words, because Texas meant more to her than he did. "Yeah, I will."

"For how long?"

"Forever."

"Oh, Tom, you can't promise me forever; that's not a promise you can keep. You'll get married—"

"Then I'll promise you now. And I'll make good on another promise I made: to make it better the second time. You had to wait a lot of years for my first promise to you to be kept, and I didn't keep it the way I planned. I think I'm going to deliver this second one a bit sooner. If you have no objections."

She angled her face up, parted her lips, and it was all he needed. He removed the trousers he'd only just put on and settled his mouth over hers. Plowing one hand into her richly abundant hair, holding her steady while with the other hand, he eased the blanket off her shoulders until it pooled around her. He laid her back, deepening the kiss as he followed. Part of him wanted to woo her with words designed to make her stay. Honest words. That he loved her. That he always had.

The young girl who had sharply criticized his bad behavior.

The elegant lady who tartly reprimanded his wicked habits.

The girl who cared about manners; the woman who cared about etiquette.

The girl who met him in the shadows of the night; the woman who did the same.

The girl whose smile had stolen his heart; the woman whose laughter kept his heart tethered to her.

The daring girl who offered him her unbuttoned bodice.

The enticing woman who carried through on the promise.

The girl who had left him behind. The woman who welcomed him back into her arms.

He skimmed his hand along the glorious length of her, over her hip, down her thigh. Silky smooth. Satin. If his mother had never taken him from England, his hands wouldn't be so rough against her skin, but neither would they be so strong. In Texas they could have protected her, worked hard for her, given her a good life. In England, they felt almost damned useless.

Groaning low, he deepened the kiss, determined to become lost in it, to have her lost in the sensations that they could stir to life together. They worked well together. Always had. He dared her to be wicked. She dared him to be good.

They complemented each other. Not opposites so much as different pieces to the same puzzle. He could only hope that they'd always come together with the ease that they did now.

Her hands stroked and teased, squeezed and pinched as she trailed her mouth down his throat along his chest, her tongue, heated velvet, leaving moisture in its wake.

With his knee, he nudged her thighs apart. A blanket against the floor wasn't nearly soft enough, but he was too lost in the increasing frenzy of desire to carry her to the bed.

He slid his arms beneath her, held her close, rolled them both over, until he was on his back with the hardness of the floor beneath him, and she was straddling him. She released the tiniest squeak of surprise, then she was looking down on him, her skin flushed, her breathing harsh and rapid, her eyes glazed with glorious heated passion.

Sweet Lord, it was all he could do not to find immediate release right then and there. Had she ever been more disheveled . . . more beautiful? Had he ever wanted her more than he did at that moment?

She didn't question him when he dug his fingers into her hips, lifted her up, guided her down until he was sheathed in her hot, velvety tightness. With a sigh, she dropped her head back. A woman on the cusp of rapture.

"You do the moving, darlin'," he rasped, as he relished the weight of her breasts in his hands. Not fully growed? The woman had no appreciation for what she was offering him.

She slowly, tentatively began to rock her hips, circling, rising, dropping . . .

He clenched his jaw, felt the sweat gathering

over his forehead. She dipped her head, planted a kiss in the center of his chest, moved up slightly, and settled her mouth over his, her tongue boldly exploring the confines. He ran his hands over her, every inch of skin that he could reach, holding her close, following her movements with his own . . . the pressure building in him, in her. He could feel her tensing, tightening around him . . .

She tore her mouth from his. "Oh, God, Tom!"

Then she was crying out, shuddering, arching back, and his body released a deeper shudder, following where she was leading . . .

She sank down on top of him, loose, limpid, and he wrapped his arms tightly around her while their hearts and breathing returned to normal.

How in God's name would he ever find the strength to give this up, give *her* up?

Lauren awoke languidly, nestled against Tom's side. He was lazily stroking her arm. She tilted her head slightly and saw that he was watching her.

"I'm going to have to leave soon," she said.

"I know."

Reaching out, she traced the scar that she'd kissed earlier. There were several others that she could see. "When did you start remembering?" she asked quietly.

Shaking his head, he shifted his gaze to the canopy. "Things come in flashes."

"But you were his heir—"

"But not perfect." He looked at her, held her gaze. "I want to leave London. Come with me."

"Where are you going to go?"

"To my ancestral estate."

Holding the sheet close, she sat up. "My family is having a ball next week, and I'll want to be here for that. Believe it or not, hosting a ball always makes my mother nervous."

"Think she'll invite me?"

"Of course."

"I'll make things right with Whithaven then. Meanwhile, let's go away."

"I'll have to get a chaperone."

"All right."

"I'll need a day to make arrangements," she told him.

"Day after tomorrow then."

Leaning over, she kissed him. "Now I need to get dressed so I can leave."

"I'll escort you home." He snaked an arm around her, laid her down, and climbed on top of her. "In a bit."

Reaching up, she placed her hand behind his head and led him back down to her. In a bit it would be. And then she'd have a week with Tom.

Would it lead her to heaven or straight into hell?

Chapter 14

❦

Tom wanted out of London. He wanted time with Lauren. And he was desperate enough that he swallowed his pride, put on his best clothes and his best manners, and made a morning call on Lydia as soon as it was fashionable—which he knew meant early afternoon, although he had yet to determine why it was referred to as a morning call when it didn't take place in the morning.

Having handed his card off to the butler, he stood in the entryway, knowing there was a good chance that she wouldn't receive him, not blaming her if she didn't. He knew he had a whole round of apologizing to do, and he had plans for all of it, but just then his main concern was having a little more time with Lauren. She'd managed to sneak away to be with him the previous night, but he needed more than that. He thought they both did.

The butler returned. "Her Grace will see you, if you will be so kind as to follow me."

Tom followed the butler down a hallway that he hadn't walked before and into the drawing room, where Lydia was sitting on a settee, pouring tea into a china cup, while Rhys stood nearby at a window, ever watchful as though he expected Tom to pounce on his wife. Lydia glanced up and smiled sweetly. "My lord, please join us. Would you like some tea?"

"No, thank you. First, I want to apologize for last night. My temper got the better of me."

"We accept your apology. I assume Lord Whithaven did the same."

He grimaced. "I haven't apologized to him yet. I think my apology to him needs to be more public."

She arched a brow as though expecting him to elaborate.

"I'm working on the particulars," he said.

"I see. Please do have a seat. I'm getting a crick in my neck staring up at you."

He took the heavily brocaded chair next to her, so he could keep an eye on Rhys while letting the man keep watch on him. He suspected the Duke of Harrington wasn't a man he'd want to meet in a dark alley alone. While he had the veneer of civilization, Tom suspected there was a bit of the savage in him as well.

"I'm assuming it was more than offering an apology that brought you here this afternoon," Lydia said, effectively turning his attention away from Harrington.

Tom nodded. "I purchased your book this morning."

She smiled with obvious delight. "Really? How are you enjoying it?"

"I don't think it was really designed for enjoyment."

"I suppose not. Did you need something clarified?"

"Chaperones. You wrote that a married cousin rather than a mother usually serves as chaperone."

"That's correct."

"You're Lauren's cousin, and you're married."

"Exactly. Which is the reason that I've accompanied you and Lauren on your outings around London. Well, that and the fact that I simply adore being out and about."

"What about a longer outing?"

She gave him an impish smile. "You mean go out of the city for the day?"

He couldn't stop himself from leaning forward and clasping his hands, transferring the strength in his grip to his words. "More than an outing and more than for a day. I want to take Lauren to

Sachse Hall for a spell. A week or so . . . I know it's asking a lot, but I'll compensate you."

"And what exactly do you think my cousin's happiness is worth?"

He studied her, trying to determine exactly where her question was leading and what it was he heard in her voice: censure or approval. "Name your price."

Laughing lightly, she lifted her cup, becoming silent only as she began to sip her tea, watching him over the rim. When she set the cup down, she said, "A pity you didn't arrive sooner."

"Why? You already have plans?"

She nodded. "Afraid so. Lauren was here quite early this morning to ask me to serve as chaperone. It seems she has a desire to accompany a certain lord to Sachse Hall. And I agreed out of love for my cousin with no financial benefit to me."

"She was already here?"

"Mm-uh. Aroused me from slumber yet again, quite eager to enlist my aid in getting her out of London for a bit. Since Rhys and I desire a little time away as well, I was only too glad to accommodate her request."

With a deep breath, he sank back against the chair. "So you're going to be our chaperone?"

"Quite."

"You might have said something sooner."

"But I like to see you squirm a bit. However, make no mistake, I shall take my duties most seriously. I've seen cartoons in *Punch* depicting young people striving to elude their chaperones. I won't be made a mockery of by being easily evaded."

"I won't take advantage."

Rhys coughed and cleared his throat, as though he no more believed Tom's words than Tom did. Tom had no plans to take advantage of Lydia, but if Lauren were available to him . . .

"We can be ready to leave in the morning," Lydia said.

"I'll have my carriage brought around at seven."

"Good God," Rhys barked. "Have pity, man, and select a more reasonable hour."

"Ten?"

"Noon."

"Eleven."

"Eleven it is."

Lydia reached over and patted Tom's knee. "Now, if Lauren can just have success convincing Aunt Elizabeth that I'll make an acceptable chaperone during a country visit, we should be all set."

Lauren watched as her mother dug the trowel around her precious rosebushes, loosening the soil, removing the few scarce weeds that had dared to invade her domain. She suspected the next few minutes were going to be very difficult, but she was all of twenty-four, old enough to make her own decisions. She was ready to exert her independence.

So why was she trembling? Because she knew she was on the cusp of a battle she might not win, even though she had her arguments lined up in a row like good little soldiers. Taking a deep, steadying breath, she knelt beside her mother, reached out, and pulled up a weed, tossing it aside. "The roses have made a wonderful showing this year."

"Indeed they have. I've been quite pleased."

"As well you should be. You work so hard on them. I swear I've never seen a more beautiful garden."

"It's been a while since you've given me this much flattery." Her mother sat back, laid the trowel on the ground, clapped her gloved hands together to rid them of the excess dirt, and slowly peeled them off. "Guilt is an awful burden to bear."

The heat suffusing her face, Lauren wondered if her mother could look at her and know exactly what she'd done with Tom last night and how many times. "I'm not feeling guilty." She grimaced at the squeaky sound of her voice. She sounded like an out-of-tune violin.

"I was referring to myself," her mother said.

"Oh, of course."

"I keep thinking if I dig up the garden enough times, it'll make everything right again, that perfection here is perfection everywhere, but I don't know if everything will ever be perfect again."

"I'm not sure everything was ever perfect. It was simply not quite so bad as it might have been."

Her mother turned to her. She looked remarkably young, incredibly vulnerable, with dirt smudged along the side of her nose. Lauren resisted the urge to wipe it away, but in the end, she couldn't leave it alone for the servants to see—her mother looking less than countess-worthy. "You have a bit of a mess here."

Using her thumb, she rubbed away the offending dirt.

Her mother laughed lightly. "Sometimes I think I like the smell of the earth more than the smell of the roses."

"I think it's the farm girl in you."

"Probably. So what brings you to my corner of the garden?"

"Tom invited me to Sachse Hall, Lydia has agreed to serve as chaperone, and I want to go." The words rushed out, one right on top of the other, as though she thought if she spoke them fast enough her mother would miss the true meaning of the message: that she was going away with Tom.

"Do you think this is a wise course of action?" her mother asked softly.

Lauren studied her dirty thumb. "Probably not."

"Well, then be careful while you're away."

Lauren jerked up her gaze, but her mother had already turned her attention back to the soil, using her ungloved hands now to loosen the dirt.

"You're giving me permission to go?"

Lauren wondered if her mother had indeed guessed about last night's excursion.

"At least this way," her mother continued, "I'll know where you are and I can pretend to believe that Lydia will prove an adequate chaperone. And having her there gives the appearance of propriety. It's the best I can hope for."

"Lydia will be an excellent chaperone," Lauren said, feeling a need to stand up for her cousin. "She, more than anyone, knows the price of scandal."

"You don't have to convince me," her mother said. "Go with my blessing."

A battle won so easily was certain to be a battle not yet finished.

"We'll leave tomorrow," Lauren said warily, waiting for some sort of indication that her mother was playing a spiteful prank on her.

Her mother's hands stilled their seemingly frantic movements. "Take care with your heart."

Lauren wrapped her arms around her mother, hugging her tightly, not caring that she might end up equally covered in dirt. "Thank you for not making this moment difficult." She kissed her mother's cheek, only then noticing that another smudge had appeared on the side of her nose as well as a damp trail left by a passing tear. She whispered, "I love you dearly," then rose to her feet and went to prepare for her journey.

Because Tom and Rhys were good-sized men and because the ladies, even for a short stay in the country, required two trunks of clothing each, they traveled in two coaches, and while it might not have been entirely appropriate, Lauren traveled alone in the coach with Tom.

"You've been awfully quiet," Tom said, once they were beyond the boundaries of London.

"My mother was too agreeable about my coming. I don't quite trust the ease with which she capitulated."

His laughter easily traveled to where she sat opposite him. "Maybe she thinks a little time in my company will convince you that you no longer have an interest in me or in Texas."

Studying him sitting there with his gray tailcoat with the black velvet collar and gray trousers, the blue waistcoat, and the red cravat, she realized that she no longer expected him to appear in his cowboy garb, that she hardly ever thought of him as being a cowboy any longer. The realization somehow surprised her, saddened her, and in an odd sort of way also satisfied her. Not that she could take complete credit for his transformation. Much of it had begun before she'd agreed to help him, but if he reshaped his mustache just a bit and never spoke, one would never realize that he hadn't been raised in England.

"You might consider trimming your mustache a bit," she offered. "It looks decidedly Western."

He placed his thumb and forefinger at the center of the mustache right above his lip and slowly outlined both sides. "You mean make it so it twists up at the end?"

She nodded. He grimaced. She laughed. "It was only a suggestion."

"I like my mustache the way it is."

"I suppose you could remove it completely."

"I'd look too young."

"You are young."

"In years, Lauren, not in experience. In some ways, I'm older than a lot of the gentlemen I meet. They've had pampered lives."

"Lives of excess can age one as well."

"True enough."

She let the silence ease in around them, before saying, "I've never been to Sachse Hall."

"It needs a good deal of work."

"I didn't realize it was in need of repair."

"Not repair so much as redoing. My father seemed to like . . ." He looked out the window as though searching for the right words, and she could see the red of embarrassment darkening the skin beneath his chin. Or perhaps it was a reflection of his red cravat, but she didn't think so.

"What did he seem to like?"

"Naked statues, that sort of thing. I thought about fixing the place up, but I decided that I should leave that to my wife, let her redo the house to suit her tastes."

Lauren's stomach knotted up at yet another mention of his having a wife. Were his continual reminders deliberate or unintended? Was he hoping to gain some sort of reaction from her, some spark of jealousy? Dear God, as much as she was loath to admit it, she was envious of the woman who would marry him. And surely he would marry.

"That's very thoughtful," she said, striving not to let the moment ruin the collection of wonderful memories she'd hoped to gather so she would have them to carry away with her when she left.

"I thought it a rather . . . civilized decision."

His perfectly delivered English accent astounded her. She stared at him. "My goodness, Tom, you can speak quite convincingly without a drawl."

"Only when I concentrate on it."

"I think you've learned the secret. All aspects of this life require concentration."

He laughed again, and she realized that he laughed much more easily than most of the men she'd been around for the past several years. "It's more than just getting rid of the slow talking," he said. "It's using words in ways I never have before." He gave her a pointed look. "It's a . . . bit of a bother."

She smiled warmly. "Frightfully so."

"I daresay you're right."

She released a light laugh. "I should be happy as a lark if you learned the proper speech."

"Happy as a lark," he repeated. "It creates a different image than pig in slop."

She laughed harder. "Oh, Tom, that's atrocious! They're not the same at all. One is refined, the other is crude."

"Which is which?"

"You know damned well which is which. If you're not careful, I shall become very cross with you."

He shook his head. "Very cross isn't much of a threat. Angry, mad, infuriated, now that might give me pause."

"Don't underestimate the unpleasantness of dealing with a woman who is very cross. I assure you the words used may give a more civilized impression, but they can mask a beastly temperament."

"I always thought speaking English was speaking English."

"Not quite, but you do speak remarkably well, and you're picking up on all the small things rather easily."

"Nothing easy about it. It's as hard as sitting on my side of the coach while you sit on yours."

"I intend to behave with a good deal of decorum during our time away from London. I don't wish to put Lydia in a difficult position."

Leaning forward, he took her gloved hands. "Define decorum."

"I have no plans to be seduced."

He narrowed his eyes. "How does one plan *not* to be seduced? I can see planning to seduce—"

"I simply meant that I shall be ever vigilant against any sort of inappropriate overtures that you might direct my way." She wasn't going to sneak into his bedroom. She absolutely wasn't.

Grinning as though he knew she'd have no will to resist, he released his hold on her hands, slid over to the corner of the coach, and stared out the window.

"What are you doing?" she asked.

"Just watching the countryside. It's so damned green."

"There's green in Texas."

"Not in Fortune, there isn't. Not like this. Come the middle of summer, everything starts to turn brown." He shifted his gaze over to her. "Don't you remember?"

"I have a vague recollection . . ." Very vague. Did she even truly remember what it looked like.

"I don't think everything will become dry here."

"You're like my mother with her rose garden. She has her little bit of land that's hers to tend . . ."

"Sachse Hall is set on more than a little bit. The tenants are farmers. You're more than welcome to join me when I ride out to see them."

"You're a man of the land, aren't you, Tom?"

"I reckon whether the land is in England or in Texas, it calls to me."

He fell silent then, as though he was listening to whatever the green and brown of the earth might whisper to him as they passed by it. She wondered if his father had ever taken him for rides over the land, if he'd somehow managed to instill a love for the land in Tom . . . whether intentional or not.

Surely there had to be some evidence of his father's influence, other than scars.

It was amazing to watch the light of appreciation in his eyes as he looked out over the passing scenery as though he would never grow tired of it, bored with it, as though seeing it all for the first time when he must have seen it before, on his journey to London.

"Do you recall your father taking you for rides over the land?"

His jaw tightened. "No. The memories that come to me"—he shook his head—"I have yet to come across one I'd like to hold on to."

"At least you'll have no bad memories associated with the land."

She scooted over to the window so she could have a similar view of what it was that he found so fascinating. She'd never truly bothered to study the countryside, to look at it without resentment because it wasn't Texas. The rolling hills here had seemed so foreign to her because Fortune was nothing more than good, flat farmland near the Texas coast. She'd seen nothing to remind her of it, and so she'd found fault with all of it.

It was only while gazing at it through Tom's eyes that the verdant greens seemed to warrant her appreciation and actually had her feeling a little guilty for her years of harsh assessment.

Tom got up and moved over to her bench, sitting down beside her, leaning over to look out the window, until his chest was pressed against her shoulder. "I prefer to see where I'm going instead of looking back to see where I've been," he said quietly, the warmth of his breath wafting along the sensitive skin of her neck, sending chills rippling through her until her toes curled.

"Shall I move to the other bench so you have a clearer view?"

"No, I like my view just fine."

"I've never looked at the countryside without a measure of resentment. Don't you resent it?"

"How can I resent it when it belongs to me?"

She twisted her head around. "This is your property?"

"No, not yet. We have a few hours to go. I didn't mean I own it. I meant it's just . . . beautiful. You can't resent land for simply existing, not when it gives so much back to us."

"It's in your blood," she said, amazed by the realization.

"Sometimes, it seems like it is. When I look out on it, I don't miss Texas quite as much."

Looking out on the land with Lauren's profile framed in the corner of his vision had probably done a great deal toward making him not miss Texas so much. Dark clouds had moved in, a light rain had begun to fall, and the lullaby of the drops pelting the roof had lulled Lauren into sleep, her head nestled against the nook of his shoulder. His jacket was draped over her to ward off some of the chill. The arm he'd placed around her to hold her steady had begun to go numb, but it was a small inconvenience when compared to the pleasure of having the weight of her body pressed against his side, the fragrance of her hair, her perfume enticing him into taking deep breaths just so he could enjoy her unique scent, memorize it for the times when she wouldn't be near.

The trip to the country was as much to get away from London as it was to have an opportunity to hoard memories with Lauren. He had estate business that he needed to take care of, but he still planned to find time for her: for walks, and rides, and sitting in the garden, for trying to persuade her to settle for a little bit of Texas, and in the settling, she could settle for him.

On the estate she'd have a more realistic view of his life. It wasn't all balls, dinners, operas, and morning rides through the park. As a matter of fact, very little of it truly was. He hoped that she might gain a greater appreciation for him, might begin truly to look at him, not as a cowboy or a lord but as a man.

The rain, thankfully, had ended by the time they arrived at Sachse Hall. And Tom damned his soul for holding his breath, waiting for her reaction to seeing his ancestral home for the first time. His claim to the place came about only because he'd emerged from the proper womb, and yet, here he was, feeling undeniable pride in being a part of something that until a few months ago, he hadn't known existed. He hadn't hammered the nails that held it together or hired the servants who crept around its hallowed hallways or stocked the wine cellar or purchased a single piece of ostentatious artwork that was displayed through the house, and yet, he couldn't deny that some part of him wanted her to be . . . impressed.

He wanted her to look at it, as he did, to see what it was, and to see the potential for what it could be.

It was only when the carriage rolled to a stop that he realized she was staring at him, not looking out the window at all. She'd removed his jacket from around her shoulders and was holding it out to him.

"You're nervous," she said softly.

"Don't be ridiculous." He snatched his jacket

from her and leaned back just enough to shrug into it without hitting her in the face.

"I wouldn't have thought you'd care about something that you didn't acquire through hard work."

"I wouldn't have thought so either," he said truthfully. "But I look at everything that I've inherited, and it's humbling to know that there's a history here that goes back six generations. What I have in Texas, it started with me, and I can't deny that I take a fierce pride in that achievement, but I'd also like to think that a few generations from now, the men who inherit what I started will feel a reverence and an appreciation for its history. They won't know me or what I went through to give them the beginning of a legacy, just like I don't know the men who passed this one down until it came to me. But that doesn't mean I can't respect what they accomplished."

Her eyes darkened, with something akin to appreciation, and as he was the only thing she was studying intently . . .

The door to the carriage clicked open, effectively shattering the mood as she gave a little jump and the tiniest of squeals, and he couldn't help but think that for those few moments, she'd been as lost in him as he was in her. The footman helped her alight from the carriage, and Tom followed, wishing the moment hadn't been lost to them, wondering what she'd been thinking, what she might have said.

"It's impressive," Lauren said.

Tom couldn't help but agree. Three floors above ground, one partially below, all almost twice as tall as the floors in the house he'd built in Texas. He couldn't help but think that his ancestors had considered themselves giants among men and had wanted the home in which they lived to reflect that attitude.

Rhys and Lydia approached, and the valets and ladies' maids who'd been traveling in a third coach were already heading toward the manor, where Tom assumed they'd begin immediately seeing to their lords' and ladies' needs.

"The former Lady Sachse had a country party here last year," Lydia said. "She had a way of always putting people at ease and making them feel welcome."

"Everyone except you, sweetheart," Rhys said.

"Only until she realized that she couldn't win you over."

Tom clapped his hands and rubbed them together. The leaden sky had begun to darken with the approaching night. "Let's get settled in."

Which he didn't think would take much effort, since several footmen had already taken the trunks and bags into the house. "Since I've never had a guest here," Tom began, not counting the previous Lady Sachse as a guest since she'd actually been in residence, "I'm a little new at this, but feel free simply to make yourselves at home."

"We'll be fine, Tom," Lydia assured him. "Don't feel that you have to impress us with any formality."

"Don't get me started with bad habits that I won't be able to continue," he told her. "I might as well learn the right way to do it."

"The easiest path is to take a wife who is capable of handling it all for you," Rhys said, which earned him a slap on the arm from Lydia.

"What? I only speak true," Rhys said. "Domestic affairs are the wife's domain."

"But not the reason to marry. One marries for love."

Rhys met Tom's gaze. "Forget I said anything."

They walked up the stone steps. A footman opened the door. The ladies walked inside, Tom and Rhys following.

The butler, stiff and formal, was waiting at attention. "My lord, welcome home."

"Thank you, Smythe." Tom had sent word that he was bringing company.

"I have had rooms prepared for the duke and duchess and Miss Fairfield in the wing that was once occupied by the former countess. I believe they'll find the accommodations most satisfactory."

"Thank you. About dinner—"

"It will be served at seven as always. I suggest a gathering in the library, where I've taken the liberty of stocking the cabinets with your best port, brandy, and whiskey."

Tom turned to his guests. "Sounds like everything has been taken care of."

"Nothing is more valuable than a competent staff," Lydia said. "I look forward to freshening up. We'll see you in an hour in the library, shall we?"

"All right."

Lydia took Lauren's arm. "Come on, Lauren. I don't know about you, but I'm ready to get out of my traveling clothes."

"I'll escort you to your rooms, Your Grace," Smythe said.

While the ladies ascended the stairs, Rhys stayed behind with Tom. "You don't want to change out of your traveling clothes?" Tom asked.

"I do, but I wanted to warn you first that Lydia is taking her chaperoning responsibilities very seriously, but as one who upon occasion managed very successfully to elude the chaperones, I take pity upon your plight and will do all in my power to distract her as the evening grows late."

Tom grinned. "I appreciate that."

"It's the least I can do. I recognize a smitten man when I see him, and having nearly lost the love of my life, I know what it is to walk in your shoes." He held Tom's gaze. "And since we've not had a chance to talk privately since the unfortunate incident with Whithaven—"

"I really am sorry about that," Tom interrupted.

"Whithaven is a pompous, arrogant arse."

Tom was taken aback by Rhys's words.

"I quite enjoyed seeing you pummel him as he once pummeled me."

"He hit you?"

"Beat me to a bloody pulp. I just wanted you to know that while the time and place may have been a poor choice, I realize that the punch was probably well deserved."

Tom shook his head. "No, I'm thinking all three were bad choices."

"As you wish." Rhys glanced around the foyer. "Interesting artwork."

"I've thought about putting clothes on some of these statues," Tom admitted.

"I'd leave them if I were you. Something about the nude form makes it quite provocative."

"I'm not used to seeing so much exposed."

"It's art, my friend. And ladies tend to appreciate art."

Chapter 15

Lauren gazed out the window on the magnificent gardens. She thought her mother would love to see them. It was obvious that they'd come about over time, and she wondered if their design had been influenced by Tom's mother or his father. His mother, she decided. They were too gorgeous to have been the desire of someone with the reputation for spitefulness that Tom's father had. All the statues of naked cavorting couples—those had no doubt been his father's influence.

"Rhys and I are just down the hallway," Lydia said. "We'll stop by your room within the hour to escort you—"

"No need. I plan to go down early."

"How early? I'll adjust my schedule."

Lauren turned from the window to face her cousin. "Lydia, you're serving as chaperone was for my mother's and society's benefit, not mine."

She walked over to the bed and studied the gown that her maid had set out for her. It would do nicely for the evening.

"You're not expecting me to look the other way while you engage in inappropriate behavior, are you?" Lydia asked.

"Of course not," Lauren said lightly. "I *expect* you to *expect* me to behave appropriately. Therefore, you'll find no need to watch me closely. You can relax, enjoy your time here with Rhys, and if we're all together, that's lovely . . . and if not, I don't want you worrying."

"You don't plan to behave *appropriately*, though, do you?"

"I don't *plan* to behave *in*appropriately, but if the occasion should arise, I'm not certain that I'd be opposed to it."

Lydia sighed. "Aunt Elizabeth will kill me if you find yourself in a compromising situation."

Lauren smiled. "I'll kill you if I don't."

"Oh, heavens, what have I gotten myself into?" Lydia held up her hands. "I'll compromise. I shall be the best chaperone to my ability, but not as diligent as I planned. Rhys no doubt will have a different view. I'll seek to keep him otherwise occupied as the night draws late."

"A fine plan."

* * *

Tom stared at his reflection in the mirror, wondering when his common sense had deserted him.

"I could thin it out a bit more, my lord," his valet said.

"No," Tom said, moving his upper lip around to see if he could make his mustache look any more presentable. "I think it's thin enough."

"We could curl the ends up a bit more."

"No, they're curled enough." Maybe he ought to shave the damned thing off completely, but he knew if he did that, he would look like he wasn't old enough to issue orders much less run an estate the size of this one. He resisted the urge to run his thumb and forefinger over his mustache and straighten it out. He didn't think he looked more English. He thought he looked . . . he closed his eyes. He didn't want to contemplate what he looked like. The next time he wanted to please Lauren he'd simply give her some flowers, not work to change his appearance.

"Shall we finish preparing for dinner?" his valet asked.

"I reckon."

"You really look quite fetching, my lord."

Fetching made Tom think of a dog with a stick. "Thanks."

Lauren arrived in the library ahead of anyone else, finding her way by asking directions of the various footmen and servants. Having been raised in the Ravenleigh household, she wasn't as awed with the grandeur or all the servants as she might have been when she first arrived in England, but she could well imagine that Tom might have found it all quite overwhelming to begin with. The library was an impressive room with floor-to-ceiling bookshelves and a spiral staircase in the corner that led up to another level of floor-to-ceiling bookshelves and a small seating area in front of a large window. She assumed it offered as breathtaking a view of the gardens and surrounding countryside as the guest bedroom she'd been given. Strange how she was suddenly viewing the green rolling hills she'd taken for granted as breathtaking.

A massive desk was set before the large fireplace, and she visualized Tom working at it, studying his ledgers and accounts. She envisioned herself curled up in the nearby chair, reading Dickens or Austen or Alcott. The room seemed peaceful as though it had retained none of the harshness or cruelty for which its former master was known. Perhaps he'd seldom inhabited the room. Maybe it had been favored by Tom's mother. Certainly it couldn't have been favored by the latest Lady Sachse as she'd only recently begun to read.

She heard the door click quietly open and turned from her musings to watch as Tom, lord of the manor, strode into the room, wearing a black tailcoat and trousers, while everything else—silk waistcoat, shirt, cravat—was a pristine white that brought out the swarthiness of his complexion. She wondered if, over time, the bronze hint of his skin would fade as he spent more and more time indoors, or would he always remain a man of the outside, even here. As he grew nearer, she realized something about him was different—

"Oh!" She slapped her hand over her mouth to prevent the bubble of laughter that she was certain would insult him from escaping.

His mustache, thinned and curling up on the ends, twitched, and the hard press of his lips told her that he wasn't exactly pleased with the results of his efforts to follow her advice. It had been a ghastly mistake. Whatever had made her suggest it to begin with? It didn't make him look more English or less Western; it simply made him look less like Tom.

Gnawing on her bottom lip, she refrained from making any sort of comment that might make him suddenly self-conscious although judging by the red beneath his chin, he was already feeling a measure of embarrassment.

"Where are the others?" he asked.

"Still getting ready, I suppose."

He walked past her to a table where several crystal decanters were lined up. "Brandy?" he asked.

"Just a bit."

She walked over to where he stood, studied his death grip on the decanter as he poured. When he set the crystal down, she touched his arm, causing him to turn toward her. "It's not that bad," she offered.

"It's damned awful. It makes me look ridiculous. Now I know how Sampson felt when his hair was cut: weak and—"

"You're not weak, Tom. Your strength has nothing to do with the hair on your face." Reaching up, she pressed her fingers to the whiskers above his lip, felt his warm breath waft over her knuckles as she slowly outlined what remained of his mustache until she reached the curled ends and very cautiously, very gingerly unfurled them until they were once again framing either side of his mouth. She watched his Adam's apple ride up and down as he swallowed. Lifting her gaze to his, she saw his eyes had darkened to the hue of a starless sky.

"It shouldn't take long to look as it did before, should it?" she asked, surprised by the rasping timbre of her voice.

"No." His voice was gravely, rough. "Not having a chaperone would be good right about now."

She backed up a step, the scent of him as intoxicating as the brew he'd just poured. "Unfortunately, I expect she'll show up any second."

Nodding, he grabbed a glass, downed its contents in one long swallow, and set about pouring another one. "What do you think of the house?" he asked, refilling his glass and filling another one. Picking up both, he handed her one.

"*House* doesn't seem like a big enough word for this place. Manor, residence—"

"But not home," he said, moving over to the window as though he realized the danger of standing too close to her for much longer, that his guests would stride into this room and find Lauren in an awkward, compromising position.

"No, not home. But it could be, I think."

"It's cold, there's always a chill in the air."

"That's common in the older manors. It's as though they absorb winter and slowly release it through the summer. I was always walking around Ravenleigh's with a shawl or blanket draped over my shoulders, and numerous fires were always going throughout the manor even in summer." She took a sip of the brandy. "You have a lovely garden."

"I can't take credit for it. I can't take credit for most of this."

"You can't take credit for what it was, but you will certainly be able to take credit for what it becomes within your capable hands."

He studied her so intently that she wondered what her words might have conveyed . . . then it dawned on her: capable hands. Yes, he had very capable hands, and well he knew it, and he was no doubt remembering what she would forever be unable to forget.

"Is that a portrait of your mother?" she asked referring to the gilt-framed painting hanging on the wall above the fireplace behind the desk, needing to turn her mind away from the thoughts that would very easily lead her back down the road to seduction.

"Yes."

"She was very pretty."

"But sad-looking, don't you think?"

"People generally don't smile when they're having their portraits painted, Tom."

"It's not the lack of a smile; it's her eyes. She looks miserable. I wonder why she didn't leave him, why she didn't just stay in America. Why she came back."

"Maybe she loved living here, thought she would miss it too much." She shook her head, even as she spoke the words. "I can't imagine her missing anything more than she would have missed her son."

"So you think she should have chosen me over England?"

His voice contained an undercurrent, and she felt as though she'd rushed headlong into a trap, a trap that she had created, set into position. Choose a place over a person? Choose a way of life . . .

She shook her head. They were discussing his mother. Not her. "Maybe she was afraid that your father would come after her, after you. My God, Tom, she told people you were dead. She figured out how to make you disappear from your father's life, but not herself." She looked back at the portrait. "You have her eyes, but without the sadness."

"I expect I have less to be sad about."

She looked over at him, his eyes, beautifully deep brown, always intense, were on her. "I remember that first day I met you in Fortune. I thought they looked sad then."

"Because your mother came around to the back of the store before I could finish unbuttoning your bodice."

"No, Tom, they contained sadness before that. How old were you when they put you on the orphan train?"

"Fourteen. When the people who were taking care of me—I always called them Mother and Father"—he shook his head—"I feel stupid now, but I never realized that the fact that we had different last names was significant. I just thought I was special—"

"You are special," she said.

"Well, that's debatable. Anyway, when they died, no one knew what to do with me. They had no other family. So the Children's Aid Society gave me a cardboard suitcase to put all my belongings in. The next thing I knew I was on a train. Most of the kids were younger, so much younger, Lauren. Crying, scared, not knowing what was going to happen to them."

"You said you walked to Fortune, but I never asked from where."

"You sure remember a lot of what I told you."

"I think I remember everything. Where did the orphan train take you?" she asked, thinking he might be trying to avoid the question. She had so many, wanted to know what she'd always wanted to know: everything about his life.

"A family took me at Arkansas."

"*Took* you?"

"Best way to describe it. It was humiliating. They'd put us on this rickety wooden stage. People would walk by, squeezing our arms to see how strong we were, opening our mouths to look at our teeth, like we were no better than livestock. And I think to some folks, that's exactly what we were. I think the Society had good intentions, wanting to find good homes for the lost children, but I think a good many people saw the kids on the train as nothing more than cheap labor.

"After they'd do their inspecting, when they were satisfied, they'd just pull a boy or girl off the stage. Bad as traveling on the orphan train was, most still went kicking and screaming off that stage."

His eyes had taken on a distant look, and she didn't think he was aware that his grip on the glass had tightened until his knuckles were almost white.

"But you got away and went to Texas."

He gave her a sad smile. "Yes, I did."

"I'm sorry they treated you badly, Tom. That you had such a hard life."

The sadness retreated from his eyes as they grew warm. "If I hadn't, I never would have met you. It was all worth it, darlin', for a night in your arms. And I sure wouldn't mind having another."

Before she could respond, he cupped her cheek with his free hand, leaned over, and kissed her, passionately, deeply, a man who did nothing in half measures.

The door clicked open, and she and Tom both jumped as Lydia and Rhys waltzed into the room, arm in arm, as though totally oblivious to the sensual tension that had begun to radiate only a few seconds earlier. Perhaps Lauren had mistaken her ability to control Tom, her conviction that she was not in need of a chaperone. Based on the dew she felt gathering between her breasts as her body heated with desire, she might very well be in need of more than one chaperone.

"Forgive our tardiness, my lord," Lydia said. "I decided to take a quick nap, and Rhys didn't have the heart to awaken me when he should have."

"Would you care for something to drink?" Tom asked, his voice sounding almost normal, only a hint of the hoarseness remaining.

"I'll take some brandy," Rhys said, walking to the table of decanters where Tom joined him.

Lauren strolled over to Lydia.

"The blush becomes you," Lydia said, her mouth twitching as she fought not to smile.

"It's the brandy," Lauren said. "It warms me."

"Considering how you both jumped as we entered, I suspect it was something else entirely warming you."

Lauren leaned close and whispered harshly, "Well, I don't believe for a moment that you were napping."

"Believe what you will."

"I'm not the only one with a red hue to my skin."

"Ah, yes, dear cousin, but the difference is that I'm married, and so a flush upon my flesh is perfectly acceptable."

Lauren shook her head. "I can't believe I once thought us friends as well as cousins."

"I'm beginning to suspect that just as one shouldn't borrow money from a friend, one shouldn't ask a friend to chaperone. I may have to include that sage bit of advice in the next edition of my book."

The men's laughter rumbled through the room.

"Do you think they're discussing what we're discussing?" Lauren asked.

"Surely, not. There was no cause for laughter in what transpired. Perhaps they're simply sharing a humorous story."

"Perhaps we should join them," Lauren suggested.

"Perhaps we should."

Dinner was a pleasant affair, dishes served as though Tom had been in residence from the beginning to oversee them. It was a testament to how well the previous Lady Sachse had managed the staff. However, when the butler discreetly informed Tom as he was preparing to leave the dining room that he might wish to discuss tomorrow's various menus with the cook first thing in the morning, he felt himself floundering. What did he know about the preparation of meals when most of his life he'd eaten a side of beef and a can of beans?

"Is everything all right?" Lauren asked as he caught up with her in the hallway.

"Apparently I'm supposed to discuss food with the cook in the morning." He extended his arm to her.

"That's a task that usually falls to the lady of the house, and while I'm not, I suspect that I'm better prepared than you are for handling it. Would you like me to see to it?"

"Would you mind?"

"Let's see . . . ensure that we have variety or risk having nothing except beef and beans served? Mmm." She touched her chin with her finger, then shook her head. "No, I don't mind at all."

"I appreciate it."

"So will everyone's stomachs."

"How did you know I prefer beef?"

"First, because you're a rancher, not a poultry farmer or a fisherman. Secondly, it's the only time your plate is practically wiped clean."

"I guess I have simple tastes."

"You should be more adventuresome. No telling what you'll discover you like."

"And what about you, Lauren? Are you adventuresome?"

"I'm here, aren't I?"

He couldn't deny that or the spark of pleasure it gave him to have her there, willing to help him out by taking care of a few of the domestic duties. He could see a definite advantage to having a lady in the house, especially this lady. He wondered if he'd be able to smell her flowery fragrance in these hallways after she was gone, if it would soak into the pillows on the bed where she was sleeping. If he slept there, would it be like sleeping with her?

"You seem to know where you're going," he said.

"Since Lydia has visited before and is familiar with the layout of the house, she gave me directions before she and Rhys went on ahead. This hallway leads to the gardens. We thought we'd take an evening stroll. Lydia and Rhys should be waiting for us outside."

They were waiting at the edge of the veranda, talking quietly, both suddenly stopping to turn to Tom and Lauren as they approached.

"I suppose we should follow you," Lydia said, "so I can more easily keep a watchful eye on you."

Rolling his eyes, Tom led Lauren up the walk,

hearing the click of heels as Lydia fell into step behind them, Rhys with her. "I don't know how these people ever figure out that they want to get married with someone watching their every move."

"They very cleverly figure out ways to evade their chaperones. Although the practice of having a chaperone is not as rigid as it once was. More and more ladies are beginning to rebel at the notion that they can't be trusted to ensure that men behave."

Tom laughed. "So, it's the men who don't behave?"

She peered up at him, and even in the night shadows, he could make out the outline of her smile, the sparkle in her eyes. "Most certainly. Ladies are always above reproach. A woman has a stronger will, can more easily resist the temptation of improper behavior."

"And what do you consider improper?"

"I don't need to define it, Tom. You know exactly what is improper."

"Smoking a cigar?"

"Definitely."

"Drinking?"

"Spirits? To excess? Most assuredly."

"Kissing?"

"Other than on the hand or cheek, yes, without a doubt."

"I don't recall you objecting to any kisses that I gave you."

"You took me by surprise, before I could object."

By surprise? His memory of each one had him taking his time, going slowly, savoring the moment. What sort of game was she playing?

He smelled the returning rain on the air only a few seconds before the downpour began. Lauren and Lydia both shrieked, and Rhys yelled, "Back to the house!"

Tom envisioned the chaperones scurrying back the way they'd come. He grabbed Lauren's hand, halting her retreat in the same direction. "This way!"

She was alternately laughing and shrieking by the time he got them under the protective roof of the gazebo. He shrugged like a dog just out of the river, thought she might have as well. The distant gaslights along the path allowed the gazebo to have some semblance of shadows rather than complete darkness, and he was able to see Lauren standing there, arms crossed over her chest, her head somehow misshapen . . .

He grinned. Her hair was falling down. The rain had managed to do what he'd been longing to do all night, release the golden tresses from the confines of pins, ribbons, and bows. He removed his thoroughly soaked jacket. It would do little to keep her warm.

"Here," he offered. "It's wet, but the inside is still warm." He draped it over her shoulders, felt her shudder beneath his fingers.

"Where did Lydia go?" she asked.

"I heard Rhys yell something about the house, so I assume they headed back."

"And why didn't we?"

"The gazebo was closer."

"Except in the house I have dry clothes. Here I have nothing."

"You have me," he said quietly.

"But you're as wet as I am." Her voice held a shiver, and he wasn't certain if it was from the cold or his words.

He moved up until they were very nearly touching. "If we're close, we can warm each other."

"I suppose you're going to suggest that we remove our clothes to generate even more heat."

"The direction your thoughts go in . . . are they proper for a lady?"

He heard a most unladylike snort and twitched his mouth, which felt funny without the full weight of his mustache. Whatever had he been thinking to change it at all?

"You've got a mess here," he said, reaching up to very slowly, very carefully begin removing the pins from her hair, his face close enough to hers that the warmth of her breath fanned over his cheek.

"You're just going to tangle it." She sounded breathless but didn't take any action to halt his actions.

"I'll brush the tangles out when we return to the house."

"And when do you think that will be?"

"As soon as it stops raining."

"Which could be hours from now."

If I'm lucky, he thought, as he removed the last pin and her hair tumbled around her shoulders. He had an urge to taunt her, to prove that he could be within close proximity of her without touching her. He had a devilish desire to push her to the edge until she couldn't resist touching *him*, to prove that it wasn't always the man who made a chaperone necessary. The lady was equally responsible, tempting a man, exposing her throat and shoulders so he couldn't help but think about nibbling that delicate skin, dabbing drops of perfume in provocative places so he couldn't help but think about leaning close and breathing in the sweet fragrance, occasionally touching her tongue to her lips so he couldn't help but think about tasting . . .

Dammit if he hadn't moved in so close that he could feel the heat radiating from her body, smell her intoxicating scent, and almost taste those lips. A whisper's breath separated her mouth from his, and his hands were tangled in her hair. So much for his resolve not to touch.

He could hear each shuddering intake of breath, not sure if it was hers or his. The rain continued to pour, tapping on the gazebo roof, splattering on the ground surrounding the structure, encasing them in a cocoon of intimacy. Resisting the urge to lean in and take what he so desperately wanted was damned near killing him. Even in the shadows he saw her lick her lips, and it almost shattered what little restraint remained to him.

He wanted proof that she wanted him with the fierceness that he desired her, wanted her to close the gap between them, wanted her almost brought to her knees with yearning. She licked her lips again, and her breathing sounded more ragged. He felt her fingers slip beneath his waistcoat, close around his shirt.

"My fingers are cold," she rasped, "and you're so warm. How can you be so warm?"

Because she had the ability to ignite a fire within him that threatened to consume him. Swallowing hard, he closed his eyes. He was going to break, dammit. He couldn't hold out, couldn't resist . . . he felt the lightest brushing of her lips over his, like a gentle wind ruffling the petals of a dandelion—

"My lord?"

His eyes sprang open, and he jerked his gaze toward the voice. Smythe stood in the gazebo entryway, an umbrella over his head protecting him from the still pelting rain.

"The duchess sent me out with an umbrella to ensure that you and the lady were able to return to the manor house without the risk of catching your death."

The rain was hardly at risk of doing him in. It was his own pride and vanity, his own need to prove a stupid point. He took a deep breath, forcing his body to loosen and settle back down so he could think clearly about something other than Lauren. His body aching with need, he strode over to Smythe and took the two umbrellas he was offering. "Thank you."

"The duchess said she expects your immediate return; otherwise, the duke might have to seek you out to ensure all is well."

Tom fought back his impatience. "Inform the duchess that we'll be there shortly."

"Very good, sir. Dreadful weather we're having this time of year. I daresay you might wish to travel slowly in order not to put Miss Fairfield at risk of turning an ankle."

"I'll do that."

"I'll inform the duchess that there will be a slight delay before your arrival."

Before Tom could respond, the butler was hurrying along the garden path that would lead him back to the house.

Turning back to Lauren, Tom could actually hear her teeth chattering. Without the warmth of his nearness, the heat of their passion, the chill and dampness were taking their toll. He opened an umbrella, held it up. "Come on."

She came to stand near him. Clutching his jacket with one hand, she reached for the umbrella.

"I'll hold it," he said. "You just get underneath it."

"I don't know that we can both fit, and we have the second umbrella."

"Don't worry about me getting wet." He wrapped his hand around her neck, drew her near, and whispered near her ear, "Good thing your chaperone interfered. I think your resistance was about to crack." Then he planted a kiss on her mouth designed to make her regret that she'd offered up any resistance at all.

With a contented sigh, Lauren soaked in the steaming hot water the servants had poured into the shining brass tub. She felt the chill leaving her bones to be replaced with a sense of euphoria, very similar to the sensation she'd experienced when she'd leaned in to kiss Tom. She'd cursed the interruption, even as she'd been grateful for it. She didn't know what had gotten into him, to just stand perfectly still like one of the statues that adorned his house—only he'd been clothed and she'd found herself wishing he wasn't, that she would have had the opportunity to see his solidly carved form in the gazebo with the rain falling around them and the pale light harkening the shadows into retreat.

She sipped on the tea that Lydia had prepared for her, wondering if it seemed too sweet because of all the sugar that Lydia might have added or because Tom's taste still lingered on her mouth. She'd barely touched his lips, but it was enough to know that he would have tasted like the delicious walnut cake that had been served for dessert. But even without the sweetness of the dessert served after the meal, Tom would have tasted divine— because he always did, always had, from the first moment that he'd kissed her.

"I hope you're not angry at me for sending Smythe out with an umbrella, but I know first-hand about the dangers that can arise within the confines of a gazebo," Lydia said, effectively bringing Lauren out of her reverie. Her cousin was sitting in a chair, on the other side of the screen, as though she thought even within this room, Lauren needed protecting.

Lauren set her teacup aside and reached for the soap. "I hope you're not planning to sleep in my bed."

"No, of course not."

Silence settled around them, and all Lauren could hear was the crackling of the fire in the hearth.

"Did you get into mischief?" Lydia finally asked.

She decided silence was the best course of action, rather than a lie. She didn't need Lydia being any more alert than she already was. Quite honestly, she was surprised by her cousin's vigilance, had actually expected Lydia to serve as chaperone in name only, especially after her instructions before dinner.

"Lauren?"

"No, no mischief." She finished washing up,

stepped out of the tub, and wrapped the towel warming before the fire around her. It too felt heavenly. Everything here seemed geared toward pampering her.

She walked to the bench and sat at the vanity. Her maid, Molly, immediately began to brush out her tangles, and Lauren was surprised that she felt a bit of regret that it wasn't Tom doing the brushing.

"I do hope it doesn't rain the entire time we're here. Rhys was hoping to do a bit of riding tomorrow," Lydia said.

"I'm sure we'll have a few days of sunshine. So tell me about your experiences in a gazebo."

In the mirror's reflection, she saw Lydia duck her head and begin sipping her own tea, as though she thought that was enough to evade the conversation.

"I'm assuming it was Rhys."

Lydia nodded. "It was at his family's estate, shortly after we met. He kissed me there."

Lauren patted Molly's hand when it came to rest on her shoulder. "Thank you. I'll finish preparing myself for bed."

Molly nodded and walked out of the room. When the door had closed firmly behind her, Lauren brought her legs around the bench until she was facing Lydia. "Then have some pity on me, Lydia. I swear you're worse than my mother. Tom's not going to take advantage unless I give him leave to do so, and do you honestly think that if I've decided I want him to take advantage, you can do anything to prevent it from happening?"

"Then why am I here?"

"Appearances. I have always felt that the notion of chaperones is silly. I want to spend this time with Tom, to get to know him again, to have a few memories to take with me back to Texas." In earnestness, she bent forward, crossing her arms on her legs. "I remember once, when you were staying with us, before you were married, Rhys bursting into your bedroom, sitting on the bed, comforting you because you were ill, and you seemed neither shocked nor ashamed, as though having him so near your bed was not unusual." She watched as Lydia lowered her gaze and her cheeks burned red. "You know what it is to be young and . . . curious, to know what it is to wonder what it might be like to be a little more intimate with a man. If you are guarding me so closely because you fear that I might travel a path you once walked, guard me only if you truly believe that your life would be better now if you'd not taken the path."

Lydia lifted her gaze. "The thing about the English is that they use so many words to say something that can be said with a few. All you have to do is say, 'Stay away.' "

Lauren rose to her feet. "Stay away. You're here to satisfy my mother and society. Not me and certainly not Tom."

"Do you love him, Lauren?"

"I don't know. There are times when I see the shadow of the boy he was . . . but there's not enough there to hold my heart. I'm trying to follow your advice and see the man he's become. If you guard me, how will I ever learn if I'm safe with him?"

Lydia sighed. "All right. Rhys and I will find ways to occupy ourselves while we're here."

"You don't have to be strangers or avoid us completely. Just don't send the butler after us if we're alone."

It was after midnight when she finally dared to venture from her room, certain that Lydia, if not asleep, at least wouldn't be scouring the hallways. The storm had increased in intensity, the claps of thunder echoing with a loudness that sometimes made her jump. She crept down the hallway, down the stairs, and came to an abrupt halt at the sight of Smythe snuffing out the candles in the entryway chandelier. It was indeed a late-night household.

Lauren pulled the sash on her robe. She gave him a weak smile and hurried past him to the stairs that led into the other wing.

"His lordship is in the library," Smythe said, in a voice that tolled as loudly as Big Ben.

Lauren spun around and headed the other way.

She intended to play Tom's little game in a way that had him reaching for her. She would be the one standing as still as a statue, the one tempting him, the one so close he could smell her scent . . .

She'd been squirming in bed with needs unful-filled, and if he was still awake and in the library, perhaps he'd been doing the same. Only she didn't know how he could sit still long enough to read.

So late at night, no footmen were about, thank goodness. She opened the door and stepped into a room that was a black abyss. A shiver went through her. Obviously Tom wasn't there. She was turning to leave when lightning suddenly illumi-nated the room, casting everything in silhouette, including the man standing on the second level before the large plate-glass window. She would have recognized his form, his stance anywhere.

He was staring out on the night, and she didn't think he'd detected her presence. She padded across the room and quietly climbed the spiral staircase to the landing that marked the begin-ning of the second tier of bookshelves. The famil-iar scent of old parchment and aged leather greeted her. She always found something com-forting in the fragrance.

Lightning again filled the sky, giving her a clearer view of Tom. He wore neither jacket nor waistcoat, only shirt and trousers, as he gazed out on the storm. She eased up beside him, wrapped her hand around his arm. "Are you all right?"

"Just remembering other storms."

Looking out the window, she watched the light-ning split the darkness. "It's a magnificent view."

"They fought here. In the library," he said quietly.

"Who?"

"My mother and father. I had sneaked up here to read; I liked being with all the books. He was yelling at her. He needed another son. He forced—"

He stopped, and she could hear the grinding of his teeth.

"She was his wife, and he gave her no choice."

"How old were you?"

Now that she was closer to him, she could see his silhouette in the shadows, could see him shake his head. "Not very old. I'd only recently learned to read. I don't think I read a book I didn't have to after that day."

She remembered him saying that he preferred being shown . . . she wondered if before this night he had any inkling as to the reason he might have an aversion to reading.

"Why did she come back?" he asked.

"To protect you. That can be the only explanation. She did love you. I believe that with all my heart."

"What if I'm like him, Lauren?"

"You're not."

"I forced you"—she heard him swallow—"to unbutton your bodice."

"You teased me into unbuttoning it. Do you honestly think that I would have carried through on the bargain if I hadn't wanted to? My God,

Tom, I got in a carriage and instructed the driver where to take me. You couldn't have been more surprised to see me if I'd strode in stark naked."

"Why did you come that night?"

"Because I saw what hitting Whithaven did to you, the remorse and humiliation you felt, the trepidation that you were a reflection of your father." She touched his hair, forced herself to offer him a slight smile. "And because I wanted to offer you comfort, and I didn't think you'd appreciate yellow roses."

"You said you planned to behave with decorum while you were here."

"And you've held yourself at bay. How in God's name can you think you in any way resemble the man who was your father?"

"His blood runs through me, Lauren."

Reaching up, she wound her arms around his neck, pressed her body against his. "His blood may, but his soul doesn't. You're your own man, Thomas Warner. Your mother ensured that you would be, and for that, I'm extremely grateful."

He kissed her softly, sweetly, as though he continued to hold himself at bay, as though he feared unleashing the hunger that had devoured them both before. She wouldn't allow it, wouldn't allow these emerging memories to destroy the passion he was capable of exhibiting. He'd never forced her, he never would, because it wasn't in his nature to be cruel, it wasn't in his nature to harm without reason. And if it was the last gift she ever gave him, she was going to erase all the doubts from his mind.

She would be the aggressor. Although she couldn't deny that she'd taken the initiative the night that she'd shown up at his house. She might have grown timid when faced with the reality of what she wanted, but she'd done nothing that she didn't want to do.

She began unbuttoning his shirt. She was aware of his fingers fumbling with her buttons. It gave her a sense of satisfaction, of power, to know that she could make him tremble.

Her gown slipped off one shoulder. He cupped her breast. With his tongue, he lapped at the tip, causing it to pucker and harden. Closing his mouth over it, he suckled earnestly, then gently. She spread his shirt wide, ran her hands over the firm muscles of his chest, his stomach.

Lightning flashed, exposing him as though nature approved of the specimen on display. She pressed kisses to his dew-coated throat, his chest.

"I'm sorry, darlin', but I can't wait."

Before she realized what he was apologizing for, he had her against a bookshelf with the hem of her nightgown up around her waist, his trousers unbuttoned. Then he was lifting her up with his hands beneath her bottom—

And plunging into her hot, moist center.

Only the tiniest bit of her scream sounded before he blanketed her mouth, capturing the rest of it, his tongue swirling and thrusting with as much force and eagerness as his hips.

Where before he'd been patient, now he was impatient, as impatient as she. To have learned what it was to be with him, then to have been without. She wrapped her arms around his shoulders, her legs around his waist, as he pumped into her.

The sensations grew like a pebble tossed into a pond, growing, growing, until she was shuddering with her release, shuddering in his arms. He tore his mouth from hers, buried his face in her hair, in the curve of her neck, as his body spasmed and his harsh groan echoed between them.

His labored breathing surrounded them as he kissed her temple, the corner of her mouth, her chin. "Next time will be slower, darlin', I promise."

She nestled her face against the side of his neck. "Ah, Tom, I'm going to hold you to keeping that promise."

With the moonlight spilling in through the window, Tom gazed at Lauren as she lay sleeping, nestled against his side, her head in the crook of his shoulder, her hand curled just below his pounding heart. Keeping his promise, he'd carried her to his bed and made love to her slowly the second time, leisurely removing her clothes, while she'd removed his.

He skimmed his finger along the swell of her

breast. Sighing, she snuggled more closely against him. He thought he'd never tire of hearing the little sighs she made while she slept, the way she rubbed the sole of her foot over his calf until she drifted off to sleep. Like a child needing the repetitive motion of a rocker so it could go to sleep.

Not that she was a child. Far from it.

It was a shame that she disliked England so much. She would have made an exemplary countess. She would have been his choice for a wife, a helpmate. But life with him would diminish her smiles, lessen her laughter until they were both miserable. He couldn't do that to her.

Her eyes fluttered open and her lips tilted up into a sleepy-looking smile. "What are you doing?" she asked softly.

"Watching you sleep."

"Aren't you tired?"

"I can sleep later." When he had nothing but his memories of her to keep him company.

She yawned. "I should probably go back to my room."

"Stay a little longer."

She started tapping her finger on his chest. "I told Amy that they didn't have chaperones in Texas because everyone behaved. They don't behave, do they?"

"Depends on your definition of misbehaving I guess."

"This here seems like misbehaving to me."

She spoke with a slow drawl that had Tom chuckling. "I like it when you don't talk so proper."

"Do you now?"

" 'Course, I like when you talk proper, too. Especially when you're getting after me. You still rile so easily."

"You still do plenty to rile me."

He squeezed her breast. "What if I do something guaranteed not to rile you?"

She stretched languorously against him. "You're insatiable, you know that?"

"Is that a problem for you?"

She laughed lightly. "Reckon not, since I am, too." She stopped laughing. "Never knew I was until now."

"That's because I'm a very skilled lover."

"Lover. I guess you are my lover. That makes all this seem so wicked."

"We're the only ones who'll know, darlin'."

She rolled over onto him, kissed his chest, moved up slightly and flicked her tongue over his nipple. Groaning, he rubbed his hands down her back, over her bare bottom. He glanced toward the window, saw a streak of light, grinned. The storm had moved on, leaving a clear sky in its wake.

He patted her bottom. "Come here, darlin'."

She lifted her head. "I am here."

"I meant move off me."

"Uh-huh. I'm awake now. I want a little loving."

He patted her bottom again. "And I want to give it to you, but let's get out of bed first."

"Are we going to do it against the wall instead of the bookcase this time?"

"Not exactly. Come on, Lauren."

"Tom—"

"Look at the window."

She raised up, twisted her head. "Was that a falling star?"

"I think so."

She scrambled out of bed, took the few steps to the window, and peered out. "Oh, Tom, the sky is so clear that the stars look like diamonds spilled on velvet. Oh, and look, there's another star falling. Why are there so many out here?"

He came up behind her. "I don't know that there are more. It's just so dark that they're easier to see."

With his hand, he scooped her hair up and over, draping it over her shoulder, so it cascaded along her chest and stomach, leaving her back completely bare. He pressed a kiss to the nape of her neck. She sighed, started to turn—

He put his hands on her shoulders. "No, keep watching the stars."

"What are you going to do?"

"Just keep watching the stars."

"But I want to touch—"

"Shh. We may never have a moment like this again."

When he laid his hot, open mouth against her neck again, and his hands came around to cradle her breast, Lauren was finished arguing. He was so very skilled at convincing her to try things his way.

She dropped her head back.

"Keep your eyes open," he said.

"I will . . . oh, there's . . . one."

He skimmed his mouth along her spine, his tongue blazing a trail, down, then up, across her shoulders, along her spine again, each swirl of his tongue, each nip of his teeth had her squirming. His hands traveled provocatively over her breasts, her stomach. She stood there, stoically accepting the torture he inflicted, moaning, writhing, wanting to turn around so she could inflict some of her own.

She could do this to him. Run her hands slowly up and down his legs. Kiss his calves, his thighs, his buttocks. She could skim her hands over his chest, tease his nipples, she could take her hands lower . . .

He was working deliciously wonderful wicked magic with his fingers.

"You're so wet, so hot," he rasped. "So ready. Keep your eyes open."

She released a tiny moan that she hoped he understood was acceptance of his order. Feeling his thrust, she gripped the edges of the window, when she really wanted to reach back and grab him. Hold him close, as close as he was holding her. Touch him as he was touching her. Ride him as he was riding her.

She felt the pressure, the pleasure mounting . . . saw the star streaking . . .

"Oh, there! There! Oh, God!"

He closed his mouth over her shoulder as he bucked against her, she bucked against him, as pleasure shot through her. His final thrust came hard and deep, then he was clutching her close, panting near her ear, and she wasn't certain how they both remained standing.

"There were stars in the sky, stars in my body," she whispered breathlessly. "That wish has got to come true."

He chuckled low. "Hope it was a good one."

"It was," she assured him, wondering why before that night she'd never seen a star fall on that side of the world. What other things hadn't she seen?

Chapter 16

~~~~~ ∽◯◯◯∾ ~~~~~

She awoke to the sound of an irritating *tick, tick, tick*. It had still been dark when Tom had returned her to her bedchamber, and she'd fallen into a deep, dreamless sleep.

Peering out from beneath her pillow, she could see a sliver of sunlight spilling in through the parted draperies. The ticking noise seemed to be coming from there. Throwing back the covers, she scrambled out of bed and padded to the window. She peeked through the window . . .

And there was Tom, waiting, with two horses saddled. He looked quite dashing in his riding attire. She waved at him, then hurried to the bed and yanked on the bellpull. She didn't think it was necessary to be dressed and out of the house before Lydia was up and about. She thought she'd made her position perfectly clear the evening before, but why risk that Lydia hadn't realized she was incredibly serious?

Molly arrived and helped Lauren dress in her favorite riding habit.

"Do you know if the duke and duchess are awake yet?" Lauren asked as she settled her hat into place.

"They haven't yet sent for their maid or valet, so I suspect they are still abed."

Lauren couldn't stop herself from smiling. "Good."

In the hallway, she found only a maid who was already quietly placing fresh flower arrangements on the various tables that lined the hallway. The girl curtsied, Lauren nodded, then proceeded to tiptoe on the thick rug that covered a good bit of the floor. Reaching the stairs, she grimaced at the first audible click of her riding boots hitting the marble. Why carpet the hallway if one wasn't going to carpet the stairs?

As lightly and silently as she could, she made her way down the stairs and was out the door, apparently without disturbing Lydia at all. Tom had brought the horses around from the back of the house. He grinned, and this morning it was barely evident that he'd massacred his mustache the night before.

"Morning, darlin'. How'd you sleep?"

"Very well, thank you very much." Tugging on her gloves, she marched over to the smaller of the horses. "Help me up, Tom, before my chaperone catches us."

His grin broadened as though he anticipated the day having very pleasant consequences. "And what if she does catch us?"

He delivered a kiss that said he didn't care if they were caught. Pushing him back slightly, she said, "If we're caught, then she'll start sleeping in my bed and how will I ever get back to yours?"

"Are you planning to come back to mine?"

"Most definitely."

She'd expected him to provide her with cupped hands into which she could place her foot. Instead he placed those magnificently strong hands at her waist and lifted her onto the saddle. She adjusted her seating while he adjusted her skirt. "Where are we going?"

"To look over my kingdom."

"You don't really consider this a kingdom do you?" She watched the ease with which he mounted his own horse, appreciating his fluid movements, the subtle ripple of his muscles as he swung his leg over the saddle, controlling his horse with his thighs as easily as she did with the reins.

"What do you call it when everyone turns to you for the answers?"

She tapped her riding crop against the horse's rump, effectively getting it to move forward. "Are there people who need answers today?"

His laughter seemed harsh as it broke through the hush of early morning. "Someone always needs an answer. This morning, we're just going to ride the land, let the tenants know I'm back in residence"—the last spoken with the slightest of British accents—"just in case anyone needs a word or has some troubles."

"Do you have many tenants?" she asked, as he guided them along the elm-lined dirt path that would lead to the road.

"Not as many as previous lords had, based on the books they all kept. They used to have a thriving enterprise going, but farming here isn't what it once was. Only ten families remain."

"Have you met them all?"

He swung his gaze over to her, and because he wasn't wearing a hat, no shadows hid his heated gaze from her. "I've met them all."

He'd done more than meet them, Lauren quickly discovered as they visited one farm after the other. He remembered their names, the particulars about their crops, any troubles they might have had in the past. He spoke to them not as though he were the lord of the manor, the man who controlled their fate, but as though they were partners trying to make the most of their destiny. He always dismounted, talked with them eye to eye, walked along beside them, listening intently as they complained about the weather as though he could do something about it, informing them that he would pay for the fixing of broken wagons, leaking roofs, and sick livestock.

And because she wanted to be with Tom, Lauren walked as close to him as his shadow, hearing not only the conversation but the respect the farmers held for their new lord, the respect he held for them, their experience, their opinions, their knowledge. "I'm here if you need me, but I don't expect you'll be needing me," he seemed to be telling them, and she thought she could actually see the farmers' backs straightening a bit as Tom gave them the confidence to carry their own burdens.

She thought she'd known the path he'd traveled to arrive at the man he'd become, but she was beginning to think that she hadn't a clue.

At one farm, a white-haired woman with rosy cheeks bustled out of the house, smiling brightly. "We had a letter from our boys, my lord," she said, before Tom had even had a chance to dismount. "They're liking the work you've got them doing."

"I'm glad to hear that, Mrs. Whipple," Tom said, as the woman's lanky husband wandered out from the barn. "I thought they would."

"Said they might have an opportunity to buy some land. Landowners." She shook her head, tears glistening in her eyes that she reached up to wipe away with the corner of her apron. "Never thought I'd see the day that my boys would be landowners."

"They're not landowners yet, Maude, and his lordship don't need to see you blubbering. He'll regret sending them, if he has to listen to you carrying on."

"Better than listening to you not being appreciative of what he done."

"I'm appreciative, and I thank the man by tending his land good and proper."

"It don't hurt to say you're thankful." She sniffed, huffed. "My lord, would you like some scones? They're warm, just out of the oven."

Tom grinned. "Can we take them with us? I have a schedule to keep."

"Of course." She turned to Lauren. "And you, my lady?"

Lauren smiled. "I'm not a *lady*. I'm simply a lady." It was confusing when the same word carried two different connotations. "I'm Miss Fairfield. And yes, I'd love some scones."

"If you'll come inside the house, I'll wrap them up for you."

Lauren followed her inside while Tom went off with her surly husband. The house was simple, neat, and clean, and had an air of warmth and contentment ringing through it. The woman laid a cloth napkin on the table in the kitchen and began placing scones on it.

"You mentioned something his lordship did for

your sons?" Her curiosity was getting the better of her, and she had a feeling getting the information here would be much easier than getting it from Tom later.

The woman bobbed her head. "Sent my two boys to his land in Texas, he did. Paid for everything himself. Said he was short on strong men to work his ranch. My boys are plenty strong, I'll tell you." She brought the ends of the napkin up and tied them together, then handed the bundle to Lauren. "I swear we were blessed the day his lordship arrived. The other lord, the one who took care of things before this one arrived, he was a good man. We had no complaints, but this one"—she nodded knowingly—"he was born to this."

Those words stayed with Lauren as she sat on a crumbling stone wall—the remnants of some ancient fortification—beside a brook, the water leaping over stones near the shore, making a frenzied yet soothing sort of noise. Tom had obviously planned for this morning to include more than visiting his tenants, because he'd brought biscuits filled with strawberry jam and a canteen of coffee. Plus they had the scones.

Sitting beside her, he looked like a man without a care in the world.

"Mrs. Whipple mentioned that you sent her sons to your land in Texas," Lauren said, biting into the cool biscuit, chewing slowly.

Tom turned his attention from the stream to

her. "Most of the young men are heading out to work in factories in the cities. Can't see that it's much of a life."

Licking the jam from her fingers, she smiled. "Because the work takes place indoors?"

"No sun, no cooling breeze, no ground beneath your feet—"

"As though you know anything about the ground. You ride every chance you get."

"All right. No sun, no breeze, no smell of cattle—"

"I never considered the odor of cows desirable."

"Better than the smell of machinery."

"Do you ever think about how different your life would be if you'd been raised here?"

"Every day."

"You'd appreciate different things."

"Sleeping late instead of getting up with the sun, sitting behind a desk all day instead of riding across the land"—he shook his head—"I can't imagine it, Lauren."

"And yet you can't deny that you bring something to your position that many lack: a true understanding of the workingman."

She'd removed her gloves in order to eat, and now he trailed his finger over her hand where it rested on the wall, her arm supporting her.

"You think that's an advantage?"

"I think it makes you unique."

He gave her one of his slow, sensual grins. "I would be anyway. You can't tell me that you've ever met anyone quite like me before."

"No, I've never met anyone quite like you."

Wrapping his hand around her neck, he brought her closer until she could smell the strawberry that laced his breath mingling with hers.

"No chaperone, Lauren, and I'm behaving, but you know what I'm thinking?"

She didn't know how it was possible for eyes as dark as his to seem to darken further, how his touch at her neck seemed to reach down to her toes, how the deep timbre of his voice could cause her nerves to tingle with anticipation, how she could suddenly have an intense desire to nibble on his lips the way she'd just nibbled a scone. She was so distracted by the confusion that his near-ness was causing her body that she could barely hold on to the words he'd spoken. What was he thinking? She hadn't a clue, but she seemed to be robbed of speech and could do little more than shake her head.

"I think that behaving is boring," he said.

"I quite agree," she somehow managed to rasp. "Why do you think I instructed Lydia to stop watching me so closely?"

His eyes somehow managed to darken further, his smile to grow even more sensual and provocative, both issuing the invitation before he spoke.

"If you want it, darlin', you're going to have to come and get it."

Want *what*? she almost whispered. But she knew exactly what he was referring to, what he was tempting her with, what he was withholding to prove his point that a lady had it within her to misbehave as easily as a gentleman did. He'd always corrupted her. She could resist the cigars, the swearing, the whiskey . . . but resist the lure of his kiss?

Why in heaven's name would she want to?

His satisfied groan was echoing around her before she'd finished melding her mouth against his. And apparently his will to resist wasn't as strong as he'd indicated. His fingers tightened their hold on her neck, as his tongue swept through her mouth, before darting back to allow her entry into his. In spite of his best efforts, his words, he could be no more passive than a tiger in the jungle when it sighted its prey. The tense quivering of his muscles told her how much he wanted her. That he was taking no more than the offered kiss was a testament to the strength of his upbringing, regardless of how much he questioned every aspect of it. Evidence of his innate goodness that he was always so quick to deny.

He kissed the way that he lived life: with purpose, with determination, with exactitude.

And his holding himself at bay made her more

daring. She swept her hand up into his hair, wondering why he'd chosen not to wear a hat. She felt the heat of passion sluice through her, swirling, stirring to life desire, want, yearning. She thought she might melt through the wall to be absorbed into the earth, might need to run naked into the brook in order not to burst into flames as ardor consumed her.

Tearing his mouth from hers, he blazed a trail along her throat beneath her chin to just below her ear, the path scalding. She could hear his harsh breathing. "You know I can hardly look at you without wanting you."

She opened her eyes to see the leaves dancing overhead. "We could be discovered here at any moment."

"Tell me to stop, and I'll stop."

And if she didn't issue that order, how far would he go? Would he remove her clothes and his? Would he take her there with the sun beating down on them? Turning her head slightly, she could read in his eyes the disappointment because she would stop this from going further. It was a heady sensation to have so much power, to know her opinion, her wants, her desires mattered to him. That he would give what she was willing to take and that he would hold back what she wasn't yet ready to receive.

Reaching out, cupping his chin in her palm, she brushed her thumb over his mustache. "I'm sorry

I'm not as wild as you'd like me to be." She flung her hand out. "But I just can't . . . outdoors."

"You're as wild as I need you to be, Lauren."

The days that followed gave her an appreciation of him as a lord, managing his tenants. One of the houses had suffered damage during the storm, the roof collapsing. Tom and Rhys had gone to work, helping to nail a new roof into place while Lauren and Lydia had helped to prepare food for the workers. Tom knew livestock like he knew the back of his hand, hard work like he knew the calluses on his palms.

The nights were heaven. Tom was an attentive lover, generous and giving. She actually began to dread the passage of the days, because it would mean that her time with him would soon be over. Oh, he made promises. He would return to Texas, he would seek her out when he did, but she knew the only promises he could possibly keep were those that could be kept immediately. She thought she had missed him when she left Texas, but the feelings she'd held for him then were paltry compared with what she felt toward him now.

It would have been easier if she'd never gone to him that first night, easier still if she'd never come to his estate, if they hadn't renewed their acquaintance to the great extent that they had. She couldn't imagine a day or a night without him in it. Didn't know how she would survive when they were no longer together.

And so she hoarded all the moments, all the little details of their time together.

The way his unruly hair would fall across his brow. At some point in his life he must have reconciled himself to the fact that it couldn't be controlled because he never swept it back. So she took to doing it for him. Often, simply for the pleasure it gave her to touch him, and in public, it seemed such an innocent touching. Yet intimate as well, because his dark eyes would darken further and she would know that he was remembering when she brushed it back after they made love.

The way he buttoned his shirt, from the bottom up. The way he unbuttoned it, loosening just enough buttons so he could pull it off over his head, as though that got him out of his clothes more quickly and into bed with her.

His impatience at getting her out of her clothes. His patience with her once he had. The way he held her as he slept, always touching her, until it was time to return her to her bedchamber.

The way she would wake up to find him standing at the window, staring out at the night sky. The way he would grin and come back to bed once he realized she was awake.

Their whispers in the dark, their murmurings in the moonlight. The many smiles, the abundant laughter, the joy, the absolute joy that had been absent from her life for so long, that she'd despaired ever again finding . . .

She found it long before she left for Texas.

And she wondered how she would survive when he was no longer sharing her days and nights.

Their time at Sachse Hall was coming to a close, and as they all sat at a round table on the veranda, enjoying afternoon tea and nibbling on cucumber sandwiches, Lauren couldn't help but wish that they had one more day, one more night, away from London. But then tomorrow she would wish for the same thing yet again. And the day after.

It was strange that in the last few days, she'd not once thought of Texas or longed for it. She'd been content simply to be with Tom. To watch him at work and at play. To enjoy the evening and the days and the nights.

"So tomorrow we leave this idyllic sanctuary and return to the reality of the Season," Rhys said.

"You're going to make me start to feel guilty for subjecting you to the rigors of the Season," Lydia said.

He took her hand, pressed a kiss to her knuckles, and smiled. "As long as I'm with you, I can endure anything."

The way he looked at her, Lauren didn't think he was enduring much at all. Had Lydia been right? Was Lauren's unhappiness a result of the fact that her heart had never been in England? Was it possible that now it was?

"I suppose we shall have to leave early in the morning so we'll have plenty of time to ready ourselves for Aunt Elizabeth's ball," Lydia said.

"Mama always gets so nervous," Lauren confessed.

"You wouldn't know it by looking at her."

"Do we ever know what anyone truly thinks simply by looking at them?"

"I suspect we shall know what Whithaven thinks," Lydia said.

"I'll take care of Whithaven," Tom said.

"Have it all planned out, do you?" Rhys asked.

"Down to the smallest detail."

"What are you going to do?" Lauren asked.

Tom winked. "Trust me. I seriously doubt it's something my father would have done."

Chapter 17

I t was all madness and mayhem when Lauren arrived home. After she said good-bye to Tom with a promise of the first dance, and the servants had carted her trunks upstairs, she went in search of her mother and found her in the ballroom, overseeing the arrangements of flowers.

Yellow roses. So many yellow roses.

She gave her mother a tight hug before glancing all around. "Whatever possessed you to choose yellow roses?"

"Tom made arrangements for their delivery before you left for the country."

She looked at her mother. "All of them?"

Her mother nodded. "He thought you might

need a little bit of Texas upon your return. How was your time away?"

"Confusing." Lauren walked to a table and pulled a long-stemmed rose from a vase, sniffed the delicate fragrance. "When Ravenleigh asked you to leave Texas, did you have no doubts that you were making the right decision?"

"Of course I had doubts."

She faced her mother. "When you come to a fork in the road, how do you know which path leads to happiness?"

"You don't. You simply make the best decision you can make and hope for the best. And sometimes you make very bad decisions, and you live with them."

Lauren nodded, sniffed the rose again. "I learned a lot about Tom while I was away. A lot about myself as well."

"And what conclusions did you come to?"

"I don't know yet."

Standing in the night shadows of a giant tree where the glow from the gaslight didn't hit him, Tom wished he had a bottle of whiskey to place between his lips instead of an unlit cigar.

He cursed Lauren for accurately predicting he would face a moment like this, a moment that would require he gather up his courage.

Tom had arrived in a carriage, one of what seemed like a hundred passing along the cobbled drive, stopping in front of Ravenleigh's house, before meandering on to park elsewhere. The procession was still going strong.

Tom observed the people in their fancy clothes alighting from their coaches and carriages. He heard their relaxed laughter. He watched as no one hesitated to walk up the sweeping steps and enter through the doors into what, for him, he was certain was going to be hell.

Music began to drift out onto the air, and he knew he couldn't put off the inevitable much longer.

He withdrew his cigar from his mouth, held it toward the light, and stared at it. He'd almost bitten through the thing, made it too nasty to return to his jacket pocket. With regret for the loss of an expensive cigar, he tossed it into the hedges behind him.

He thought about the first time he'd faced a stampede, the way he'd trembled in his boots, because he hadn't known what to do. In the end, he'd let his gut instincts guide him. He figured he just had to do the same at the ball.

He took as deep a breath as he could—which wasn't much considering the snug fit of his clothes. Lauren was on the other side of those doors. He was doing this as much for her as for himself.

The last time he'd attended a ball, he'd acted like a cowboy. This time he intended to act like the nobleman he was.

* * *

Lauren was beginning to think that Tom wasn't going to come, and she could hardly blame him. She knew what it was to attend a ball where she would be the object of gossip, and while Tom might have done something this afternoon to make things right with Whithaven, he had no guarantees that anyone else would hear of his apology.

She was standing beside her mother and stepfather at the foot of the sweeping stairs that led down to the glittering ballroom. The ballroom was packed. It had been a while since anyone had arrived and walked down the stairs.

"Well, I suppose we can begin to mingle," her mother said.

"I know Tom was going to come," Lauren said.

"I'm sure he'll find us once he arrives."

Then Lauren noticed a quieting, a hush falling over the room, the music ceasing to play, people turning. She looked toward the stairs, and there he was standing at the top: proud, bold, regal. His gaze never wavering. He allowed enough time for everyone to notice him before he began his slow descent of the stairs.

When he arrived at the bottom, he bowed to her stepfather, then took her mother's hand and pressed a kiss to the back of her gloved hand. "I appreciate the welcome into your home."

"I'm certain I won't regret it."

A corner of his mouth hitched up. "If you do, I'll hand you the horsewhip."

He stepped over to Lauren, kissed her hand as well.

"Tom, if I'd known that you planned to stand up there alone—"

"I'm not finished yet, darlin'." He winked. "Save a dance for me."

No one had yet to move although Lauren heard the first hint of whispering when Tom turned away from her. People parted in silence as he made his way through the crowd, straight toward the tallest and gangliest lord among them. She halfway expected Whithaven to turn on his heel and run. But he didn't. To her surprise, he stood his ground, although looking a bit nervous, and at that moment, she thought she might have gained a bit more respect for him. These men lived a much less harsh life than the men she'd known in Texas, and it was often easy to overlook the fact that they had steel in their backbones. She thought she could even detect a bit of admiration for the earl mirrored in Tom's expression as he came to a halt before him. The poor man's nose was slightly swollen, and the bruising around his eyes had faded to a ghastly yellow.

"Whithaven," Tom said, his deep baritone throwing his voice out for all to hear. "I owe you an apology."

"I daresay you do."

"I had no call to punch you, but that's the way we do it in Texas. Cowboys are men of action more than words, and we don't take well to having our ladies insulted."

"Well, I meant no insult, of course; I was simply trying to spare you . . . I didn't realize that you considered her . . . well . . . already your lady," he stammered to a stop. "My apologies as well."

Tom held out his hand. "Accepted."

Looking somewhat like a startled raccoon with the flesh around his eyes still discolored, Whithaven took Tom's hand. "Jolly good."

There was a general murmuring as Whithaven turned and walked away, a smug smile on his face as though he'd somehow managed to win. Music started playing and with tears in her eyes, Lauren didn't wait for Tom to return to her side. She strolled through the crowd until she reached him, this man who had felt he had something to prove and had just proven it. She studied him, scrutinizing the face that she knew so well, the man she'd thought she'd known, who'd held her, kissed her passionately, made love to her . . .

She couldn't have held any more admiration for him.

"May I have the honor of this dance, my lord?"

He grinned. "Darlin', you can have as many as you want."

"Considering you shall be the object of speculation and gossip this evening, I might consent to give you more than two."

Laughing, he took her into his arms.

"You handled that remarkably well, Tom."

"The one thing I've always been is honest in my dealings with other men. These men here deserve no less."

"I heard your words. Am I your lady?"

"How could you doubt it, Lauren? For as long as you're here."

Then what, she wondered. Would she ever again be anyone's lady?

They danced a scandalous four dances in a row. Tom didn't care about rules. He didn't care what others thought. She would be leaving soon, and as he told her repeatedly, he was saving up for the time when she was gone.

She grew tired of arguing with him.

"At least dance with Mama and my sisters," Lauren said. "I'm going to take a few moments to see to my toilette."

"Don't be gone long."

"I won't be." She wanted to reach up and kiss his cheek to reassure him. Instead, she simply patted his arm.

She walked up the stairs to the main salon, greeted ladies in passing as she strolled down the hallway to the main entry. There she took the grand sweeping stairs that led up to the next level.

Her dance card remained unmarked, but she wasn't bothered by that. She suspected all her dances would be with Tom and as much as she was scolding him, she really didn't mind. Like him, she wanted to hoard their moments together for after she had left.

She reached the next landing and smiled at the woman who'd spotted her and had waited for her arrival before starting her descent.

"Hello, Lady Blythe."

"It's not fair," Lady Blythe said in a mean-spirited whisper.

"What's not?" Lauren asked, leaning in.

"You stole Kimburton from me. I've loved him forever, and now he won't even come to London for the Season. Sachse shows the least bit of interest in me, and you snatch him away as well."

"His interest—"

"Was on me. He repeatedly called me darling."

"He calls all ladies darlin'. It doesn't mean anything."

"It means *everything*. You think his apology to Whithaven makes everything all right. But how will you feel when all of London knows that you have stayed in his residence through the night?"

Staring at her, Lauren shook her head. "You can't—"

"Know? I do know. I was watching from my carriage after Harrington's ball. Then you went off to the country with him—"

"You've been spying on him?"

"Spying on him is innocent compared with what you've been doing."

"You have no idea what I've been doing, and it's none of your business anyway."

She started to walk by, and Lady Blythe grabbed her arm. "I'll ruin you. I'll make it so no gentleman will dare to consider marrying you. Not even Sachse. You had your chance with Kimburton. Sachse belongs to me."

"You want him only because of the coins in his pockets and the titles that he wears. I want him because I love—" Lauren stopped. Dear God, but she did love him. All the plans she'd been making hadn't been to return to Texas, but to return to Tom. She'd simply refused to recognize it, to acknowledge it, because for a time she'd thought he'd abandoned her. But he hadn't. In a way, by not trusting him, she'd abandoned him.

She had to tell him, tell him what she felt. She wasn't going to go back to Texas. She wanted to stay in England.

She turned for the stairs. She had to find him. Immediately.

"No, you can't have him!"

She heard the shrill cry, felt the shove at her back, lost her balance, screamed as she tumbled down the hard marble steps, as pain ricocheted through her head and blackness descended.

Chapter 18

"**M**y lord, I must ask that you leave."

Tom didn't bother to look at the doctor they'd sent for. Sitting in a chair he'd pulled up to the bed, he just kept his gaze on Lauren, his hand wrapped around hers. Why didn't she wake up?

He'd only just arrived at the stairs when he'd heard the echo of her scream and seen her tumble, and he'd been powerless to do anything to prevent her fall. All he'd been able to do was lift her gently into his arms and carry her to her bedchamber.

"I'm not leaving her," he said.

"Tom—" her mother began.

Tom twisted his head around and glared at her. "I'm not leaving her."

He put enough force behind the words so he left no doubt that he meant every word spoken. Lauren's mother and the doctor exchanged glances, and the doctor sighed. "Very well."

Tom turned his attention back to Lauren, rubbing his thumb in a circle over the top of her hand. She didn't react at all: not a sigh, a murmur, a whisper. Nothing. She just lay there, cool to the touch and so incredibly pale.

He heard the footsteps as her mother walked to the window. The doctor cleared his throat. "Truly, my lord, I could examine her much more quickly and efficiently if you would be kind enough to move aside. We want what's best for her now, don't we?"

If they wanted what was best for her, she'd be in Texas already. Why hadn't he simply purchased her passage, let her go sooner? Why had he insisted on keeping her with him when it hadn't been what she wanted? Why had he been so damned selfish? He was no different than his father: caring about his own needs and to hell with anyone else. All the incessant questions and doubts simply served to plague and frustrate him.

With a nod toward the doctor, Tom stood, walked to the window, and leaned his shoulder against the wall. With the draperies pulled aside, Lauren's mother was looking out on the night. She didn't bother to look at him, just kept staring out.

"She'll be all right," Tom said, feeling a need to

comfort her as much as he needed to be comforted. But without Lauren, he found no comfort. She was the one who could see into his soul, who could overlook the dark in favor of the light.

"You can't know that," her mother said.

No, he couldn't but he could hope . . . hell, he could wish. If he could only find a star . . .

He knew where plenty could be found and a woman could wish all night long. "I'm taking Lauren back to Texas."

Her mother looked at him then, and before she could speak, he said, "Whether she wakes up or not, I'm taking her back to Texas."

His voice held command and authority, years of issuing orders, years of being obeyed without question, years of being the one everyone turned to for the answers, the one everyone still turned to.

Tears welled in her mother's eyes. "I did what I thought was best for her."

Tom nodded with sympathy and understanding. "I know, but now it's time for me to do what's best for her."

He turned as the doctor came to stand beside them. "She's definitely sustained a blow to the head."

Tom had to move away from the bed so the doctor could make that diagnosis?

"Which means what exactly?" Tom asked.

"Which means that we have to wait—"

"Wait for what?" he asked impatiently.

"To see if she wakes up. It could happen any

moment. It might never happen at all. It's impossible to tell. And if she does wake up, well, quite frankly, I can't tell what sort of damage might have been done until she does wake up."

"There must be something you can do," Lauren's mother said.

"I'm afraid not, unfortunately. The good news is that nothing else appears to be broken or damaged. I would suggest you have someone watch over her and send for me immediately if you detect any change."

Lauren's mother wiped the tears from her cheeks. "We'll do whatever we have to do."

"I would begin by having her maid undress her and put her in a nightgown, so she is more comfortable."

"I'll see that it's taken care of," her mother said.

"I'll stop by in the morning to check on her."

Lauren's mother nodded. "Thank you, Doctor." She turned to Tom. "There's no reason for you to stay. I'll send word when she wakes up."

Tom shook his head. "You're not listening. I'm not leaving."

And he didn't. For the sake of propriety, he kept his back to the bed, staring out the window searching for that elusive star while Lauren's maid removed her clothes and put her in a nightgown. When she was finished and Tom finally turned around, Lauren was beneath the covers, her hands folded on top. A chill swept through him.

He couldn't lose her.

Her mother hadn't left the room, but stood vigil at the foot of the bed, her arms crossed over her chest, guarding against the arrival of the angel of death. Tom reconciled himself to sharing the room with her. He sat in the chair beside the bed, took Lauren's hand, and wrapped both of his around it.

"I don't know if you can hear me, darlin'," he said, his voice low, "but I lied to you. That first night when we were lying by the river and I told you that I wrote about cattle in my letters . . . that wasn't true, and I remember every word I wrote.

"My darlin' Lauren,

"It about killed me today to watch the wagon take you away. I know you didn't see me standing at the edge of your place watching, but I was there. I was afraid if your mama saw me, she'd get mad at you. I figured leaving was hard enough on you without having your mama mad at you, too. So I did my watching in secret. I know you were wearing the hair ribbon I gave you. Someday I'm going to buy you another one, a fancier one. Lord, I already miss you so bad that I don't know how I'll make it through tomorrow. But if I don't make it, then I'll never see you again, so I reckon I'll find a way.

"Yours forever,

"Tom."

Reaching out, with his fingers, he combed a few wisps of her hair back from her face.

"My darlin' Lauren,

"There's an ache in my heart that I reckon will be here until we're together again. It makes the day long and the night longer. Even when thinking about you makes me smile, it hurts. I can't figure out why it pains me when I like thinking about you. I lay out by the creek tonight, alone. I saw a star fall from the sky. If I believed in wishing, I'd have wished that you'd come back to me. But I know that won't happen, so there's no point in wishing for it. But I will come for you, just like I promised. You don't have to wish for it, when it'll happen without wishing.

"Yours forever,

"Tom."

He didn't look over when her mother sat in a chair on the opposite side of the bed. "She cried every night on the journey over here," she said quietly. "But then so did Amy and Samantha. Uprooting them was hard, but I knew my girls well enough to know they'd adjust. Children are resilient that way. As a parent, you do what you believe is best."

"I never held it against you for bringing her here."

"If you insist upon staying in this room while she recovers, you'll have to marry her."

Tom knew that she thought she was once again doing what was best for Lauren, was maybe even letting him know that she would approve of their marrying.

"I'm staying," he told her.

She rose. "I'll let my husband know that you'll be asking for her hand—"

"I'm not marrying her."

She looked as though she was on the verge of searching for a gun so she could shoot him.

"Who Lauren marries is her decision to make, not yours, not mine," he said.

"How long do you anticipate staying here?"

"Until she wakes up."

"My darlin' Lauren,

"I bought some land today. It brings me one step closer to you. Now all I need is the livestock and the buildings and a few good cowhands. I figure another year, maybe two, and I can come for you. My biggest fear is that you grew tired of waiting. That you're married. I don't know why I keep writing, why I keep thinking of you. In some ways, it doesn't seem like so many years have passed. In other ways, it seems like you've been gone forever. In all ways, you still own my heart . . ."

Lauren heard the scratchy voice. It seemed it had been with her forever, fading in and out. She'd wanted to respond to it, to tell it to keep saying the lovely words, but whether she responded or not, it continued. Always there when she awoke, always there when she drifted off to sleep. Although little difference was apparent between one action and another, because she never opened her eyes. She was so terribly weary and her head hurt something fierce.

She tried to force her eyes open, tried to force her voice to work. *Don't stop. Don't stop. As long as you talk I have something to hold on to . . .*

"You're not doing her any favors by making yourself sick. You look awful, you sound awful."

Rubbing his unshaven face, Tom looked up at Lydia. She, Lauren's sisters, mother, and stepfather all took turns spending a couple of hours in the room. But he had yet to leave except for short stretches of time to eat or throw cold water on his face. His voice was as rough as sandpaper, but he was afraid if the room filled with silence, Lauren would just drift away.

He got up and walked to the window. It was night again. He'd missed its arrival. Was this the second or third night?

"Maybe you should go home for a few hours," Lydia suggested.

"No."

"Then at least lie down for a while. Ravenleigh has extra bedrooms—"

"No."

"I do believe you are more stubborn than Rhys," she said.

He peered down at the street. "There's no fog tonight."

"Is that significant?"

"The stars will be more visible."

"So?"

He spun around. "I need to take her to the river."

"Aunt Elizabeth isn't going to allow—"

"We won't tell her."

He crossed the room, knelt in front of Lydia, and took her hands. He knew he was close to collapse, so weary that he could hardly hold the tears at bay. "It'll mean something to Lauren."

"Tom, she's not aware—"

"You don't know that. Help me bundle her up, help me get her into a carriage. You can even go with us if you want. Serve as chaperone one more time."

"As though I've ever been any good as a chaperone. Don't think I don't know what was going on at your estate—"

"I love her, Lydia. I've always loved her. Sending her to Texas is going to kill me. But I'm going to do it, but she has to be awake first. Trust me to know what she needs."

"Aunt Elizabeth is going to kill me."

"Only after she kills me."

"If this doesn't work, Thomas Warner, you have to promise me that you'll go home and rest before you collapse."

He looked at Lauren, so peaceful, so still. He shook his head. "That's a promise I can't make."

"You are the most stubborn man," but even as she chastised him, she got to her feet and began to help him wrap Lauren in a blanket.

When he had her bundled in his arms, she led the way down the stairs, found the butler, and had the carriage brought around.

He knew he was a desperate man, but he didn't know what else to do.

Lydia had decided to stay in the carriage, but Tom wanted Lauren outside. Holding her close, he walked toward the river, stopped by a nearby tree, and as carefully as he could, sat on the ground with his back against its trunk.

He cradled Lauren tightly. She seemed so frail. It had been three or four days. He'd lost count.

"It's not Texas, darlin', but there's the river and above us are the stars. You know I worried that I was like my father, but you made me realize that I'm not, because he wasn't the kind of man who could love as deeply as I love you."

He looked up at the sky, so vast, so black . . .

"There's a star, Lauren. Falling. I sure wish you'd wake up."

"You don't believe in wishing."

His heart jumped, and he looked down at the woman in his arms, surrounded by shadows. "Lauren?"

"Hello, Tom."

Laughing, he felt the tears burning his eyes. "Hello, darlin'."

There was a good deal that Lauren didn't remember. She didn't remember actually falling or hitting her head. She didn't remember any pain.

What she did remember was the constant raspy voice, the words, and the love. She remembered the love most of all.

So she was surprised, a week after she woke up, to find herself holding a ticket for passage on a steamship that would take her to New York, where she would board a ship that would take her to Galveston.

"You've taught me everything I need to know," Tom said, sitting across her, looking extremely formal with his top hat on his thigh. "I can't see any reason for you to have to stay until the end of the Season. The doctor says you're strong enough to travel."

"You told Lydia that it would kill you when I left."

He stared at her. "You heard that?"

"I heard a great deal. You told her that you love me. Tell *me* that you love me."

To her surprise, he got up, crossed over to her, knelt in front of her, and took her hand. "I love you, darlin'. I always have and I always will. I can only give you a little bit of Texas, but I can give you a whole lot of my heart. I'd ask you to marry me if I thought it was what you wanted—"

"It's what I want."

"Are you sure?"

"I was sure before I fell. I just didn't get a chance to tell you." She cradled his beloved face. "I love you, Thomas Warner. I've loved you forever."

She was suddenly in his arms, being held tightly, being kissed deeply. And she knew that he was the only part of Texas that she'd ever need.

Chapter 19

"They say he fell in love with her when they were children in Texas."

"I've heard that he wrote her a letter every single day, of every year that they were separated."

"I daresay I find that incredibly romantic."

"Have you seen the way he looks at her? He can scarcely take his eyes off her."

"I would love to have a gentleman look at me with that same sort of intensity."

"He doesn't look at her as though he's a *gentleman*. He fairly looks at her as though he's entertaining *barbaric* thoughts."

"How fortunate for me," Lauren said.

The three ladies spun around, their eyes wide,

their mouths agape. It was odd seeing them without Lady Blythe, but her parents had ushered her off to the country in shame and embarrassment for her inappropriate behavior at the Ravenleigh ball. Lauren actually felt rather sorry for the lady, as it was unlikely she would garner any gentleman's fancy. Lauren had even sent her a bouquet of flowers with the sentiment, "No hard feelings."

She could afford to be generous in her forgiveness. After all, without Lady Blythe's conduct, Lauren might never have learned the true words that had been written in Tom's letters, might never have known how strong and constant Tom's love had remained over the years.

"Lady Sachse, we didn't hear you approach," Lady Cassandra said. "We meant no insult to you, dear friend, but one can't help but notice . . . well, that your husband looks as though he can't wait for the wedding breakfast to be over so that he can get on with the wedding trip."

Lauren smiled, not bothering to hide her anticipation. "Again, how fortunate for me."

Her wedding to Tom had been the most-talked-about event of the Season. Lauren didn't think there had been a vacant seat in the church, nor a spot of grass in the churchyard that wasn't being stood on by someone wanting to catch a glimpse of the newly wedded couple. Her half sisters had strewn flower petals from the church to the carriage that had brought Lauren and Tom to her parents' home. The wedding breakfast had followed. After all the toasts to their health, Lauren's sisters had led her away so she could change into her departure dress. She'd only just returned to the drawing room, where she planned to begin saying her good-byes. But the gossipmongers had caught her attention. She held them no ill will either. It was the happiest day of her life, and she wanted everyone to be as filled with joy as she.

"Where are you going for your marriage trip?" Lady Anne asked.

"We're going to Texas for a few months." Tom's wedding gift to her, as though she needed anything at all from him.

"Oh, how delightful," Lady Priscilla said.

"We shall no doubt spend a good deal of our time there, since my husband owns a ranch and several other businesses. You must visit sometime. I'll introduce you to some cowboys."

"Oh, my word. Would you really? That would be lovely," Lady Cassandra murmured, rather like a contented cat.

"If you ladies will excuse me, I think my husband and I are going to begin the preparations for our departure. I do thank you for coming to the wedding and the breakfast. I have always treasured your friendship." She leaned in, they leaned in. "I think he looks at me as though he intends to ravish me quite unmercifully."

"Indeed he does," Lady Cassandra said breathlessly.

Smiling, Lauren winked at them. "Ladies, I can hardly wait."

They were still gasping and fanning themselves as she went to join her husband, where he was standing on the other side of the room talking with her parents. Her mother was actually smiling broadly and laughing. It seemed that she and Tom had somehow managed to put aside their differences. She wasn't quite sure what all had transpired within her bedchamber while she'd slept on for three days, but obviously her mother had gained an appreciation for Tom during that time.

It was a little strange, but now that the moment had finally arrived, Lauren wasn't quite certain that she was ready to leave after all. Tom put his arm around her, drawing her up against his side. "Are you all right, darlin'?"

She nodded, surprised by the hoarseness of her voice when she said, "I'm just not quite ready to leave, although I know we must."

"Lauren, it's your wedding. If you want to stay here all day, that's what we'll do."

"You're going to spoil me, Tom, letting me do whatever I want."

He suddenly looked incredibly serious. "That's my plan, darlin'."

Stretching up on the tips of her toes, she kissed

his cheek. "I like your plan." She squeezed his arm. "I'm ready."

She turned to her mother. "Can you believe it? I'm going home tomorrow."

Her mother smiled sadly, caressed Lauren's cheek. "I'm hoping you'll discover that home isn't a place. It's wherever your heart happens to be." She shifted her gaze to Tom, then back to Lauren. "I thought you were too young to really leave your heart in Texas, and I'm so sorry—"

"Mama." Lauren touched her gloved hand to her mother's lips and shook her head. "All of that is in the past. I'm happier today than I've ever been. And I already know that you're right. Whether my home is in Texas or England will be determined by whether or not Tom is beside me."

"Are you ever going to leave?" Amy asked.

Lauren looked over her shoulder to see her sisters standing there, wondering when they'd sneaked up on her.

"Yes, I am."

"Won't you miss it all?" Amy asked. "The balls, parties—"

"We'll be back," Lauren assured her. "Before next Season. Now that I'm married, it's Samantha's turn."

She glanced over at Samantha, but her sister hardly reacted to her declaration.

"I think she already has someone," Amy said.

"And I think the article on the front page of tomorrow's newspaper recounting this affair is going to mention how unfashionably long it took the bride to say *adieu*," Samantha said.

Following a round of hugs and additional best wishes, Lauren found herself fighting to hold back her tears. She was certain that they were tears of happiness rather than sadness. This was what she wanted, what she'd always wanted. She couldn't be sad, even though the tightness in her chest felt a good deal like sorrow.

Then she turned to face her mother, and she knew the tears gathering in her mother's eyes *were* tears of unhappiness.

"I always only wanted what was best for you," her mother said.

Lauren hugged her tightly. "I know, Mama."

"Who would have thought what was best for you would have turned out to be a cowboy?"

Laughing, Lauren hugged her mother more tightly, before stepping back. "A cowboy and a lord. I'm so glad that I didn't have to choose between them. I love you, Mama, and I'm going to miss you."

"Lauren, darlin', we probably do need to be going. Folks seem to be getting restless," Tom said.

Lauren spun around, with one more good-bye to give. She wound her arms around her stepfather's neck. "Thank you for the life you gave me."

"It has always been my pleasure."

"Don't let Samantha get married before I get back."

He laughed. "As though I can stop any of my daughters from doing what they set their minds to doing." He touched her cheek. "And you are my daughter, not of my blood, but of my heart."

Lauren felt the tears rolling down her cheeks, Tom pressing his handkerchief into her hand. "I love you, Papa."

She hugged him one more time, hugged her mother, and her sisters. Guests began crowding around, to offer final best wishes. She placed her hand on Tom's arm, allowed him to lead her through the throng. So many smiling faces, so many people offering her warm wishes.

It was an odd thing as she was leaving, at long last to realize that she belonged.

They arrived at Tom's ancestral home by late afternoon. While Lauren's things were moved into the house and arranged in her bedchamber, she and Tom walked over the grounds discussing the plans for their wedding trip. The next day they would leave for Liverpool, where they could board the steamship that would take them to Texas. For only a few months. In the event she became pregnant with the Sachse heir, Tom wanted the boy born in England, and based upon how he planned for them to spend most of their time, Lauren couldn't help but believe that she would indeed be presenting him with an heir incredibly soon. She knew that nothing would please her more.

Following dinner, they retired to their respective bedchambers, and Lauren couldn't help but feel a slight fluttering in her stomach at the prospect of her first night with Tom as his wife. She knew what to expect and as she'd told the ladies, she could hardly wait.

Sitting at the vanity in her bedchamber, having dismissed Molly after she helped Lauren prepare her for bed, Lauren brushed her hair, remembering the ladies talking that first afternoon about how the American-raised lord wouldn't have an appreciation of his heritage. Lauren was learning that he had an incredible appreciation for tradition, whether it involved that to which he'd been born or that to which he'd been raised. He was a complex man, a combination of all he'd experienced, of all he'd ever lost, and all he'd regained. A man who would never take any aspect of his life for granted. She loved him for it, and for so much more. For being the man he was, a man who had never given up on their love. It humbled her at times to know that he'd continued to write faithfully long after she'd stopped. She only hoped that she'd always prove deserving of him.

Setting her brush aside, she reached out and wrapped her hands around her jewelry box, set upon the vanity by Molly earlier when she'd unpacked Lauren's possessions. She placed the box on her lap. Very slowly she opened the gleaming wooden box and smiled at the contents nestled within. Perhaps she'd had faith as well, but had chosen to express it in a different way.

Looking up, she saw Tom, wearing a black silk dressing gown, standing behind her, reflected in the mirror. The nightgown she wore was nothing at all like the ones she'd worn when she'd clambered out of windows. This one was a diaphanous material that revealed much more than it covered, and, based upon the heat in Tom's eyes, she wouldn't be wearing it for long.

"What have you got there?" he asked, the raspy rumble of his voice indicating the depth of her affect on him, causing her toes to curl into the thick carpet at her feet.

Crooking her forefinger, she wiggled it. "Come here."

He knelt beside her, his gaze roaming over her face as though he was having a difficult time believing she was actually with him now, as though everything he'd ever wished for were in danger of disappearing. As though he feared that their time together now would be as temporary or short-lived as everything else in his life.

He'd begun his life here and been taken from it. He'd had a life in New York that hadn't lasted. A life in Arkansas that while short had still been too long. Finally, a life in Texas with a girl who had left him. Then a ranch that he'd had to leave behind in order to return to what he'd never known he owned. His entire life he'd been lost, and she desperately wanted him to know that what they had now would last forever. That she would never leave him. That they would never again become lost.

She combed her fingers up into his thick hair. "I love you, Thomas Warner. I've always loved you."

She turned the jewelry box so he could see inside. She watched as the corner of his mouth hitched up.

"Is that what I think it is?" he asked. He lifted his gaze to hers. "You said—"

"I didn't say I didn't have it. I simply asked where you thought I would find one in this country."

He reached into the box, removed the quarter, and laid it in the palm of his hand. It seemed so small and insignificant, and yet it meant so much. "Is it the one I gave you?" he asked.

"Of course." Out of the box she lifted the worn blue hair ribbon on which it had been nestled. "And I kept this, too."

Grinning, he held the quarter between his thumb and forefinger. "But this you could have given back to me. At any time, you could have canceled the debt."

Smiling warmly, she snatched the coin from him and arched a brow. "I could have, but what woman in her right mind would choose to give you a quarter when she could have you unbutton her bodice?"

The deep rumble of his laughter echoed around them as she dropped the ribbon and coin back into her jewelry box and set it aside on the vanity. Tom unfolded his strong, lean, tall body and lifted her into his arms.

She wound her arms around his neck. "You're what I've always wanted, Tom. I don't know why it took me so long to realize that you're the part of Texas that I always missed. Not the land or the creeks or the smells. Not even the stars at night. Only you."

He carried her over to the bed, set her feet on the floor beside it. Then he did the most remarkable unexpected thing. He sat at the foot of the bed, leaned back against the thick post, crossed his arms over his chest, and hitched up a corner of his mouth. "Unbutton your nightgown."

She stared at him. "Tom, I not only paid the debt and unbuttoned a bodice, but I've proven I can give you back the coin—"

"Do it not because of any debt, but because it brings me so much pleasure to watch you, to watch the way the blush creeps along your skin, the way your eyes darken with each button loosened, the way your lips part, and your breath begins to shorten with the anticipation of revealing yourself to me, of me finally touching you."

She swallowed hard. "Did you want to extinguish the lights?"

Both corners of his mouth hitched up. "No."

"Tom—"

"Lauren, do you know that the sight of you takes my breath away?" he asked quietly, solemnly. "It always has."

Reaching up, she loosened a button.

"You make me tremble deep down inside where a man has no business trembling."

She released another button.

"You terrify me because I think if you ever leave me—"

"I won't, Tom. I'll never leave you."

Button. Button. Button.

"Tom, did you know the sight of you takes *my* breath away? It always has."

Button. Button.

She watched with satisfaction as he slowly came to his feet, untied the sash on his robe, and shrugged out of it, the silk shimmering down his body to land on the floor.

Button. Button.

She eased her nightgown off her shoulders, felt it slide down her body, to pool at her feet. He took a long sigh as appreciation ignited his eyes.

"I don't think I'll ever grow tired of looking at you," he said.

"I know I'll never grow tired of looking at you."

"You're my wife, Lauren."

She nodded, hardly knowing what to say, as he was taking far more time to get her into the bed than she'd expected. Was this another one of his trials, his tests, to prove he had more willpower than she did?

Obviously not. Obviously it was simply a matter of him relishing the moment. He stepped forward, cupped her face between his hands. "You can't begin to imagine how much I dreamed of this. That a time would come when every night would be spent with you. I never want another night in my life without you. I never want another day when I can't see you anytime that I want. From this moment on, nothing will come between us. From this moment on, we will be together forever. I give you my word on that."

"Are we going to shake on it?" she asked.

"Darlin', you know how I close a deal with a lady."

"Then get to it, cowboy."

His mouth swooped down to blanket hers, one arm snaking around to draw her up close until they were touching, thigh to thigh, breast to chest, the passion stirred to life, the heat consuming, beginning as a spark and igniting into a full-fledged flame. His mouth, hot and wet, left hers to journey along her throat, branding a trail that she thought would be visible for days to come. His mouth went lower, until his face was buried between her breasts, and his tongue was lapping at the inside swell of one and then the other, slowly, slowly, his breath fanning her flesh.

She heard herself whimper as her head fell back and her fingers dug into his shoulders. Purchase, she needed purchase before she executed a perfect swoon.

As though aware of her thoughts, he lifted her into his arms and laid her on the bed before stretching out over her, his hips between her thighs. Dear Lord, but she loved the weight of him, the sturdiness, the rippling muscles and hardness that was such a part of him. She wondered how different he might have been if he'd not traveled the road away from England . . . and just as quickly she realized that it didn't matter. They'd both gone on a journey that had brought them to this destination, this moment, this destiny.

If she'd never come here, she'd have been the awkward wife of an English lord. Instead, she possessed the confidence and wherewithal to stand with poise and self-assurance at his side. All of the long-ago lessons, no longer seemed as tedious or pointless or resented. They'd prepared her for his arrival long before either of them knew the incredible life that awaited them together.

He glided his hand along her side, down her hip, and back up, cradling her breast, molding and shaping it, lifting it in order to offer her hardened nipple to his questing mouth. She moaned low as desire stampeded through her, from the tips of her toes to the top of her head to the tips of her fingers. Stretching languidly, she stroked his calves with the soles of her feet and took delight in the feel of the coarse hair that covered his legs.

There was nothing soft about this man as he stirred her passions with his talented tongue and skilled fingers. All the years they'd been denied the celebration of their love would pale when compared to all the years that remained to them.

He rasped his love, her beauty, his desire . . . and she sighed with pleasure and contentment.

She whispered her love, his strength and power, her yearning . . . and he groaned and shuddered.

He rose up above her like the conqueror his ancestors must have been, he entered her with the sure thrust of a man who is confident of his ability to wield a sword mightily. He cupped her face and kissed her deeply as his body began to move in an undulating rhythm that released the wildness in them both.

Everything within her centered on him, on the incredible sensations he was creating, on the madness . . .

She was thrashing and screaming—

Suddenly he rolled her over, managing to stay buried deep within her, his fingers digging into her hips. "Ride me, darlin'," he ordered, his voice hoarse with need, his body coated in dew, his muscles quivering with the force of his straining to hold back his own release until she'd been granted hers.

And London considered him a savage, this man

who always, always was civilized enough to put her needs above his. She thought it was impossible to love him any more than she did, and even as she thought that, she realized that she couldn't quantify what she felt for him, it was as rich as the history of England and as vast and untamed as Texas.

She rocked her hips against his, felt the pressure build, threw her head back as he cupped her breasts, taunting her nipples, sending shards of pleasure shattering throughout her body . . . until she felt as though she were riding a shooting star across the heavens, until she exploded into a thousand brilliant points of light—

He bucked forcefully beneath her, his guttural groan music to her ears, his fingers tightening and loosening as he shuddered and jerked one last time. She dropped down, nestling her head in the crook of his shoulder, listening to his thundering heartbeat, inhaling the musky scent of their lovemaking. She couldn't stop herself from smiling. She would have the miracle of him and what they shared . . . forever. Until she was frail and gray. Until his stride was not as bold or his muscles as firm. But always their love would be strong.

Eventually, he raised his hand enough that he could begin lethargically to stroke her back.

"Every time that happens, I feel as though I'm seeing a black Texas sky filled with shooting stars," she said contentedly.

"Darlin', that's a little bit of Texas that I'll be happy to give you anytime you ask."

Laughing softly, she held him tightly. She'd told her mother wrong. She wasn't *going* home tomorrow.

Home was here, now, right beneath her.

Epilogue

~~~❦~~~

Near Fortune, Texas
1889

"**Y**ou're English!"
   "Am not!"
   "Are too!"
   "Am *not!*"
   "Are, too!"
   "*Am not!*"
   "Boys, that's quite enough!" Lauren called out in exasperation.
   She glared at Tom, who was stretched out beside her on a quilt beneath a towering oak tree near the creek, grinning broadly, refusing to get

353

into the middle of their sons' all-too-familiar hotly debated argument. He merely gave her an innocent shrug that seemed to say "boys will be boys."

"Mama, tell him, tell him, please, that I'm not English. I was born here, so I'm Texan."

"Sam—"

"I'm not English. I don't want to be."

"If you're not English, you can't be the spare," Edward said haughtily, sounding so frightfully English at the age of eight.

"Can, too. But it don't matter anyway, 'cuz I don't want to be the spare. When we grow up, you can be the earl, and I'll be the rancher," Sam told him. He was two years younger, and whenever they were in Texas, he tended to leave behind everything English, including any semblance of being exposed to the slightest bit of an education.

Sam dropped down on the ground beside Tom. "I can be the rancher, can't I, Pa?"

Reaching out, Tom ruffled his son's black hair. "Reckon so. Ward *has* to be the earl because he was born first, but you can be anything you want."

Sam wrinkled his brow. "That ain't hardly fair to Ward, that he don't get to choose."

Lauren rolled her eyes as he continued to massacre the English language. The odd thing was, as soon as they stepped on British soil, his "ain'ts" would disappear. He was a chameleon in that regard, adapting to his surroundings so he blended in unnoticed. It was really quite remarkable.

"I don't mind," Edward said, as he sat on the quilt, never forgetting for a moment that he was the young lord who would one day step into his father's shoes, while it seemed that Sam had definite plans to step into his father's boots. "I want to be the earl. And I can do other things, too. Like Father. I don't have to be *just* the earl. Isn't that right?"

"That's right. You don't have to be *just* the earl, and Sam doesn't have to be *just* the rancher. Both of you can do anything that you damned well want to do," Tom said, winking at them.

Falling back dramatically, the boys laughed, their differences forgotten as they found something to agree on. Their father was going to get into trouble later with their mother for his use of profanity.

"I can do anything that I want, too."

Smiling with all the love he felt for his four-year-old daughter mirrored in his eyes, Tom winked. "That you can, darlin'."

She wound her arms around Tom's neck and hugged him tightly. "I love you, Papa."

"Love you, too, darlin'. Love you all."

"Come on, we've got fish to catch," Edward said, sensing that things were about to get too emotional. They always did when it was time for them to return to England. Picking up their poles, he led his younger brother and sister back to the creek.

Tom sat up and leaned against the tree. He patted the ground between his legs. Lauren moved over and sat within the circle of his arms, her back to his chest, welcoming the feel of his lips pressing against the sensitive skin just below her ear.

"Sorry we're leaving tomorrow?" he asked, his voice a low rumble.

"It's only for a few months. Then we'll be back."

It had become their habit, a few months here, a few months there.

"If you want to stay longer . . ."

She shook her head. "It wouldn't be fair to Ward. He loves England. He'll make an exemplary lord."

"Sam's going to be a good rancher."

She twisted around slightly until she could look at him. "Thank you, Tom, for giving me this little bit of Texas every now and then."

"Thank you, darlin', for giving me a little bit of your heart always."

"Oh, Tom, you have more than a little bit, and you damn well know it."

She cut off his laughter over her use of profanity with a kiss that would have led to other things if the children weren't nearby. She was amazed that after all these years, his slow, lazy kisses still had the ability to melt her bones and stir her desires.

When she pulled back, he said, "I'll meet you here later tonight to search for a falling star."

"I have nothing left to wish for. I have everything I could ever possibly want."

"Meet me anyway," he said. "I have some wishing of my own to do."

"What could you possibly wish for?"

He winked at her. "An unbuttoned bodice."

Sighing, she snuggled up against him. "You can have that without wishing for it."

"But, darlin', if you've taught me one thing, it's that a man ought to believe in wishing."

In the years that followed, Tom and Lauren divided their time between England and Texas. Half of their children were Texan by birth. And while the Lonesome Heart ranch was distributed equally among all their children, it was kept intact, passed down from generation to generation.

During both world wars, their descendants, based upon their place of birth, would serve in the British and American armed forces. Several would receive commendations for their bravery, including the Victoria Cross and the Congressional Medal of Honor.

Sixty-two years after they were married, Tom took Lauren back to Texas for the final time, laying her to rest in the rich Texas soil, near the creek where they'd fallen in love. He visited her every day, until six months later when he was laid to rest beside her. On their joint headstone, beneath the particulars of their lives, was carved a single word: *Forever*.

Tom had promised his Lauren forever. It was a promise he kept.

Coming in May from
Avon Romance

Duke of Scandal by Adele Ashworth

An Avon Romantic Treasure

Lady Olivia is a wife in name only, returning to London determined to confront her dastardly husband. But the man who stands before her is her husband's twin, the Duke of Durham, and now Olivia must make a scandalous choice.

Vamps and the City by Kerrelyn Sparks

An Avon Contemporary Romance

Can the undead really find love on Reality TV? Producer Darcy Newhart thinks so. But this sexy lady vampire is distracted by a hot, handsome contestant named Austin . . . who just happens to be mortal, and a slayer! What next?

What to Wear to a Seduction by Sari Robins

An Avon Romance

Lady Edwina is putting on clothes . . . only to take them off again! But she's determined to seduce notorious rogue Prescott Devane, the one man who can help her find a blackmailer . . . and also steal her heart.

Winds of the Storm by Beverly Jenkins

An Avon Romance

Archer owes his life to Zahra Lafayette. Now, in the days after the Civil War, he needs the help of this beautiful former spy again. Posing as an infamous madam, Zahra is willing to help in his cause, but she's unwilling to grant him her love.

Avon Romantic Treasures

Unforgettable, enthralling love stories, sparkling with passion and adventure from Romance's bestselling authors

Avon Romances
the best in
exceptional authors and unforgettable novels!